COMING THROUGH IN WAVES

COMING THROUGH IN WAVES

CRIME FICTION INSPIRED BY
THE SONGS OF

PINK FLOYD

EDITED AND WITH AN INTRODUCTION BY

T. FOX DUNHAM

GUTTER BOOKS
www.gutterbooks.com

TRIGGER WARNING

I feel it necessary to warn any reader who has an emotional trigger that there are elements in these stories that may be upsetting. I was careful not to include any stories of sexual assault. I felt they weren't in the spirit of the book. However, there are elements of violence, gun violence, robberies, drug addiction and murder. If you are vulnerable to any of these triggers, read with care.

—T. F. D.

I dedicate this anthology and all of my efforts to all the good doctors who battled a dehumanizing system, putting themselves at risk to put the patient forward. I especially honor Doctor Gerald J. Hansen. My oncologists preserved my life, but without Doctor Hansen, I would not have been able to live it. Without him, none of my books would be possible. All my work is thanks to him and his dedication.

Also, I extend my gratitude to all the authors who submitted to the anthology. This was my first time at the helm as an editor, and the job turned out to be bigger than we expected. I received seventy stories, and I had to reject authors for the first time. Also a thank you to my friends, Jon Prive, Michel Garrett, Crystal Judy, Kyle Thoms, Cindy Hermann and Jon Foster for keeping me sane once a week when we played D&D remotely on Roll20. Of course, I thank my wife Allison Ledbetter for her constant companionship and for taking up the brunt of the errands, since I've had to stay in our apartment. And finally, I thank a young man from the South who met me most nights on the D&D online game to run adventures. You were very kind and helped me through a lot of painful nights, Jessie LaMartiniere.

Contents

INTRODUCTION

BY T. FOX DUNHAM

I was watching an episode of *Deep Space Nine* late at night when I felt along my chin, making sure I had properly shaved. After a year of dealing with previously undiagnosed Lyme disease, I prepared to return to school and my life. I felt good. I felt like it was over. My favorite episode of Star Trek Deep Space Nine played—*The Die is Cast*. I always loved the character of the Cardassian tailor, Garak, played by Andrew Robinson. I checked my chin and jaw, then my fingers brushed against a lump the size of a golf ball below my ear. When I had shaved, not more than an hour before, that part of my skin had felt flat. Whatever it was, it had grown in an hour.

The next day, I rang a specialist who had treated me. Over the phone, he said it was probably just a cyst. I went to see him the following day. He looked annoyed and ready to move on, but then he felt it, and in a moment, his demeanor shifted to concern and urgency. The doctor ordered immediate surgery. In two days, he cut it out. It took months to identify the mass as cancer because a rare phenomenon had grown in my flesh: two different cell-types of lymphomas had grown in the same malignancy—a disease that had only been recorded fifteen times before me.

Sometimes you tell a story enough that you become the story. And sometimes you tell a story again and again and again because you are trying to escape it. I never wanted this to be my story, and I'm tired of telling it. I wrote two books based on my experience: *Destroying the Tangible Illusion of Reality or Searching for Andy Kaufman* and *Mercy*. Both stories told different aspects of my experience. Once they were done, I threw them into the seas of Amazon like a message in a bottle. Then, I waited to die.

You see, I was ready to die. I was the first person to survive my type of Lymphoma, and by the time they discovered, I had malignant masses all down the upper half of my body. The cancer was aggressive, and I endured a vigorous summer of chemo, then radiation treatments on my face, neck and chest each day for the autumn months. In order to live, I accepted extreme damage to my body that would disable me for the rest of my life. My radiation oncologist, feeling that no one had properly explained the side effects, gave me a choice. He was right, of course. My mother was a nurse who worked with the doctors who had treated me. She controlled the information that was coming to me. She needed me to live. I told him I'd go through with it. It wasn't a decision I made for myself. Everyone in my life looked so heartbroken. I couldn't let them down.

After the chemo and two months of radiation, I joined friends at Pyramid Comics to dungeon master a Ravenloft adventure. I couldn't lift my head up off the table. I went home that night and my mother took me to the hospital. She thought I was going to die, and I nearly did. When they let me go home on Halloween, they declared me in remission.

But I was warned. I was told I could never consider myself cured. I would need scans every six months. They expected it to return. And I stopped trusting life. I stopped trusting time.

Then a bunch of stuff happened in between the early nineties and last February.

Matt Louis, editor at Gutter Books, approached me to do this anthology. I hadn't heard from Matt in years, and I always felt like I owed him something. I was familiar with the previous anthologies inspired by music. I always swore I would never edit an anthology.

I've watched author friends buried by slush piles, and I wanted to be writing my own stories and not reading the stories of others. However, this offer came at a difficult time in my life.

Covid-19 hit. By then, I had reached out to talented authors whom I had come to respect over the years, and I didn't want to do the anthology without them. For the next six months, I continued to extend the deadline until I got a majority of the authors I wanted. We expected to get about twenty submissions. We actually got seventy. I planned to read each one and offer constructive criticism if I could not use the story. I kept a keen eye. I focused on the story. I am sure I rejected some respected authors, but my allegiance was to the story—always to the story.

Each of the stories you are about to read delighted me. What drew me most to an acceptance was unique character voice. From the souls of these characters, the authors created a world. It was my hope to generate a table of contents from a diverse group of voices, which is why it took me so long to complete the anthology. It's the editor's responsibility to reach out to a diverse group of authors, and I did my best. I was selective. I had a vibe going, a feeling that threaded through the book. I didn't want stories that would upset the reader. There's a place for that in fiction, but I wanted fun stories, stories with a bit of wit, characters that would make the reader smile. There are a couple of intense stories in the mix but most possess a sense of fun. They will uplift spirits and not crush them.

Also, thanks to the band I picked, we have contributions from the United Kingdom, the United States, Australia and more. This is a truly international anthology. The stories are fun and compelling. They will grab you from the first sentence then drop you at the end. I have edited every story, helping the author create their vision. Some of them are new authors looking to get their foot in the door. Others are veterans to whom I reached out. I am happy Paul D. Brazil has a story in this. Paul wrote a blurb for *The Street Martyr* years ago, and I wanted to return the favor.

Cancer is the plague of humanity. It isn't a virus. It's not bacteria.

It's a malfunction within our cells. And it affects all of us. I write this witnessing a new wave of Covid-19 in the United States, and it's important we fight it; however, we must not let the urgent be overshadowed by the immediate. Charities like the National Leukemia and Lymphoma Society suffer to make fundraising goals this year. When the Covid fire has been extinguished, cancer will still be rampant. We've just gotten used to it. We must remember these important organizations when we can once again gather in public or hug our friends. Cancer will keep killing us long after the next plague and the next. Covid is the plague of the 21st century. Cancer is the plague of human history. That is why I selected the National Leukemia and Lymphoma Society to benefit from the purchase of this book.

So I present to you *Coming Through in Waves,* with stories inspired by the music of Pink Floyd. Pink Floyd wrote songs about cultural issues, the disconnection of humanity and the destruction of the soul, but they also composed music that inspired and uplifted. The band always communicated with me, and after reading these stories, I can tell the authors experienced the same. Some of these stories are literary crime stories, but read carefully. At times, the stories transcend the genre much like the music did.

And so I thank you reader for joining in my battle. I humbly offer these tales in recompense for your patronage. And if you like a story, search for that author on Amazon and find their work. Write reviews. We live and die off of reviews.

THE WALL

BY T. FOX DUNHAM

Author's Note: I debated whether I should include a story. We had limited space. I decided to include a flash piece. I didn't do it out of a desire to be published. I did it because none of the stories include non-violent crimes, crimes committed by the apathetic. My topic, as you will read, is a personal one.

Cliff hunted along the stone wall that separated the Penn Medical Center from the dens of South Street, searching for his prey. Three days of constant rain swelled the Schuylkill River, and it roared below the 76 overpass, cutting Philly in half. A fine mist still sprayed, and Cliff yanked his hood over his face, giving himself just enough clearance to see. Headlights on the highway flashed light on the wall, and he'd pause, merging into shadow. He followed the wall around the Penn Hospital emergency room complex, passed the Katzman Center for Diagnostic Testing, and crossed Quaker Avenue until he reached the back-alley catacombs where business transpired behind the hospital cafeteria. He knew the area and had seen the regular nightlife. It wasn't long before he spotted his target—two figures huddled near the rusty dumpsters. He stalked closer, blending into the wall shadow, making sure it wasn't a couple of techs on a smoke break. They usually took their breaks in the walled gardens around the hospital, but he couldn't be sure. Cliff had one shot at this. He couldn't fail. Failure meant an agony he couldn't bear. He had to have it.

"Yeah, I got it," a female voice said. She carried a child's book bag at her waist. He caught a putrid scent on the air and spotted two infected sores festering on her arm—a common enough mark of heroin users who shot up with dirty needles. He'd seen it many times before and knew she needed IV antibiotics or risked sepsis, maybe amputation. "Ten pops," she said, and he sighed in relief. He had hoped for percs or other synthetic opiates, but tonight he'd won the junkie lottery. Ten could cover the distance, get him through the month.

Cliff stepped out of the curtains of shadow and found his mark. He pulled out the .22 from his coat pocket. The cold metal of the gun chilled his hand, and he aimed it to the left of the dealer.

"The candy," he said to the woman. This close, he could see she was just a girl, maybe seventeen—his sister's age. Sis had taken off a year ago when their mom got sick. Her customer took off toward South Street, nearly knocking into him.

"Don't you come back to me, Leon," she called after him.

"Give me the fucking bag," he said, imitating some of the clockers he'd heard at Franklin High. His arm trembled, and he fought to keep the gun steady.

He'd been handed a few months ago. *Dude, take this. Hide this. I'll get it later.* The kid hadn't been more than fifteen and had bled out that night in surgery. Cliff didn't know what to do with it, nearly chucked it into the Delaware a few times, but kept it, hoping he could pawn it one day.

"It's just candy," she said, acting calm, in control, but he heard her breathing increase from the adrenaline dumped into her blood. "Lollipops. My sister is raising money for a school trip to the art museum."

"I'll give you ten dollars for the whole box," he said. His hand ached from squeezing the gun. The hood kept sliding down and covering his eyes. This was taking too long. He should have been crossing the bridge right now. "Anything for an art fan."

Cliff's mind wandered, and he remembered when his mom had

taken him to the museum when he was twelve. She was so healthy, so strong. Nothing could take her down. She said she wanted him to have an appreciation for the finer things in life. The paintings overwhelmed him. Cliff had no idea the world could contain so much beauty, and there it was all under one roof.

He lost focus and nearly dropped the .22. She sensed it and took off, banging her arm on the dumpster and ripping her coat as she ran. A junkie always looked for the advantage. He followed her, running along the stone wall—the barrier that protected the doctors and patients from the trash on this side. She turned left, running into Franklin Park and ran down a gravel path. Her sneakers kicked up the stones, slowing her down. He caught up, meeting her in front of the ivory angel standing in a dry fountain. Spray paint decorated its wings.

"You don't gotta do this," she said, trying to catch her breath. Cliff heard an asthmatic wheeze or maybe an early stage of pneumonia. "I owe somebody. You take this bag, and I'll owe."

"We all owe," he said. "We never make good." He shook the .22. "It's just your time on the other side. If it makes you feel better, this is going to a good cause." She still wouldn't let go, and finally he grabbed the strap and yanked it out of her grip. She yelped and struggled, but he got it from her.

"At least leave me some for my itch." He sighed. Cliff knew it wouldn't be long before she was hurting. Somewhere in this world someone loved this girl, and he had seen too much of suffering. He kept the gun on her and reached into the sack then tossed the lollipop into the air. When she dropped down to pick it up, he slipped away.

"You think you're good and shit?" she yelled. "You ain't good."

He ran from her, ran from the hospital complex, ran from the river and made it to a BSL underground platform just as the train pulled in. He swiped his card, pulled up his mask and slipped onto the train.

—

Cliff rode the subway to Suburban station and got off at City Hall. When he got off on the platform, he adjusted his mask and slipped on his glasses from a case in his pocket then pulled down his hood. Since the second lockdown, the subways had been light. He climbed the steps into the courtyard and crossed the street, walking along the walled park where vendors had been setting up for the Christmas Village, though it was much smaller this year due to Covid. He tried not to attract attention to himself until he got to the apartment building. He fished the keys out of his jacket, opened the door and climbed the stairs. Somewhere in the depths of the building, a couple yelled, and he hoped the noise would fade away by the time he reached the fourth floor. Through the thin walls, you could hear the drone of every television, the conversation of every couple and the cough of every sick man, woman and child in the broken-down and derelict building. He turned the corner and stepped into the apartment.

"Clifford, is that you?" his mom called from the bedroom.

"Who else would it be, Mama?" he replied while kneeling down and taping the gun under the sink.

"Could be the angel of death come to end this at last," she said. Cliff pulled off his coat then tossed it onto the table, knocking over a stack of medical bills. Before going into see her, he grabbed a cold can of Ensure and poured her some water into a chipped mug. Then he took a deep breath before going in to see his mama. He dreaded this more than robbing dealers. Finally, he stepped into the room his mother had shared with her husband for thirty years. The Lord had taken him fast but designated his mother to slowly rot. The desiccated little woman lay twisted on the mattress and clutched her abdomen, hugging a pillow. Sweat dripped down her shorn head.

"Mom. I got to the drugstore," he said and pulled out one of the lollipops.

"You talked to someone at the Medicare?" she asked. "They helped us out?"

"Yeah Mama," he said, lying to the woman he'd promised never to deceive. He hadn't even tried to call those people again. When the pharmacist had first told them about the co-pay, he'd spent hours fighting them. First, they kept you on hold for two hours. Then they fed him the same shit about percentage and deductibles, throwing him back and forth between customer reps. The answer was always the same. Sometimes a sympathetic operator would suggest a charity to help with the medicine costs but it never amounted to a solution. These people had built their walls to guard against compassion or sympathy. They brainwashed their staff and never let them stay on the phone too long. He didn't blame them. They were just trying to survive too.

"That's good, son," she said. "I try to be strong, but no matter how hard you try, it's just too much. My body's burning up. I don't know why Jesus hasn't taken me yet."

He offered her a lollipop but she hesitated. "It's Fentanyl, Mama. You lick it. It'll help the burning and you'll be able to sleep."

"Well look at that," she said. He helped guide her hand until she got the candy to her mouth. "It just burns so bad," she said. "I never once felt tempted to break God's law in my life but this don't make sense." He thought about taking her back to the hospital, but the oncologist had exhausted her options. They needed the beds and would refer him to hospice care again, which was a laugh in the middle of a plague.

"Bless you," she said, closing her eyes. "I knew they'd help. You have such a grim outlook on the world, but you'll see yet. There's good people everywhere."

"You're right, mama," he said and pulled up the blanket over her thin frame. Cliff turned off the light, then slipped out to the living room. Sitting on the couch, he counted the pops. He set them on the coffee table in front of him. If they rationed out doses, he could probably get his mama through the next three weeks as long as the cancer remained in her GI tract. If they ran out, he'd have to take the train to Camden or maybe even go down to Trenton. He dreaded the idea of robbing another dealer, but he couldn't take watching her writhe in pain. It twisted up in his chest until he felt his own helpless agony.

Cliff fell asleep for an hour before his phone alarm woke him. He dragged himself off the couch, took a quick shower, then pulled out yesterday's scrubs from the laundry. Before heading to work his shift at the emergency room, he looked in on his mama. She trembled in her sleep but she slept. Tonight, she slept. He took the partially melted lollipop out of her hand, set it next to her on the table, then kissed her head. Then he grabbed his keys, secured his mask, and headed out for another night stacking patients against the walls in the halls of Penn Hospital.

COMING THROUGH IN WAVES

COME IN NUMBER 51, YOUR TIME IS UP

BY DBSCHLOSSER

"Ain't you awake?" The cop banged his club between two bars. "Quit dreaming."

He'd been dimly aware of being not asleep for some time. No watch, no phone, no clock. *Some* was his best estimate under buzzing greenish lights. His best estimate without windows.

"I'm not." His mouth was dusted dry from using it, instead of his nose, for breathing. From using it to escape the moist green stink of the overflowing toilet in the middle of the back wall.

A slow trickle of cloudy water dribbled over the rim. It followed a glistening mossy furrow to a drain in the middle of the floor. It dripped metronomically to a puddle somewhere below. The *pah pah pah* ticked off seconds, minutes, hours in the absence of other methods for tracking time.

"I don't know why I'm here."

The cop said, "Why is anybody where they are?"

He pushed himself off the bench, vertical for the first time since he'd awakened. Since inventorying his injuries—ribs painful on

1

each breath, left eye swollen nearly shut under hot skin, bruised forearms tender where he'd tried to protect his head. "Instead of a hospital."

"Zabriskie." The cop looked at a clipboard. "What kind of name is that?"

He shook his head. "How would I know?" His brain sloshed inside his skull after his head stopped moving. He thought he could hear it.

"End of the line for you."

A sharp jolt of adrenalin flushed away his dull aches. "What—end of what?"

"Zabriskie. Z. Always been at the end of the line." The cop tapped the clipboard with his index finger. "In school."

"My name's not zebra—whatever."

"I got one page on my clipboard. Zabriskie." The cop thumbed the single piece of paper into a curve. "I got one body in my cell. Zabriskie."

"That's a mistake." Exhaustion amplified his dull aches as the adrenalin drained away.

"They'd've told me if there was a mistake."

"I'm Smith."

"You and me, Zabriskie, we'll get on better when you stop pretending to be something you ain't." The cop glanced at the clipboard. "Anthony Zabriskie. Aggravated assault."

"Jon Smith." He raised his chin and flinched at the *snap snap snap* in his neck. "The one who got assaulted."

"John Smith. Don't think you ain't the first what tried that with me."

"Not John. Jon." His dad thought it would be funny. "Jonathan Smith."

"Be that guy." The cop shrugged. "I was gonna let you choose margarine or mayonnaise on your sandwich. I'll just scoop out some food loaf for you."

"Wait," he called after the cop as he heard the crash of a door opening and closing. "Come back."

—

He stood when he heard the door open. He went to the bars across the front of the cell when he heard the door close.

"Step back." The cop carried a tray made from the same almost-cardboard material that eggs came in.

"You gotta believe me," he said. "Jonathan Smith."

"Step back from the bars, Zabriskie." The cop raised the tray. "Food loaf has a high water content. This tray ain't plastic. Longer you don't step back, more likely it'll melt through. You don't wanna eat it off this floor."

"I shouldn't be here."

"Step. Back."

"The guys who jumped me—that's who oughtta be here."

The cop put the tray on the floor outside the cell.

"I oughtta be in the hospital."

"After this tray softens up a little bit more, if food loaf don't kill the hunger, you can kinda fold it in the middle and pull it through the lower bars."

A little paper cup perched on the tray, the kind his grandmother kept in a spring-loaded dispenser in the bathroom. A tiny white spork sat next to a coruscating lump of colorless mush that still showed the ridges and seam in the can the cop had dumped it from.

"I don't need to eat. I need to—what day is it? I gotta call my boss, tell him why I'm not at work."

"My experience?" The cop was already halfway back to the door. "When the boss hears why no one showed up at work, you don't gotta worry about showing up at work no more."

—

He'd thought himself hungry until he saw what the cop called food loaf.

While he waited for the cop to come back, the lump lost consistency. It melted into a mounded puddle. It crept over the spork. The cup floated on it. The cup moved imperceptibly to the edge until it tipped off the tray on the floor.

The decohered meal trickled toward the drain on his side of the bars.

"Not hungry?" the cop said. "Most important meal of the day."

"It's morning?"

"Any free meal is the most important meal of the day."

"Margarine. Next time I'll take margarine."

The cop faked a smile. "Now that's the Zabriskie I've come to know and love."

"How—what—I mean, I can prove I'm Jonathan Smith. I gotta make a phone call."

"You want to call the lawyer? Paperwork says you got a PD."

"I don't have a lawyer."

"Ain't that the reason you got a public defender?"

"I can call my boss," he said. "My landlord."

"Pay phone down here's been busted a couple weeks."

"Someone who can tell you I'm Jon Smith."

"Pay phone's the only way to call."

"Someone who knows I am who I am."

"That don't help as much as you think."

He blinked at the cop.

"What you need," the cop proclaimed, "is someone who doesn't know who you are to tell them you're not Anthony Zabriskie."

"I don't—"

"Someone who knows you? Someone helping you outta the jam you're in? Why would they believe someone you ask to tell them you're not Anthony Zabriskie?"

—

"Zabriskie," the cop shouted as the door opened. "PD."

He'd been standing at the bars since the cop dropped the food loaf because it was the furthest he could get from the sulfurous stench of the dribbling toilet.

The melting food loaf trickled to the drain in a chunky stream between his feet. It tumbled through the grate, splashing below with a *boimp boimp boimp*.

The ache of his injuries hadn't faded, but he'd grown less aware of the steady pain. He'd grown more aware of his head, his brain, the dull throb that alternated with his pulse.

"I think I got a concussion," he said.

"Step back from the bars."

"I said I think I got—"

"Puke?"

"No."

"You ain't got no concussion. Step back."

"But my head—" He squeezed it between his hands to make the throbbing stop.

"Step. The fuck. Back."

"—and I'm not—I don't feel myself."

The cop swiped his club from his belt and pounded it on the bar closest to his face in a single motion.

He stepped back.

The cop replaced his club and extended his palm to the door. He made elaborate motions with his fingers.

After a click and a buzz, the bars slid aside with a *clank clank clank*.

"Turn around," the cop said. "Hands behind you."

He turned around and put his hands behind him.

The cop wrapped cold metal cuffs around his wrists. "Behave, and I'll take these off when you talk to the PD."

"I stepped back."

"Keep up this identity illusion, wear the shiny new jewelry the whole time."

The cop grabbed his collar and guided him from the cell down the hall to the door. They waited for a *click-buzz*. The cop pushed him against the crash bar to open the door.

They passed a desk with a clipboard sitting in the middle of an otherwise empty surface. The cop pushed him into a beige cube with a table and two stools bolted to the floor. As the cop unlocked his cuffs, a door opposite the one the cop has pushed him through opened and a man with a cardboard folder stepped in.

The cop pushed him down on a stool.

The man sat on the other and said, "Mister Zabriskie, I'm the public defender."

The cop left. The doors clanged shut. Both clicked and buzzed.

"You gotta help me," he said.

The PD opened the file. "That's why I'm here."

"I'm not Zabriskie." He rubbed his wrists. The skin was cold where the cuffs contained him. "I'm Jon Smith."

The PD looked at the single page in the folder. "Anthony Zabriskie. Aggravated assault."

"I know that's what the paperwork says. But the paperwork isn't who I am. I'm the one who got assaulted."

The PD held up one finger. "No." He used another to trace lines of text on the paperwork. "This says you assaulted Eric Fletcher, who is ... mmm."

"What?"

"He's the headmaster at Dodgson. Where Governor Lutwidge's children go to school."

"I didn't assault anyone. Look at my eye." He held out his bruised arms. "I got assaulted. Then I woke up in that cell."

"They advised me of this story."

"This is not a story."

"If you can prove this story isn't a story," the PD mused, "I might be able to help."

"Let me use a phone."

The PD frowned and smiled at the same time. "You, of all of us, should know I can't bring a phone in here."

"My wallet—my phone. What I had with me when they brought me here."

The PD consulted the paperwork again. "No personal effects."

"They stole everything." He looked at the pale skin on his right wrist. "My watch."

"An auto registration?"

"I don't have a car."

"Motorbike?"

"I ride the bus," he said. "The train."

"To and from work."

"Yes—work. My boss. My boss will tell you this is not a story."

"Tell?" The PD frowned with no smile. "A boss should have paperwork. To show."

He shrank around his lungs. "I'm ... off the books. Right now, I mean."

"Oh, dear." The PD took a pen from behind his ear and made a mark on the page in the folder. "All other options take longer than the preliminary hearing."

"Anthony Zabriskie's preliminary hearing."

"Yes."

"Not my preliminary hearing."

The PD shook his head. "The preliminary hearing."

"You're telling me to go along with this."

"Isn't that the most logical way to proceed with the proceedings?"

"It would be if I wasn't Jon Smith."

The PD made another mark on the paperwork. "Perhaps what you're asking for is a psychiatric evaluation."

"I'm not crazy."

"It might help resolve this identity complex."

"I don't have an identity complex. Anthony Zabriskie isn't my identity."

"Well." The PD tucked the pen behind his ear and closed the file. "None of us feel quite ourselves when we've been through an ordeal like this, do we?"

—

"I gotta use the bathroom," he told the cop as the cop handcuffed him.

"Good thing you got a toilet right there in the cell."

"It's backed up."

"You got no company." The cop grabbed his collar. "Plenty of privacy."

"I can't use that toilet."

"It ain't good enough for someone in your circumstances?"

They waited for a *click-buzz* at the door to the hall to the cell.

"What's your name?" he asked the cop.

"It ain't Anthony Zabriskie." The cop pulled open the door and pushed him through.

"Please."

"You ain't still Jon Smith, are you?"

"I'm—that's my name."

The cop turned him to face the cell. "Don't step on Zabriskie's meal."

"That's my meal."

After the *click-buzz* and the *clank clank clank*, the cop took off the cuffs and pushed him into the cell. "Exactly."

—

That was when he puked.

The contents of his stomach forced water over the edge of the toilet and settled at the bottom of the bowl. His bile glowed yellow there. It seemed to pulse.

He'd hoped vomiting would make the throb in his head stop.

It didn't.

In addition to the acidic slime now sizzling in his mouth, he had the same headache, throbbing, and still needed to use the toilet.

He tried and failed to sleep. The yellow glow pulsed through his eyelids.

When he couldn't hold it any longer, he took off his pants and underwear, stepped back into the black plastic sandals they'd put on his feet, and squatted over the toilet. The water brimming over the edge of the bowl splashed the insides of his legs as he emptied himself.

He no longer felt his pulse throbbing in his head, he no longer saw the glow pulsing, after he'd relieved himself.

After a few minutes, the surge over the toilet's rim returned to its dribble.

He drifted off when the *pah pah pah* returned to the cadence he'd grown used to. He dreamed, but he did not remember his dreams when he opened his eyes.

He felt unrested, as if he'd done the opposite of sleeping. His eye was less swollen. The skin over it was less hot. The bruises on his arms yellowed at the edges. He wondered how long that took to happen.

He was thirsty.

The paper cup that floated to the edge of the tray on melting food loaf still lay on its side in the hall to the door. He reached through the bars before he realized he had no way to fill it.

He heard the door open, then close.

"Somebody made a mess."

It was a cop. A different cop wearing the same uniform and carrying the same clipboard.

"How can you have any pudding," the cop said, "if you don't eat your food loaf?"

"I didn't understand."

"You're not the only one, are you?" The cop glanced at the clipboard. "Kinda rare for a weekend like this."

"Is there a note on there?"

The cop held up the clipboard. "On here?"

"About the mistake."

"They'd've told me if there was a mistake."

"I'm not Zabriskie."

"I got one page on my clipboard. Zabriskie." The cop thumbed the single piece of paper into a curve. "I got one body in my cell. Zab—"

"My name isn't Zabriskie."

"I'm saying it wrong?"

"What?"

"That ain't how you say it?"

"There's no note?" he pleaded.

"About how to say Zabriskie?"

"About the mistake."

"They'd've told me if there was a mistake."

"I'm not Zabriskie."

The cop made a point of looking into the cell. "I see three brick walls. I see two wooden benches. I see one steel toilet. And I see you." The cop jabbed the clipboard with an index finger. "Zabriskie."

"I keep telling people I'm Jon Smith."

"Bucking for a psych eval?" The cop looked at the paperwork. "Tough play if all's you got's a PD."

"He didn't tell me when he'd be back."

"Not 'til Tuesday at least." The cop barked a laugh. "Nice work if you can get it."

"What day is it?"

The cop cocked his head. "How long you been in here?"

"I don't know."

"Don't know the right name. Don't know the right day. Maybe that psych eval ain't so far outside the realm of possibility."

"I'm not crazy."

"Sure." The cop shook his head.

"I'm thirsty."

The cop glanced at the paper cup. "You can't reach that?"

"I don't have any way to fill it."

The cop jerked his chin at the toilet.

"I—you want me to drink out of that?"

"The sink is on the top of the tank."

He turned away from the bars and noticed for the first time a little spout on the back of the toilet. He turned back to the bars.

"Push the foot pedal," the cop said. "Like a drinking fountain. Ain't nobody show you nothing?"

"I've been alone since I got here."

"Stir crazy. That's all. You'll get some company soon. Three-day weekend and all."

"What weekend is it?"

"Payday." The cop turned to the door. "Full moon."

—

The *click-buzz* smothered the *pah pah pah*. Two sets of footsteps approached in the hall to the door.

"Told you you'd get company," the cop said over the *clank clank clank.* "I'll be back when the paperwork comes down."

"When will that be?" said the new prisoner.

The cop pushed the new prisoner into his cell.

"Long weekend," the cop said over the *clank clank clank.* "Everything's running behind." The cop turned to the door. "Island time."

The new prisoner sprawled on his bench.

"That's my bench," he said.

"There's two benches."

"That one's mine. Take the other."

"Look the same to me."

"I think I got a concussion." He took the other.

"Puke?"

"Yeah."

"That's a concussion."

"I'm not supposed to be here."

"Ain't that what we all say?"

"I'm Jon Smith."

"You and all the other John Smiths that ain't supposed to be here." The new prisoner laughed once. "I'm Tony Z."

"You're thirsty."

The new prisoner looked at him. "I am?"

He went to the bars. "You get confused." He retrieved the paper cup from the floor in the hall to the door. "When you don't drink enough water."

The new prisoner took the cup from him.

"The sink is on top of the tank." He took his bench. "Push the foot pedal."

The *pah pah pah* eventually got to the new prisoner. "Guess I am."

The new prisoner stepped over and began pushing the foot pedal.

He approached and circled the man's neck with his bruised arms.

He pushed the man's head into the bowl.

The head hid the yellow glow.

He held the head in the water.

The dribble became a splash before it became a dribble.

And because he pushed so slowly, such an exquisitely measured exertion that so serenely syncopated with the tempo in his head, the *pah pah pah* ticked no faster as he followed the glistening mossy furrow to the drain.

After the door opened, the cop called "Zabriskie."

Before the *click-buzz* and the *clank clank clank*, the cop said, "The paperwork came through."

A Saucerful Of Secrets

by Paul D. Brazill

A bitter, cold dawn gasped for life and seagulls screeched. Craig Ferry sneezed as he snaked his battered, black Jaguar along Marine Road, listening to a phone-in show on Radio Seatown. A former footballer with a high-pitched voice whinged on about having to go into rehab and Bryn Laden wished He'd bloody well stayed there. Craig changed stations and found an old Rolling Stones song he used to play to death when he was a kid.

"This is more like it," said Craig.

"Nostalgia's exactly what it used to be, eh?" said Bryn.

"I like what I like. I am what I am."

"Well, Popeye, did you call your sister about the happy talc?" said Bryn.

"Nope," said Craig. "I thought I'd give her a bell later. I've been thinking, like … maybe we should shop the stuff around a bit. See if anyone can up our Bev's offer. It doesn't always pay to put all your eggs in one basket, you know. And you can't make an omelette without breaking eggs."

Bryn groaned. The last thing he wanted to do was piss off Bev

Ferry. Bev had always been a bit of a wild card but since her dad had died it seemed like Bev had really lost the plot. Craig had always been jealous of his big sister's position as head of Seatown's top crime family and regularly tried to undermine her. His attempts usually left a lot to be desired.

Bryn knew that he'd have to talk Craig out of his plan, at some point. Or maybe get him so drunk that he'd be incapable of wheeling and dealing. He decided to change the topic in the meantime.

"Ere, I see the waste disposal pipe at the Chicken Licken Factory has burst again," he said, nodding toward the sea front. "The beach is full of chicken heads and legs."

"Oh, that's all part of the Seatown charm, that is," said Craig. "I bet you never had that when you lived down the smoke, eh?"

"Yeah, like John Revolting said in Pulp Fiction, it's the little differences. A lotta the same stuff you've got up here, they've got down there, but some things are particular only to Seatown. The Chicken Licken factory being case in point."

"Well, the North of England's not had the advantages of the south, has it? When the docks and the factories closed town, there weren't exactly scores of marketing companies and PR firms rushing to Seatown. That's what you lot forget."

"What do you mean by 'you lot'? I was born and bred in Seatown."

"Aye. But you moved to London as soon as you got the chance though, eh? It's like you chose your friends not you family. The place where you actually choose to live is where you're actually from, actually, and not and the accident of birth place. Actually."

Bryn groaned. He wasn't in the mood. Craig's pub philosophy was fine enough when they were actually drinking in a pub but there in the cold light of day, and stone cold sober, it was like fingers down a blackboard.

"Yeah, if you like," said Bryn.

"'Ere, speaking of the Big Smoke, I heard there was another terrorist attack down London last night," said Craig.

"Yeah?"

"Yeah. Another twat in a Transit van went mental. Nobody was killed but a few were hurt."

Bryn shook his head.

"Well, unfortunately it's par for the course and a sign of the bleedin' times, these days," he said. "Mind you, London's always had its terrors. Jack the Ripper, The Blitz, the IRA … Chas n Dave, Spandau Ballet, Danny Baker, jellied eels …"

Craig tutted.

"I'm quite partial to a plate of jellied eels, as a matter of fact," he said.

Bryn grimaced.

"Well, that does surprise me. I didn't know you were into foreign food," he said.

Craig sniffed.

"There's a lot you don't know about me, lad. And, for your information, Chas n Dave had some top tunes under all that Cockney Pearly King cobblers. Anyway, don't you ever miss living down London, then?" he said.

"A bit but not a lot. That said, on a day like today upping sticks seems more and more attractive …"

He ran a hand across his shaven head.

"What about you," he said. "Don't you ever think about just pissing off out of Seatown and starting afresh? Maybe even going abroad. Fancy far-flung foreign lands?"

"Nah. What about you?"

"Well, when the weather's like this you could say the idea has its appeal. If I had the dosh I might well scarper off to sunnier climes."

"Money's too shite to mention, eh?"

"Ain't it always?"

"Myself, I doubt I could ever leave this place," said Craig. "For better or worse Seatown's too much a part of me. It's in my blood, in my lungs. And anyway I've never lived anywhere else, unless you count Darlington …"

Bryn snorted.

"I don't, actually. Have you ever even been abroad? To Greece or Spain?"

"I have, as a matter of fact. I went to Majorca once, with me gran. Before she died, like."

"I bloody well hope so!"

Craig tutted.

"I've been to France too, mind you," he said.

"Really. You do surprise me. Once again"

"Yeah, I went a booze cruise to Calais back in the nineties. I picked up a VHS bootleg of Reservoir Dogs when it was still banned in Blighty. Swedish subtitles and all."

"Good film, that was, for its time. What did you think of Calais?"

"I didn't reckon much to the place, to be honest. It reminded me of Darlington," said Craig.

He shuddered. Bryn laughed,

"Maybe you'd be better suited to Spain, then," said Bryn.

"Well, apparently, one of my old schoolmates is living out in Spain. Marbella to be precise," he said. "A bloke called Dougie Cronk. He was a tidy boxer in his day. He could have been a contender and all that but he boozed his chances away."

"Float like a butterfly, drink like a fish, eh?"

"Aye, a bit and that. He owns a bed and breakfast or something. I hear he's supposed to be writing his memoirs, though, the amount of booze he's put away over the years I doubt he that remembers much at all."

"Things change. People change."

"True enough. The man who sees the world in the same way

at sixty as he did when he was thirty has wasted thirty years of his life."

"Very profound. Who said that, then?"

"I did," said Craig. "Didn't you hear me?"

Bryn sighed.

"No, you clot. Who said it originally? Nietzsche again?"

Craig sniffed.

"It was Mohammed Ali, would you believe," he said.

Craig chuckled and snaked the car through the rain-soaked streets listening to Lana Del Rey sing about being "Young and Beautiful." Bryn didn't exactly feel like he was either. He was completely knackered. He'd spent the night waiting down by the docks for a shipment of cocaine to arrive and it hadn't been a particularly pleasant experience. Being stuck in a stinky old rust bucket with Craig wasn't exactly his ideal pastime, although it seemed to be becoming a more and more frequent occurrence.

They drove past a piece of waste ground that had been given the nickname Dogging Lane. Dogging Lane had earned itself a bit of a national reputation recently via the very popular YouTube clip of a couple of well-known kids, television presenters, who were filmed there making a spit roast out of a six-foot-six transvestite known locally as Ella The Fella.

A couple of bag-heads were at the end of the pier feeding sweetcorn and lemonade to the seagulls. They both laughed as they watched the birds scoop down for a drink of seawater and then explode mid-air.

They stopped at a zebra crossing. A fat woman shuffled across pushing a double buggy that was stuffed with two chubby kids. A skinny man in a purple shell suit followed her, smoking a cigarette and jerking on the arm of a lagging, screaming toddler. "Look at that lot," said Craig.

"That's life in the 21st century, that is. Shit people living shit lives and shitting out shit kids to live even shittier lives."

Bryn laughed.

"Yeah, not everyone has made the informed life choices that we have, eh?" he said.

The car started up with a splutter.

"I assume they'll be draining the state to support their shit life choices," said Craig.

"Assume makes an arse out of both of us.

A small group of football fans, watched by an equal-sized group of bored policemen, snaked out of the train station, through the streets and toward the high street.

"That lot are a hell of a lot quieter than I expected," said Bryn. "Mind you, I"ve never been much of a football fan, even as a kid and I always assumed supporting a football team was something you just grew out of."

"It looks as if a few of those fans have grown a bit too much. Especially around the stomach area," said Craig.

Bryn laughed.

"But really, you're right, it is ridiculous," said Craig. "What the bloody hell is a football team? Just some people you don't know, who are all paid to wear the same shirt and kick a ball around. And if they win a game all the suckers think their lives have improved. It's just reflected glory for underachievers."

"Young and Beautiful" ended and was followed by an Amy Winehouse tune. Bryn groaned inwardly. It wasn't so much the song. He didn't mind it, in fact. But he knew it would set Craig off on one of his rants. His musical knowledge was as exhausting as it was exhaustive.

"Aye, she was one of them, eh?" said Craig. "That thing I was telling you about last night. Remember?"

"Unfortunately, I do," said Bryn.

Craig shrugged.

"Well, then. 27," he said. "Twenty bloody seven."

"And you're saying you really believe all that Curse of Robert Johnstone bollocks, do you?"

"Well, all I'm saying is that it's a bit of a weird coincidence, isn't it?" said Craig. "I mean, Robert Johnstone sold his soul to the devil …"

"Allegedly …"

"… and he died when he reached 27. Jim Morrison, Janis Joplin, Jimi Hendrix, Brian Jones, Kurt Cobain, Amy Winehouse. They all snuffed it at the age of 27 and all of them were full-blown musical legends."

Bryn checked his reflection in the smudged rear-view mirror. He certainly wasn't a 27-year-old, that was for sure. In fact, he had to admit that he was looking a bit haggard these days. He was definitely no longer the pretty boy of his youth and no amount of expensive designer clobber could disguise the fact, unfortunately. When his salt and pepper hair had started to err too much on the side of Saxa, he'd decided to shave his head and had regretted the decision almost immediately. It had made his face look bloated. And since he'd moved back to Seatown, He'd definitely put on weight.

"What about David Bowie, then?" he said. "He was as old as the hills when he croaked. And Elvis Presley was no spring chicken when he bit the dust either."

Craig lit a cigar.

"I'm just saying that it makes you think, is all," he said. "You've got to keep an open mind, Tommy. That's the problem with most people these days. They're too narrow in their worldview, like. Their experience is limited by their lack of imagination and their imagination is limited by their lack experience. Know what I mean, like?"

"Oh, yeah," said Bryn. "Clear as crystal, that is. Maybe we could listen to some more modern music for a change?"

"Aye, alright. I think the cassette player still works."

"Have you actually got any cassettes?"

"Aye."

Craig shuffled in the glove compartment and plucked out a cassette. He slammed it in the cassette player and Adele started to warble about chasing pavements.

"It's not over till the fat lady sings," said Craig.

Sweet cigar smoke filled the car and Bryn coughed. Craig turned right onto Starling Lane. As he turned the corner toward the seafront, a big black SUV suddenly screeched in front of them and blocked their way. Craig braked but his reactions were slow.

"Judas Priest on a bike," said Bryn.

"What an idiot," said Craig. "What the bloody hell is that arsehole up to?"

He reversed the car but another SUV turned the corner and slammed into him, stopping his exit.

Within seconds a punk rocker and a skinhead staggered out of one of the SUVs. Bryn immediately recognised them.

"That's Han and Solo," said Bryn. "Which means …"

"What the bloody …?" said Craig. His cigar fell from his mouth into his lap.

The door to the other SUV opened and a woman dressed in black leather got out. She had a raven black hair, a slash of crimson lipstick across her mouth and carried a cricket bat that she swung loosely.

"Shite," said Bryn.

"Oh, buggeration," said Craig. "It's our Bev."

"It most certainly is."

Bryn squirmed in his seat as Bev walked over to the Jag. She placed the bat on the roof of the car and gestured for Bryn to wind down his shattered window, which he did with alacrity.

"Alright, Bev," he said.

"Morning, sis," said Craig, weakly. "What can …"

Bev slammed a hand on the roof of the car.

"I'll keep this short-n-sweet, ladies," said Bev. "We're only having this conversation as a courtesy to Bryn's mother. If it wasn't for her, you'd both be up at Jed Bramble's farm, feeding his pigs. My boys are going to unload the stuff from your car and take it over to The Red Herring post-haste, okay?"

"Well, we were actually on our way to the pub, Bev," said Bryn. "We were just taking the scenic route."

"Be that as it may, I'm fully aware of our Craig's propensity for distraction and side businesses. I'd rather have the gear in the hands of those two simpletons, just in case."

"Should I feel offended?" said Craig.

"Probably," said Bev.

"Well, they do say lack of focus is another form of multi-tasking," said Craig.

"Is that right?" said Bev.

"Probably," said Craig. "Maybe."

Bryn turned and watched as Bev's goons opened the car boot and unloaded wooden boxes, which were packed with bags of cocaine, into one of the SUVs.

Bev slammed a hand on the roof of the car again. Craig almost jumped out of his seat.

"Best practice, eh, lads?" said Bev.

They nodded their heads in unison.

"Yeah, sure," said Craig. "Sorry, like, I …"

"As you were," said Bev. "Oh, I might have a bit more work for you over the next few days, Bryn, if you're that way inclined?"

"Sure," said Bryn, groaning inwardly. "Fire away."

"Good. I'll give you a bell when I want you."

Bev picked up the cricket bat and patted it. She walked back to her SUV. She turned and pointed the bat at the Jaguar. She nodded and Bryn nodded back. Bev got back in her car.

In a flash, the SUVs had driven off but Craig and Bryn just sat in the car, stunned. The dropped cigar burnt a hole into

Craigs leg. He looked down and brushed it away as if it were a mosquito.

Bryn grimaced.

"Did that hurt?" he said.

"Aye," said Craig, distracted.

"Oh, well. Shit happens," said Bryn. "Let's bugger off."

"Yes, Miss Daisy," said Craig.

He tried to start the car and it made a whining sound but didn't start.

"Oh, great," he said. "That's all we need. It's cream crackered."

Craig rubbed his forehead. Sirens wailed in the distance.

"We'll have to bloody well walk then, won't we?" he said.

"It certainly looks that way."

"I'll phone Mikey The Mechanic to come and pick it up," said Craig. "He might get something for the scrap if it's completely knackered. And I'll have to get the old Zephyr Zodiac out of mothballs."

As they got out of the car and started to walk toward the bus terminus, lightning flashed, and thunder rumbled.

"Oh, bloody great," said Bryn, looking up at the sky. "As if things couldn't get worse."

"Well, a tactical pub stop it is, then," said Craig. "I think it's time for a little eye opener anyway. Breakfast of champions and all that."

"Great minds drink alike," said Bryn.

"And I'll tell you my latest scheme. Sure-fire winner, this one is."

"Oh, I'm sure it is," said Bryn, drowning in Sisyphean resignation.

MOTHER

BY KIMBERLY GODWIN

Beyond a splintered dark wooden door, a vivid shade of magenta stained apartment 148. Copper and bile assaulted Detective Hill's nostrils, making his stomach heave in revulsion as he fought down his lunch. "What could have done this, Doc?"

"This much blood reminds me of an explosion, Ethan." Maeve knelt down to examine the long bloody streaks that led from the doorway deeper into the apartment.

Hill stepped back, taking a deep steadying breath, and closed his eyes. He imagined the weight and feel of rosary beads in his hand as he silently counted to ten before opening his eyes again. A creak pulled his attention to the middle of the room as an overturned wheelchair's tire lazily turned under the roving illumination of a ceiling fan. He frowned and wondered: *Is there any place here not coated in blood?*

Maeve navigated the blood trail on the cream colored carpet. Her technicians diligently documented the scene in front of them. Heavy, white, blood-stained curtains blocked all natural light on either side of an empty TV stand in front of a stained floral couch.

Shards of glass glittered across the red puddles. "What a mess. Who lived here?"

Hill pursed his lips together. "Misty Nocturne." He walked closer to the few pictures hanging on the wall, noting long drips of drying blood that went from above the frame and down. "We haven't seen one this bad in a while."

"Reconstruction in the lab will be interesting," she paused as she glanced at him. "It's been a while. Are you going to be okay?" Maeve moved from the overturned wheelchair to beside Hill.

Hill hesitated before he shrugged. "Yeah. I'll be fine. Medication and therapy do wonders." *The nightmares have mostly gone away,* he dryly thought before he continued. "Call was about the door. Isn't it weird that there aren't any footprints in the blood? Think that's why the fan was on?"

"It's possible that it's on to dry the blood," Maeve speculated. "Diaz and Miller walking through here without leaving a footprint means that it was dry when they entered." She tilted her head flicking frizzy black hair from her face.

Hill ran a hand over his blond crew cut before he followed the dark smear into the open bedroom. "Why drag her from the wheelchair? Wouldn't it have been easier to grab it and move her?"

"You'd think. But we may never know." Maeve shrugged as she took some more notes.

He cautiously stepped into the room and marveled. Sweet rose perfume permeated the air. Sunlight streamed through white lace as well as the heavier pink curtains over a neatly made bed covered with a white comforter. A white and gold dresser scattered with bottles and a face-down, gold picture frame sat to the left of the door. He gently lifted the frame, observing the faces of a stern older blonde woman standing beside an unamused pretty young woman through cracked glass. *Must be Misty and her mother? Reminds me of pictures with my mom.*

He returned his attention to the blood trail that led into an open closet with bare, cheap, wire shelving smeared with bloody handprints. "Looks like you guys might have at least a partial in here, Maeve."

Hill searched the room. Maeve moved past him and looked up at the ceiling. She clicked her pen as she pointed up at some fine crimson spots. "There's more spray on the ceiling, but that comforter is still fairly clean."

He shivered in the soft light of the room. "None of this makes sense. It's like they vanished into thin air."

—

Joyce Nocturne wailed. Mascara ran down her cheeks in black streaks. Hill sat uncomfortably behind his desk, waiting for her to finish so they could continue. When she finally looked up from the mangled handful of tissues, her gray eyes were bloodshot. "Why won't you let me see my baby? I promised her that I'd … and now …"

Hill cleared his throat, pushing forward a box of tissues. "I can't go into detail about what we found in Misty's apartment. If you're willing to provide a blood sample, it'd help us determine if anything we found belonged to her. Forensics is trying to sort it out but I can't make any promises."

Joyce sniveled as she took another tissue. "Anything you need. I'll do anything for Misty." Her voice trembled on the edge of a new breakdown.

Hill leaned forward in his chair, making a couple of notes. "Do you remember if Misty said anything that might indicate where she might be? Who she might be with?"

Joyce twisted the wad of tissue in her hands. "We … had an argument about some worthless boy she met."

"Tell me more about the boy. You get his name?" he coaxed.

"Jesse, uh, Lovegrove. White trash artist type. I warned her! She didn't listen and look at what happened."

Hill felt the onset of a migraine as he forced his expression to stay neutral. *Christ, is this my mother?* He inwardly grimaced as he continued his questioning, "Why is that so strange?"

"All she needed was her momma! How was he going to support her? He's only in school on pity money," she fumed. "My Misty was a nightingale! He's not even low enough to be a crow. He's a vulture eyeing a wounded bird." Her face twisted into a fierce scowl.

Hill noted the trappings of wealth that Mrs. Nocturne covered herself with—from the impressive size of her diamonds to her immaculately tailored pink Louis Vuitton dress. He shifted uncomfortably. He felt bad for Lovegrove, who might not have had anything to do with his girlfriend's disappearance. "When did you talk to her last?"

Joyce sniffed, dabbing her eyes with a fragment of tissue as her voice mellowed to a more conversational tone, "Yesterday."

"What college did you say they went to?" Hill patiently asked. *That's strange, why is she talking in past tense?*

"Miski U," Joyce replied with a huff. "Her idea, not mine."

—

Ancient brownstones leered down at Hill as he climbed out of his unmarked black Crown Victoria. Gray clouds hung heavily above barren white birch trees bordering what would be lovely gardens when spring showed up. He pulled his jacket closer as he hurried down a red stone path to the arts building.

Abstract twists of wood and patinaed metal reached skyward in the center of the large foyer. Colorful canvases edged the room with small paper placards under them. He checked his watch and nodded, knowing he had a few minutes to admire the student gallery. The sculpture centerpiece drew his attention.

The patina was a mix of green and black, which reminded Hill of a raven with its wings covered in moss. "Are you a patron of the arts, Detective?" mused a husky, feminine voice from behind him.

Hill turned to face the older woman with a polite smile, "Does the badge mean I can't appreciate art, Professor Lynn?"

"Please call me Edith. I thought you might've been getting to know your subjects better," she replied with a dismissive shrug. Edith's tone was polite, though she folded her arms across her chest. "Since Jesse and Misty are both missing."

I haven't earned her trust yet, he noted.

"Then please call me Ethan." His eyes turned towards the placard in the middle of the sculpture. Hill squinted but could only make out that the title was "Mare." "Lovegrove made this?"

"Miss Nocturne and Mr. Lovegrove did. Named 'Mare' for 'Nightmare.'"

He let out a low whistle. "I didn't realize she was a sculptor. With how her mother was talking, I thought she was a singer."

"Misty was, but she said something about finding a new muse. Most of these paintings are hers." Edith gestured towards one of the frames on the wall.

Ethan approached the painting and stopped. He opened his mouth to speak though no sound escaped. *Red! So much red!* Within the painting was the familiar sliver of silver over a glittering of black and red. His heart leapt into his throat as the visceral memory of the stench filled his mouth. "When … when did she paint this?"

"Three months ago. Why do you ask?"

—

Ethan sat on his living room floor, surrounded by photos of Misty's paintings and her apartment. He furrowed his brow in concentration. The search of Lovegrove's apartment revealed nothing new, and he had no leads. Two college students were missing and the only person who had an issue with either of them was Joyce Nocturne. He frowned, clicking his pen absent-mindedly as he mulled it over.

His eyes returned to the painting of the living room and

compared it with the photo. It was so close. *Did someone stage the crime scene after her paintings? Would her mother do that out of spite for disobedience?* He noticed that one painting stood out from the rest. He squinted and lifted the picture to get a better look. "Suicide," read the caption beneath the painting of a bloody handprint on a fogged glass shower stall. *The implication is clear. What does it mean? It feels like it's happening again. Like when mom… I need to take my pills and clear my head.* He set the photo back on the floor and rubbed his eyes. *Visions of the future where you can only foresee your own death? I can't build a case on that.*

The way Joyce talked about Lovegrove. It was hostile. Against her wishes, her disabled child was dating him. Misty had changed her major. They had an argument. Joyce started talking like she knew Misty was dead, even though I implied that the girl might still be alive. The lines around his mouth deepened into a frown. *She knows something. It feels like she had something to do with this.* He sighed and looked up at the clock. "It's after midnight. I'll talk to her again tomorrow," he said out loud as he rose. He carefully navigated through the ring of photos and went to bed with his thoughts swimming.

—

"Ethan," a voice whispered.

Hill snuggled deeper into his blanket, his breathing even in the darkness of the bedroom.

"Etha … Wake up," a distinct male voice insisted in his ear. Ethan startled awake, narrowing his eyes into the empty space beside his bed. He turned, sitting up to look at the other side to find that he was very much alone. He shivered as he swung his legs over the side of the mattress. His feet pressed against cool hardwood as he reached over to turn on the lamp.

Out of the corner of his eye he saw something flutter past his open bedroom door. He grabbed his gun from his nightstand. Straining to listen, he heard nothing but the low rattle of his heater.

Quietly, he crept toward the door, peering around the corner before continuing down the hallway. His uncertainty cast the familiar shadows into hostile shapes. *Where are they?* Sweat beaded along his brow as his body tensed with anticipation. His gun was loaded and ready. The rattle faded to soft feminine sobs. He stopped and craned his head at the noise. *It's coming from the kitchen.*

A lone beam of moonlight spilled through a crack in the curtain and illuminated a small figure in the middle of the linoleum floor. Piteous sobs racked her frail body. A girl with soft, honey-blonde tresses and wearing a thin white dress sat with her back to Ethan.

Is that a ghost? Am I dreaming? My meds are supposed to stop this from happening.

"Momma. Momma, why?" the girl sobbed.

A figure cloaked in darkness responded in a harsh whisper, "He's not good for you. It's better this way." Ethan could tell it was an older woman as he hid behind a wall, trying to remain unseen. *Joyce?*

"Jesse… is… you're wrong, Momma," the girl insisted as she looked up from her hands. "I'm not your doll anymore."

Ethan couldn't see "Momma," but he could feel her frown in the heavy silence in the seconds that followed.

"I've done nothing but make your dreams come true. It's time to wake up and come home, Baby." Momma sounded closer.

The hair on the back of his neck stood on end as he felt her breath against his neck. *This is real.*

"Games are over." A hand clamped down on Ethan's shoulder as he spun to face two piercing orbs of light in a void of a face. "Did you think I wouldn't notice you prying, boy? Trying to take my baby from me. Even in death, she's *mine.*"

Ethan's fear froze on his tongue as the light dragged him deep into the abyss until he was drowning in despair. All the colors bled into nothingness.

—

The whir of camera flashes interwove with the distressed murmurs of the crowd. Maeve stood in the doorway of the bathroom with tears in her eyes. *I can't believe it. Suicide? Why, Ethan?* A bloody handprint dripped down on the fogged glass of a small shower door. The body of Detective Hill was slumped against the back of the stall with blood trailing from his wrists.

Have a Cigar

by Fraser Massey

I taste blood as he hits me a good one in the mouth. All I know is I gotta stay on my feet. Things'll go bad for me if I don't.

He hits me again. And the ringing in my head drowns out the bloodthirsty cries of those who've been urging him to give me the beating of my life.

There's every chance they'll get their wish.

This guy's at least eight inches taller than me and maybe twelve pounds heavier. Last time I saw anyone his size, it was in a children's storybook and he was living on top of a beanstalk.

I reach up and clasp my hands behind his neck to keep myself vertical. Then I push down, making him take all my weight. Just-Call-Me-Harry taught me that little trick.

The guy's carrying on, hitting me as best he can in the ribs. But he don't have enough room now to get any power into his punches. I've earned myself the few seconds I need to recover. Then I stand on his feet to put him off balance and stick a thumb in his eye. When he jerks his head back from that, I thump his right temple with my right hand.

There's a stunned silence before I hear Just-Call-Me-Harry yelling, "Finish him off, boy. You always gotta finish 'em off."

Next thing I know the referee's lifting my arm in the air. Just-Call-Me-Harry's dancing round the ring and I'm being declared Heavyweight Champion of Great Britain.

Back in the dressing room, Harry's fussing around. There's a medic looming over me, dealing with my split lip and a cut above my eye.

"I'm proud of you, boy," Harry tells me. "Always said I'd make you champ if you did what I told you and built yourself a ruthless streak. Now that you've learned to finish them off when you're on top, there'll be no stopping you."

Harry's taught me a lot. Not just the finishing them off thing. Or the making the opponent take you weight on his neck bit. That standing on their feet to put them off balance and the sticking a thumb in the eye maneuver? They'd come from him too. As well as some handy hints on more conventional boxing skills.

"Here, boy, I got you a present to celebrate."

With that he opens the back door to the dressing room and in skips this blonde twenty-something in a kid's size version of a Spurs football shirt. She's wearing it as a minidress, even though it's too small for her.

Taking no notice of the doc, who's still dealing with my face, she kneels between my knees and pulls down my shorts.

She looks puzzled when she sees the protective cup I'm wearing underneath, but she soon pushes that aside and takes me deep in her mouth.

She stops just as I'm getting to the good bit and I hear Just-Call-Me-Harry yelling from the other side of the room, "Finish him off, girl. You always gotta finish 'em off."

One of the other things Harry taught me was that to deliver maximum power you've got to breathe out as you punch. It seems it works just as well when you're shooting your load.

When she's done, the girl leaves by the same door she came in through, with Harry helping himself to a little 'thank you' pat on her butt as she goes.

"Pull up your shorts, boy," he tells me. "We've got other people who want to congratulate you."

—

The party in my dressing room's a blur. Somebody fetches my mum. She won't watch me fight, but she likes to come afterwards to make sure I'm not hurt. There are reporters, well-wishers, friends and lots of hangers-on from Harry's stable of others on his books.

Most of them I figure are invited guests. But every now and then I hear my manager introducing himself to a new arrival with his time-honored greeting, "Just call me Harry."

I spot a couple of footballers, a soap star, one or two models, some dancers (well, strippers really) and a lot of musicians.

The bulk of Harry's clients are musicians. He manages my brother Zach's band, the Dunning Kruger Effect. Has done for quite a while, though even now he'll occasionally say to them, "Remind me again, which one's Dunning?" Or, "Which one's Kruger?"

If you're there when he does that, you'll see Zach and the boys exchanging knowing looks behind his back.

It's because of the band I first met Harry. I went backstage to see Zach after a gig and this middle-aged figure in a tweed suit put out a hand, saying, "Just call me Harry."

A couple of weeks later he asked me if I needed a manager. I didn't know what experience Harry had in the boxing world, but I knew from Zach he was a hustler and I figured that's probably what I needed most then.

—

Harry loves being a manager. Although he's happy to diversify, it's the rock manager stuff that's closest to his heart. He styles himself after what he calls "the greats": Brian Epstein, Peter Grant. People I'd never heard of when he first mentioned them.

Get him in the right mood and he'll tell you story after story of managers from way before my time. One of his favorites is about a member of some '60s band or other. A bass player, if I remember right. The muso's querying his royalty payments, so the manager invites him out for a day on his yacht. When they're on the open sea, the bass player gets turfed over the side and then the manager starts lobbing chunks of raw steak at him and only hauls him back on board when the first fin of a circling shark appears.

Most times he tells that one, Harry laughs for ten minutes solid.

—

Mum's sticking to the shadows in the corner of the dressing room. It's her way of avoiding Harry.

She's never liked him. Told me and Zach we should steer clear of him from the get-go. Reckons he pretends to know more about what he's doing than he really does. "That one's got beady eyes," she says.

He has too. There's something about the way they flicker from side to side that makes my flesh creep.

If Zach and me had only listened to her, things might not have turned out the way they did.

"You don't normally stay this long," I say, as I go over and join her.

"I thought I'd wait 'til your brother turns up."

I must admit I'm disappointed that Zach's not here already. I wanted him to receive his share of the praise. I'd have never got this far without him. Dad left when I was fifteen and Zach fourteen. Money was tight. We had a family meeting. Mum couldn't afford both my boxing training and Zach's piano lessons. So Zach insisted the money went on me because he reckoned I was better at boxing than he'd ever be on the piano. I was so proud when he achieved his dream and the band started to make it, even though he thought his untutored playing was holding the rest of them back.

But an hour after the fight finished, there's still no sign of him.

"He says he's bringing someone for us to meet," Mum says. "I bet it's a woman."

"If there's a new one in tow, it's the first I've heard of it."

As if on cue, there's a commotion at the door and there at last is my missing brother. "Sorry I'm late,'" he calls out, beating a path towards us. "I lost this one earlier in the crowds and it's taken 'til now to track her down. Don't know what she's been doing. Everybody say 'Hi' to Jodie."

"Hi Jodie," Mum and I chorus.

"I told her it's time she met the family. This is not just a big night for you, bro'. Ten minutes ago, Jodie did me the honor of agreeing to be my wife."

"C-c-congratulations," I manage to get out. I'm in shock and not just 'cause Zach's gone all fancy with the way he's talking. Nobody else says anything. So to fill the silence I ask the blonde wearing the too-small Spurs shirt, gazing lovingly at my brother, "How did you two meet?"

She tears her attention off Zach for a moment to stare me down. "Harry introduced us."

Fast forward two years. My career's stalled since the night I became British champion. I'm still winning, but I'm not getting the big fights I need. And no, in case you were wondering, Jodie's never again popped into the dressing room afterwards offering her own unique way of helping me celebrate.

She and Zach had a big white wedding last year. I got to be best man. They still seem blissfully in love with each other.

Despite what I do for a living I'm not much of a one for confrontation. So I've never said a word to her about how we met.

This whole unwillingness to face up to difficult situations has also resulted in me not dealing with Just-Call-Me-Harry.

Until today.

It's a warm summer's evening. Harry lives in a penthouse in a glass tower that stretches up into the London sky above Spitalfields.

I take a gentle stroll there from Liverpool Street station, enjoying the sunshine and running over in my head what I'm going to say.

The doorman greets me as I arrive in Harry's building. "Go on up, sir. You're expected."

When the lift pings to announce its arrival on the twenty-first floor, Harry's standing in the doorway to his flat waiting to greet me.

"Come on in, boy. You know you're always welcome."

Just-Call-Me-Harry has a glass in his hand. Gin and tonic, I imagine. "Get you something?" He gestures for me to sit down as he walks towards his bar. "Your usual?"

I could do with something stronger to get me through what I'm about to do, but I nod. He returns with a cocktail glass containing the mixture familiar to every boxer in training. Tonic water, with three drops of angostura bitters, topped with ice cubes and a wedge of lime.

Harry removes a cigar from his humidor. "I guess you won't join me in one of these," he says.

He strolls outside to smoke on the terrace. I take a sip of my drink and follow. It's been a while since I've been here. Last time was before he'd had the swimming pool put in.

"Something here that'll interest you, boy."

He walks towards the deep end of the pool and points. I look at the bottom, but can't work out at first what's embedded in the floor of the pool.

I peer more closely at it.

It's my Olympic silver medal. I'd wondered what had

happened to that. Harry had said he'd put it somewhere safe for me.

"When I look at it, I always remember how far we've come together, boy." He sucks in a lungful of smoke.

I seize the moment.

"We've come as far we can…" I go through my well-rehearsed speech about how I want a shot at the world title and for that I'm going to need management with bigger and better international contacts than Harry could ever offer.

He sits patiently and hears me out. Then he sighs and goes all business-like on me. "Don't forget we've got a contract, boy."

I've got my response ready for this. "There'll be lawyers somewhere who can get me out of that."

He settles down in a chair poolside and urges me to do the same. I can tell he's going into storytelling mode.

"When Elvis Presley got uppity about making all those junk movies that his manager Colonel Tom Parker signed him up for, do you know what the Colonel did?"

I guess he's going to tell me anyway, so I keep quiet.

"The Colonel goes to his safe and gets out this old document he keeps in it. It's a copy of Elvis's dad's prison record. The Colonel threatens to release that to the press if Elvis doesn't do as he's told. And Elvis thinks about the shame on his family and how his beloved mama won't like it and he caves in."

One more from Just-Call-Me-Harry's never-ending stock of tales of old-school management techniques.

It must be all those blows to the head I've had in the ring that makes me so slow on the uptake I can't see what's coming next.

Harry's eyes dart around, without settling on anything. Like they do when he's about to get devious.

"Get you another drink, boy?"

I shake my head and he pops inside with his own empty glass. When he returns with a fresh G&T, he's got something else in his other hand. There's our contract and a package sealed in bubble-wrap.

He undoes it and shows me an antique-looking smartphone. He delves into his pocket and puts a battery in the thing.

When it's working, he scrolls through before finding what he's looking for.

Then he hands it over. It's a film of me on the night I became British champion. My shorts are around my ankles and there's a figure in a Spurs shirt, arse in the air kneeling between my legs while her blonde head bobs up and down on my groin.

Mostly you can only hear me groaning. But there's a moment when she pauses, which is filled with Harry's distinctive voice shouting encouragement. "Finish him off, girl. You always gotta finish 'em off."

When she stands up, she wipes her mouth on the back of her hand and then she looks straight at the camera phone. Nobody could fail to recognize her as Zach's Jodie.

My mind's reeling. Harry smiles smugly. "She was a good girl, Jodie. Had a thing back then for wanting to get up close and personal with famous people. She'd help make sure lots of my clients really enjoyed triumphant moments in their careers. That's why I introduced her to your brother on the night he and the band signed their record deal. Didn't expect him to want to make an honest woman of her, as we used to say back in the day."

He takes the camera from me and removes the battery. He puts bubble-wrap back round the phone and taps the piece of paper. "You and me have got a contract, boy," he says.

Harry puts his drink down and goes back inside. I watch through his French windows as he returns the phone and the contract to his safe.

He comes back and picks up his drink again, as he sits down. "It would be a moment's work to upload that bit of footage and send it to your brother and maybe the rest of his little band too. Dunning and Kruger and whatever the other one's called."

"You know none of them are really called Dunning or Kruger, don't you?" I ask, for want of something better to say while I work out my next move. "The Dunning Kruger Effect. It's a thing, right? They named themselves after it."

Harry puts his cigar back in his mouth and looks disappointed it's gone out.

I watch while he deals with that and I think about what he's just said.

"It would be a moment's work to upload that bit of footage."

He hasn't already done it.

So far then, that's the only copy.

Harry's still busy lighting-up the cigar again, so it's a bit of shock when he finds himself sprawled on the floor of his sun-deck, rubbing the side of his head where I just punched him.

I stand over him. "What's the combination of the safe, Harry?"

He's keeping schtum. I could beat it out of him. But I get the urge to be more creative. He deserves that much at least. I think about dumping him in his swimming pool, but for that to work properly I'd need a live shark and several lumps of raw steak.

And then I remember another of Harry's favorite old-time management technique yarns.

I haul him up by his shirt front, and drag him to the low wall that surrounds the penthouse sun-deck. I lift him up and dangle him over the side, hanging on to his ankles. As the contents of his pockets fall past his ears and land twenty floors below, I hear him whimpering.

If I remember right that was a move some old beat group manager carried out when a rival impresario tried to poach one of his bands. I should really remember which one, what with the number of times I've heard Harry tell the story.

Harry's shaking when I bring him back up. He can barely make it to the safe to hand over the phone and the contract.

As I'm leaving, I hear him shout, "I taught you everything you know, you ungrateful bastard. You'll regret this. I'll wash my hands of your whole family. I'll tell the band their American label wants to drop them unless they find a better keyboard player. They won't know if it's true or not."

I go back and deliver a left-hook that sends him sprawling again, remembering to breathe out as it connects.

I pick him up off the floor, drag him out to the terrace and dangle him back over the side.

"You know what, Harry? The biggest lesson I learned from you was to be ruthless and always finish people off when I'm on top."

Then I let go of his ankles.

FEARLESS

BY LINDA SLATER

While standing at the bathroom mirror in Room 102 of the Inn north of Haddington Hill, England, Matt O'Leary used a comb to brush away the clumps of hair from his brow. The digital clock behind him glared 8:30 am. He was anxious to get behind the wheel. He wondered if this day was truly to be *the* day.

I can still drive a lorry. You chided me, Trina McCord.

He continued to talk to his wife of ten years as though she was there, sitting on the bed, against the light of her cell phone, impatiently waiting. He sighed.

I always take longer than you. That has not changed. Strutting up to me with your incandescent hair, stroking my cheek, wiggling that nose full of freckles on my neck, to gain my attention…

He missed her calling him a poser. With a pronounced Irish brogue, she would remind him. "You're a bee on a hot brick, dashing around. Stop being so vain. Nobody cares, Matt."

I don't miss your bluntness. But the lad we met from Cork warned me you were a fiery ginger. I can spot you in the dark…

A blue tinge flowed up to his face from his phone. It was a steamy glow, ready to engulf his chin and pull it down into the abyss under the screen. Beads of his sweat sizzled on the surface. With one hand, Matt pulled the charger out of the wall.

Bloody Hell. Cheap phone. I'll throw it in a tip in London.

He checked for messages. None. He wanted to believe the effort to find Matthew O' Leary had ceased. Now, if folks were getting on the horn, they were talking to Heath Barker, just in case.

—

He clutched his chest. Heart palpitations were a daily occurrence ever since Catriona was struck down by a car in London two months prior. He remembered peering over the bonnet of their car to see her head, with few red filament streaks of hair exposed from an unraveled scarf. Her contorted, petite frame looked as though someone had shoved her right leg into her mouth. Her dead black eyes faced sideways, his way.

But when I tried to look away, your pupils widened. You wished to go through the length and the breadth of "the nefarious plan"! I wasn't ready. We promised each other we would never walk alone. But what good was your instruction to kill if we could not be together now?

He pinched his eyes closed and forced himself to concentrate. There was a lorry sitting in the parking lot. The keys, covered in blood, were on the dresser.

Got me in a bit of a bother. Don't remember parking it. The driver—he had a gammy leg…

Matt worried a tad. He had not driven a lorry since 1973, when he was a trucker in America.

April of that year was a humdinger.

—

Matt remembered the day he received the handle from the delivery service where he worked. His teeth clenched so hard he broke a tooth as the supervisor told him the news. They were cutting back his hours due to the oil embargo. He only just delivered cow carcasses to a processing facility off Highway 421 in Frankfort,

Kentucky. After a pickup outside Nashville, Tennessee, he would return to Georgia.

The chance at a new life seemed unreachable. He'd fled to America from Canada and had been driving at his current job for only six months.

To stay calm, he got on the CB radio and sang a song. Matt hogged a frequency. "Breaker. Breaker. Psychedelic Moon here to sing 'Fearless' by Pink Floyd on this overcast morning. Cheers!"

The song had a slow chugging tempo, mimicked the heavy-duty diesel engine's hydraulics, distorting vibrations, and a dreamy sequence that imagined the driver floating. His surprisingly smooth cockney accent liberated the power underneath the 18 wheeler's hood. The song oozed hope and energy. In the end, Matt whispered into the microphone, "You will never walk alone. From your die-hard Liverpool football team fan. Peace out!"

Truthfully, he did not give a shite. The newly enforced 55 mph speed limit only irritated him.

Fuel conservation's not in the plan. I'm climbing. After a few Quaaludes, I will find the clouds.

He reached Tennessee in half the time required and did not expect to meet the love of his life there. As he pulled up to the loading bay, he savored a glimpse of her. Catriona carried a stack of envelopes. Matt wondered if she were an employee.

The neon bandana around her face highlighted her doe eyes with luscious eyelashes. Catriona sang an unusual tune; her euphoric voice, supercharged by the wind, grabbed Matt's attention. He followed her inside.

Matt walked through a large metal unmarked door into a room no larger than the cab of his truck. The walls shook violently from the weight of the cows body-slamming each other. They were corralled inside the garages near to him, and as he walked, they whined from the sound of stun guns firing bolts between their eyes.

Like sonic booms, the ruckus. The sobs. My best buddy told me that he flew sorties in the RAF in the 1950s, dropping bombs on Oman's insurgents in the Dhofar Rebellion. He had bad dreams. One day with fog as dense as trifle pudding topping, the heat intense as a poker in a fire pit, we enjoyed tea on his porch. The fan above us crashed down on the table and slashed Buddy's neck. His body twitched, and a bloody fountain came from his lips. I made it easier for him. He no longer suffered. It was an easy kill. He thanked me later. I no longer longed to join the forces.

Catriona hummed over the cows' muffled cries as he followed her through a series of doors. He passed severed limbs in an overflowing metal cart left abandoned in a corner. Flies circled above the mess and charged at Matt. The swarm nipped at his cheeks and rammed into his mouth. With an exaggerated spit, he unloaded insects into a makeshift sink nearby and used his arm to mask himself. Spatters of blood caked the ceiling. Remnants of body parts left behind were reduced to fine particles and powdered his boots by the meat grinders. Drawn to the prickly blades, he lovingly recalled Buddy again when he slipped in blood puddles. Matt almost lost his footing

The musings stopped. Down a hall, Catriona congregated with employees short of the dismembering wing. Snapping and tearing behind the wall to the right startled her when she spoke. In a steady voice, she said, "The funds are not there." She clenched her hands together, took a deep breath, and continued. "My internship here will terminate."

Terminate. Such a perplexing word. So final.

Matt listened inquisitively. "My Mum thought it was unusual that I'd carry out my internship studies here. I am quite chuffed. You all have been brilliant." Catriona smiled.

Matt adjusted his posture. He watched Catriona lean up against a desk with quivering legs. As he walked up behind her, the smell of flesh in his nostrils turned to sweet perfume, sending mixed messages to his senses. He stared as she turned around, tilted her head ever so slightly, and turned out her trembling hand to him.

A sign of vulnerability, perhaps?

He offered her a gentle handshake.

Yes. She was hauntingly beautiful, even inside this slaughterhouse.

"We will miss you," the lead supervisor said.

Matt watched her wave her hand in front of him so he would walk first. "After you," she insisted.

They exited quietly and faced each other. Catriona ripped the bandana off her face. Matt looked up to the shadows hovering over them from the birds perched on the electrical lines. She began humming again.

Not at all bemused, he joined her. Their meshed voices followed the music note placement of the crows on the wires. They ended the acapella at the last electric pole in a high octave. Straining, Matt, and Catriona both laughed.

"Well done," said Matt.

"Now that's calling the cows home," Catriona replied, in the literal sense.

"Yes. But my Irish grandmother once told me that means that you are ready to tackle anything."

She blushed. "I have heard that. Not sure where. In a Limerick, possibly?" She paused, looking into his eyes. "Where are you from?"

"Ulster, but I lived in London," Matt responded proudly. "And you?"

"County Cork. Never been to England. Our musings, it's as though you could read my mind." She hesitated, then fluttered her eyes at him.

"I thought everyone who sings, does this." He winked at her. "Their eyes are watching us."

Hungry, they ate their own lunches inside the semi-truck cab.

Finally, Matt held her in his arms and said, "Your voice is extraordinary."

"That's the nicest thing anyone has ever said to me. Now give over…" Catriona replied sheepishly and tossed her head down on the pillow next to him. They fell asleep, and their meshed bodies released at the break of dawn.

That morning, Matt loaded up his final cargo and put Catriona's light suitcase into the semi-truck.

He went inside to call the dispatch and returned spewing at the tone used by his supervisor to explain the reason for his official termination.

The word of the day. Terminate … the word of my life.

On the trip to return the semi-truck, they listened to veiled lingo on his CB radio and code-talk from truckers who secretly planned invasive convoys in protest. Matt's truck traveled down the road with others who planned opportune moments. Catriona looked interested when the semi behind him urged him on by flashing its lights.

"Oh – let's do this!" Catriona reached for Matt's hand across the seat.

"Are you sure, Trina? We have no other means of transportation. Are we not thinking clearly?"

"On the contrary, Love. Come on; let's leg it. Do it for me."

He parked the semi-truck horizontally on a highway with three others and tossed the keys. Traffic surged, and there was a backup to Atlanta for miles.

Matt stacked three ball caps onto Catriona's head at once. They walked away hand in hand, dragging their belongings.

"Give me your knife," she insisted.

"I …I don't have a blade."

"Oh, yes, you do."

He pulled it out of his sock, then paused. Matt stared at the reflection of gold and yellow with hints of red speckles warming the steel. From the sunset. From blood.

"Watch me." Matt watched Catriona cut her bell-bottomed jeans off her body, up to her thighs with hardly any effort.

No slashes to skin … oh Trina … short shorts …

Catriona walked haphazardly in her wedge heels on the rocky shoulder and stuck her thumb out at a T-junction up the road. They hitchhiked for miles until they were able to change course.

Matt pulled the brim down on his Paddy hat as they saw the first sign to Nashville. He pulled out a joint. Tripping on reefer, they continued onward, and when they tired, they stopped at a motel. The next morning another trucker going their way obliged.

Dropped at a truck stop near a honkey-tonk bar, they squatted. They sang hits from billboard charts for the regulars at the counter for tips only, using the bar's piano for the week. Matt tended bar if needed, and Trina washed dishes in the back kitchen.

By the time he could be apprehended, they were on a plane back to their homeland. The music clung to their souls. Matt and Catriona married at her parents' home in East Cork and lived an uneventful life in London until recent events brought him to the Inn.

—

Although Matt was still in England, he kept a low profile. Disguising himself in baggy denim and flannel, he grew a long beard to hide his cleft chin. He swooped his long, curly hair over his shoulders.

His obsession with laundry mats nearest to truck stops had ceased. Washing pieces of bone fragments rolled up with his clothes became routine. He discarded what he could retrieve into wastebaskets afterward then poured bleach into the tubs before leaving the premises.

All I wanted was to love you forever, Trina. I am ready. I regret what I have done. But it was all for you. Don't say the hill's too steep to climb.

It was their car that hit and killed Catriona. It was his keys stolen.

Left the car home that day, Trina. Walked to the pub and had a shandy. Thought the bartender would vouch for me, remembering my first drink request. I ask…who flippin' drinks scorpion vodka here? Got it? Buy one for yourself too. You are my everything, Trina. You are my electric charge.

Matt's breath warmed.

The heat of the room is making me a bee on a hot brick. There. I said it. You chuffed now?

He flipped a fag between his fingers, leaning low to flick on the lighter. Pursing his lips on the lighted cigarette, drawing it in like he was gulping a double shot of whiskey.

Grabbing a bottle of Crown, he stepped outside and closed the balcony. A fly landed on top of his free hand and cocked its head at Matt, ready to meet its demise. He gasped at its wonderment.

Aye, I can almost see the fear in its tiny eyes. They are looking for me too. I could be squashed in an instant.

He felt one with the lowly insect, exposed. But with an uncontrolled impulse, he slapped it away. The bottle of whiskey slipped from his hand. One of its wings snapped. In a rocking motion, he watched it blend with the glass shards. During its plummet, tiny arms stretched out to hug the crown jewels depicted on the sticker. Spilled whiskey stung the fly's feet when it landed in a puddle. Matt felt the brutality. His throat burned.

We are both louses.

He went back inside to gather his belongings, ready to go.

Wait ... My cap. Trina? It was right here near my bag.

She always hid his hats. It was her way of delaying the inevitable. She didn't like Matt to be gone from their home much, even to work.

Trina, I am attending your funeral. Today is the day. Stop messing around. I will be there soon.

He was in no shape to drive but did anyway, knowing he could maneuver the lorry better than most. He smiled. Truckers in America laughed when he'd call a truck a lorry.

Lorry ... Laurie ... I knew where you moved after Trina broke the relationship off with you. Just following instructions. SHE demanded it. Your bloody accounting firm in jeopardy. You're whacked. Couldn't have your reputation ruined, huh? What about mine?

The swooshing noise in his left ear increased—tinnitus in the form of numerous washing machines

Tossing, turning, tumbling.

Matt jumped on the rocker panels, slammed the door, started the lorry, and headed towards London.

Oh. But it feels good to be back in the cab.

A few minutes down the road, he rerouted from the M40 to a back-road detour—he changed gears, preparing the lorry for the climb up Chilton Hills.

It is not too steep…I can do this…I am climbing…I am fearless.

A pair of wedged heels appeared bundled on the road in front of him, just as the lorry gained traction. He drove over them. One skipped over the pavement and landed in a ditch past the barrier. He stretched his neck out the window.

You skipped stones in those. I am only 30 minutes away.

In an instant, a large brick crashed through the windshield, tossed from an over-bridge and hit him square in the forehead. Crimson blood drained from his face into his mouth. He squinted to adjust his vision. In the corner of his eye, he thought he saw her.

Damn, that hurt. Lovelylegs. Yes. I've got the knife. I am climbing.

He looked over his shoulder to his weapon in the sleeping area of the cab.

Suddenly he could hear the force of Catriona's voice calling his name. Her once steady cadence gently rose and fell with his, entwined.

Was now drowning in the blood of her lover … of the cows … of the dead crows on the wire.

Lost in her voice, the truck barreled down a hill well above the speed limit. Matt's eyes swelled with tears from pain and regret. His right hand clenched the steering wheel as he braked hard to avoid a collision with a hearse. He swerved and jammed the controls into neutral.

Fly-infested Nibley Fingers—Matt's favorite chocolate—flopped on the dashboard in a pile. He tried to grab them as he headed straight for an embankment, missing a tree. The blade flew to the front, slashed his ankle, the same time the remnants of the windshield glass grounded into his forehead. The lorry slammed to its side.

Matt's head was violently forced forward into the dashboard. One by one, each stick of chocolate slid down out of the cab, out of sight. He pinched a single wing sticking out of a single piece of larvae and felt the coolness of the tiny maggots encrust beads of his lover's phlegm.

I am a louse. I am worse than a fly. I forgive you, Trina, for having an affair with Laurie. But you bribed me with candy? After everything we went through? It's quite a feeble way to gain my love back.

The sounds of sirens entered the area quickly. The police arrested Matt. He was defeated, but complied.

And now you leave without me…

The hearse on the highway arrived at the cemetery without a body.

—

Weeks later, after sentencing, Matt left the courthouse in shackles, to be transported to a holding facility. He could feel the amplified depth of anger from the crowd at the bottom of the stairs.

First, Laurie's laugh echoed.

Stop Cackling!

Buddy's voice roared behind hers, escalating, "No! No! No!" in an angry tone.

You wanted me to do it…

Then, the stolen lorry driver's intense clapping perforated his eardrums.

Oh, drooling one, with the crackling crepitus. Your wheelchair chugged too.

Finally, Catriona's voice rose above them all.

Hum with me, my Trina. Birds are here…superimposed in my mind.

He began humming after studying them in full view, hanging on the electrical wires across the street.

The magistrate had found him guilty of murder. Blood under his fingernails matched the victims.

But I am fearless. I am okay. I want to climb. Climb to you, Trina.

When the current entered his ears, he hadn't time to process it. The powerful flash blinded so strongly it hurled everyone to the ground. With the acrid smoke on his tongue, Matt could not hear his own scream. And for a moment, the air hummed without accompaniment.

Matt's love for Catriona was incandescent, much like the color of her hair. It shined in filaments and its fragments in the grass of the aftermath from the lightning bolt.

Matt fell to the ground, face down, into a steamy hole.

Only in the afterlife could Matt hear Catriona's hum along with his.

I looked down to join you in song … in death, not above the tree line … but far, far, below.

HEY YOU

BY PHIL THOMAS

The crush of seagulls tweaked Warren's senses as he absorbed the audible silk that poured from his fresh 1980 Panasonic boom box. The words were familiar, yet only heard a few times by him. He rose from the bench and splayed his fingers across the riveted wooden railing that rested at the edge of the pier. The fish were not biting for him, nor his friend, Jacob, but after eight Budweisers that afternoon, he hardly noticed or cared. The foamy July waters struck the unstable bulkheads as he listened to the song.

He finished the rest of his beer. A buzz warmed his insides just as the sun baked his bronze skin. And as he looked out across the vast ocean, he thought of Luna. It had already been three months, and he'd stopped fearing the worst and accepted the truth. She was gone, lost, probably forever.

Jacob was dozing on the nearby bench, dripping beer down his chest and losing grip on his fishing rod, when a sharp jolt startled his eyes open. "I think I have something!" he said in a daze, tossing his bottle aside. Standing to rush to the pier's edge, he spun the reel, the thin line bowing the rod downward.

Warren watched from the sidelines, raising his beer but doing nothing to help. As the fishing line buckled, a shadowy object struck the base of the pier, causing enough of a disturbance to throw both men off-balance.

The object systematically thumped against the base, causing a rhythmic drumbeat that remained in-time with the song's percussion. It soon rose to the surface, and the young men visored their eyes to gain an unobstructed view. Warren mirrored Jacob's expression, but he felt a sinking feeling inside, like the world had just slipped out from under his feet. By the time Warren and Jacob made their way off the pier, the object washed onto a beach. A spool of copper wiring wound tightly through the opening where a padlock should've been. Seaweed draped the chest. Its hinges were lime-rusted, and moss spotted its wooden encasement.

 Jacob grazed his hand over the slimy surface and glanced at Warren. "I wonder what's in it," he said, picking at the wire. "At least it isn't locked."

"We should push it back," Warren replied. "What if we aren't meant to see what's inside?" The tide rushed past his bare feet, and his vision pinpricked as he watched Jacob ignore his suggestion and unwind the copper coil, each layer closer to the chest's contents. The familiar initials, C.S., were carved into the side of the softened wood. He recognized the trunk and knew who it belonged to. It should have never been seen again, but it was here, and Warren recalled the last thing *she* said to him: *I'm coming home.* It couldn't be a coincidence.

Jacob discarded the wire and stood behind the chest. "You ready?" He shifted his weight and pried the lid. The interior was empty, save for an RC Cola bottle that housed a scrap of torn notepaper. "Well, I guess neither of us will be retiring any time soon." He uncapped the bottle and recovered the paper from its container. A diamond ring, wrapped inside, slid out and fell to the sand. But Warren hardly noticed. He could only focus on the message scribbled in red across the notepaper: *I'm coming home.*

—

It was past 8:30 when Jacob left the police station. Typically, there'd be no reason to report an RC Cola bottle in a washed-up trunk, but this was a unique circumstance. Upon initial retrieval of the diamond ring, he noticed a peculiarity. Around the outer edges were the engraved words: *Luna and Charles 9-15-80.*

The date had been his sister's planned September wedding to a person he despised. The ceremony hadn't happened yet, and it probably never would because she'd been missing since the twenty-fifth of April, last seen over three months ago on the beaches of Wildwood New Jersey—the same beaches he had just occupied. The police had never closed the case, but now there was renewed interest. It was too much for even them to ignore.

During those first weeks, Jacob and his family had become frantic, searching usual hangout spots and questioning the people last seen with her. That included Charles, who'd been with her that morning. There had been plans to take one of Charlie's power cruiser boats out—yes, he owned more than one—and Warren was to accompany them for an afternoon of drinking and, well, more drinking on the open water, but she supposedly never made it that far. Her best friend and Warren's girlfriend, Sandy Cormac, a hostess at the Hitching Post, went on record that she seated Luna for lunch that afternoon and paid her tab with cash. And apparently, whatever Sandy Cormac says is gospel to the locals.

Jacob never had much reason to doubt anyone, but new questions were swirling in his mind as he approached a payphone on the busy boardwalk. He dropped a quarter and dialed a phone number. As the buzzing tone rung through one ear, he listened to the surrounding laughter of children and the distant rumbling of waves with the other. The sound of his brother's voice interrupted his gaze on the nearby rollercoaster—dozens of arms raised to the sky, tempting the fate of secure seatbelts and giving death a middle finger.

"Yeah, Trent?" he said. He then explained the trunk and the engagement ring and everything that had transpired that day practically in one breath. "Don't tell mom and dad yet," he added and hung up.

As his quarter dropped into the pool of change, he watched the sunset far down Fourteenth Avenue. He checked his watch— just after nine—and proceeded down the boardwalk towards Hunt's Pier, past the funnel cake shops and tee-shirt depots.

He hadn't eaten since noon and found himself at Sam's Pizza Palace, resting down on one of the many empty swivel seats at the front counter and ordering two slices of pepperoni pizza and a jumbo-sized Coke. The temperature had dropped significantly, and the numbing winds leaked through the open doorways. Most bystanders wore long pants and sweatshirts in contrast to Jacob's maroon Adidas tank top and sandals.

The first slice washed down quickly, but halfway through his second, Jacob looked to the left of the counter and spotted a face he had particularly avoided since Luna's disappearance. And worse, that face noticed him too and was heading over.

Shit.

"What are you doing here?" Charlie Stockton asked, sitting down on the stool next to him.

"I should ask the same thing. Have you decided to see how the other side of the boardwalk operates?" It was an entirely legitimate question because Jacob's would-be brother-in-law owned Mariner's Landing, a pier on the opposite end of the beach. It would also explain his multiple power cruiser boats, 1980 Ferrari Testarossa, three beach houses spanning Jersey to South Carolina, and the womanizing that nearly derailed his engagement to Luna on more than one occasion. But she had always stuck by him through the countless infidelities, mostly out of denial. Jacob's sister might have turned a blind eye, but he never had, and made it a point to confront Charlie on many occasions.

"I just needed a walk," Charlie continued. "Besides, I'm meeting someone here in a few minutes." Jacob assumed it was a woman but kept his mouth shut. Instead, he reached in his pocket and retrieved Luna's engagement ring. Charlie's smile fell away.

"This washed up on the shore today inside a soda bottle." Jacob paused and took a sip of soda. It was inside a trunk with the initials 'C.S.' carved on the outside."

Charlie cleared his throat. "I've already given my statement to the police. I don't know anything about a trunk or bottle."

"Is this the ring you gave her?"

"It looks like it," Charlie said. "The damn thing cost enough. If the police have any more questions, they can contact my lawyer."

"This is the ring you gave her, Charlie. She showed it off enough. You bribed her to look the other way when you banged some college student who was working the summer at your bar."

"That ring could have come from anywhere," he said. He started to sweat, and his skin looked clammy. "How do I know you didn't have something to do with her disappearance? She never took it off, and somehow you now have it in your pocket."

Jacob didn't respond. They both knew it was bullshit, but he couldn't prove it. Jacob finished eating, stood up and dropped some crumpled money on the counter. "I'll see you around," he said.

"Hey," Charlie said, and Jacob stopped, keeping his back turned. "You can count on it."

—

Warren recognized Jacob, and he waited for him to leave the pizza place. The salt air whipped past Jacob as he stepped outside, heading left towards Hunt's Pier. He vanished into the flock of bystanders, and thankful that their paths hadn't crossed, Warren entered Sam's Pizza Palace a moment later, then approached the counter, sitting on a stool next to Charlie.

"You're late," Charlie said.

"We have bigger problems." The men found a secluded booth in the back and placed their food order. Once it was safe to talk, Warren started first. "She's not dead."

"What are you talking about?"

"What do you think? The trunk that we, correction, you put her body in washed up today. And guess what wasn't in there?"

"Could you keep your voice down?" Charlie insisted. "Yes, I heard, but so what? There's no way—" The waitress approached the table and placed their slices in front of them. She smiled and walked away. "As I was saying, there's no way she could be alive."

Beads of sweat formed on Warren's forehead as he lifted his pizza, his hand shaking, and his complexion flushed. "This is your fault. If you hadn't given her those pills in the first place, none of this would've happened."

Charlie slammed his soda cup on the table but kept his voice calm. "It was an accident. She wasn't having a good time. We took the boat out to party, and I didn't see the harm in slipping her something extra."

"It caused plenty of harm. I have to speak with Sandy before…"

At that moment, another customer passed by on her way to the restroom. She sang the Pink Floyd song that was on the radio earlier, informing him that she was coming home. At the front of the shop, standing before the doorway, Warren noticed the outline of a woman. She was translucent and wore a yellow sundress with a daisy slid into her long golden locks. He blinked, but she remained steadfast as patrons seemingly passed through her as they entered. Spooked by her appearance, Warren left without a word and slipped out the back.

—

Jacob palmed the diamond ring as he parked his 1979 Pontiac

Firebird in front of his brother's two-story beach house. Trent had rented it for the summer and allowed Jacob to come and go as he pleased, mostly on the weekends. Warren had also lived there during the earlier summer months, but his constant drunken behavior had forced Trent to kick him out. Now Warren lived with Sandy two blocks away on Tenth Avenue.

Since Trent rarely allowed visitors, Jacob was surprised to see a dark silhouette on the porch bench. While he made his way up the steps, he blinked to adjust his eyes to the darkness, but the outline remained. It then moved right to make room, and Jacob sat next to it, holding up the ring. "I guess you heard by now," he said. Sandy nodded and sat silent. "Is there anything else you'd like to tell me about that day?" he asked. "I assume that's why you're here."

"I never seated her at the Hitching Post," Sandy explained. "Luna was on the boat, and I was there when they sailed off, but she never got off as Charlie claimed. I watched it disappear into the distance right from the dock. It's the last time I saw her."

Jacob assumed he'd be angrier while listening to Sandy's confession. But he mostly experienced relief that he finally had the truth. According to Warren's firsthand account, she explained that Luna had an adverse reaction from the Quaaludes that Charlie slipped in her beer.

"The guys panicked when they thought she had overdosed," she continued. "But after they placed her body in the trunk, Luna regained consciousness and realized they were about to dump her in the water. Charlie, having already gone too far, decided to finish the job and suffocated her with his bare hands."

Jacob's relief gradually turned to anger, as he imagined Charlie's hands wrapped around his sister's throat, snuffing her out. "I'm afraid for my life," Sandy added. "I never bought their story because I *knew* she was on that boat, and when I confronted Warren one night when he was drunk, he admitted everything and threatened me if I ever talked. But here I am, talking."

"Where is he now?" Jacob asked calmly.

"He arrived home a while ago and was acting crazy, calling out my name, running around the house looking for me. Charlie showed up too, and I hid behind the dining room table, right before I slipped out the back door and came here. I saw what they did to her. I'm sorry, Jacob."

Jacob had heard enough. Warren, a person whom he called a friend, had betrayed him by protecting Charlie. And now, if he didn't act quickly, Sandy could be next on their list.

—

"Stay in the car," Jacob said as they pulled up to Sandy's beach house.

"Maybe we should call the police," Sandy suggested as she watched the movement of silhouettes through her living room window. "They're both inside, probably looking for me."

"I need to do this now," he said, checking his watch and noting it was eleven o'clock. Electricity crackled overhead and fat rain drops splashed his windshield. "Now, stay put," he instructed and retrieved the .22 from his glove compartment, then checked the chamber to make sure it was loaded. He got out of the car, leaving her in the passenger seat. The rain quickly soaked him. He found the front door ajar, and a faint melody slipped through the opening. Cautiously, he stepped inside, then checked each room. Red streaks led from the parlor to the basement steps.

The wind pushed the front door open, and the chandelier lights flickered over the dining room table but Jacob didn't flinch. He was distracted by the shape of a woman slumped against the back wall, bruises on her face, her familiar turquoise GAP tank-top smeared in blood from a rip in her neck. Lightning flashed through the windows, and Jacob caught a sharp glimpse of her features.

It wasn't possible.

Another flash bounced off her pallid face, and there was no mistaking her identity. Jacob fell back a step at the sight of her stock-still expression but never broke focus. The wind and rain continued to pour in, spattering his back and shoulders.

"What happened here?" a soft voice behind said.

Jacob spun and, after anther flash, caught the same face and turquoise tank-top standing in the open doorway.

Jacob waited for a moment, assuming he'd lost his mind. "Sandy," he said, moving in front of the body to obstruct her view. "I told you to wait in the car." She walked into the room and looked around.

"I shouldn't have let you come in here alone, and I also realized that I don't remember how I got to your brother's beach house." After her last few words, lightning strobed through the room. It bounced off the walls, hitting Sandy's limp body, which rested behind the table, brightening it to recognition. Her expression fell. She placed her hand over her mouth and stumbled back at the sight of her own corpse.

"Don't come over here," Jacob said, slowly moving towards Sandy.

She looked up to him and said, "They got to me."

"I'm sorry."

"Now go get *them.*"

Jacob took another glimpse down at Sandy's body and directed his attention to the four-inch laceration across her throat, recognizing the pattern. It didn't matter which one had done it, it was ending that night. "Can you tell me where they are?" he asked, but when no answer came, he turned to the other Sandy, the one standing by the doorway. But she was gone too.

The faint music continued to circle the room, seemingly from the basement in the same direction the bloody floor streaks pointed. Jacob cocked the trigger because there was only one place left to go. The trail persisted down the staircase, and with each step Jacob took, the music levels rose. But under the guise of the melody were quiet moans of anguish that quickly morphed to blistering screams. The screams faded, and he hesitated, pausing to take a deep breath. Then, gripping the pistol, he pressed on to the base of the staircase.

When he saw the bloody scene in the basement, he lost his nerve and dropped the gun. It fired off a bullet, and the sound of the gunshot echoed against the basement walls. The streak down the stairs split into two trails, leading side-by-side to Charlie and Warren. They rested against the wall, their screams silenced. Standing between them was Luna. She had painted the words *I'm home,* in large strokes of blood on the stone wall. And she held both of their hearts, one in each hand.

She was home.

ARNOLD LAYNE

BY BILL BABER

If you asked any of the cons locked up at Pleasant Valley State Prison if they could name one thing pleasant about the joint, they'd either laugh out loud or stomp the hell out of you. Severely overcrowded and situated among large swaths of agricultural land at the bottom of the San Joaquin Valley, it was hot as hell in the summer and stank of manure used as fertilizer on the nearby rows of peach trees. Flies constantly flew about the cells. The bastards were everywhere.

The moment Arnold Layne walked through intake, I would have bet anything Pleasant Valley wouldn't be a picnic for him. He might have been five foot four, a hundred and twenty-five pounds and thin as a rake. His boyish looks—with a tousled mop of jet-black hair—guaranteed him a hard time. Bugs McRae immediately staked a claim that no one was going to dispute. Bugs was a giant, a lifer who had committed four murders outside and at least one after being locked up.

As Arnold walked by, Bugs called out to him," Get used to it bitch, you're mine."

Arnold turned to him, smiled and replied with a Cockney accent, "Bugger off mate."

Bugs just laughed. It didn't take him long to make his move. After morning chow the next days we were being marched to the yard and Bugs made his way alongside Arnold and shoved him into a supply closet. I felt sorry for the little guy.

Moments later, Arnold strolled into the yard. Ten minutes passed with no sighting of Bugs. Arnold lit a smoke, walked to the center of the yard, and announced: "Mates, just wanna make it clear, I'm here to do my time. Not going to bother anyone. Don't want anyone to bother me."

He crushed out his smoke and headed toward the cell block.

An hour later, they found Bugs in the closet. He had been gutted like a fish.

That earned Arnold mad respect. But it didn't mean his troubles were over. Sooner or later, someone else would try him. That's just the way it is inside.

I got to know Arnold. Man, he was a different breed of cat. Prison populations are segregated. The Aryan Brotherhood, Mexican Mafia, the Bloods and the Crips. Most cons choose an allegiance. Some can get away without doing so but they needed to watch their shit every minute. Anything seen as a challenge could get them killed in a heartbeat. I stayed independent. I just wanted to stack my time and get out. Arnie wanted the same.

That's why I liked Arnold. He was the only English cat in the joint and no one knew quite what to make of him.

We were on the yard one blistering morning, trying to ignore the stench of the nearby fields. We could hear Mexican farmhands talking and laughing—the sounds of freedom. I imagined they might have a cold *cerveza* after a grueling day in the heat, picking the sweet fruit that grew in those putrid fields. I tried to put it out of my mind. Arnold came up alongside me. He lit a smoke, then offered me one.

"How ya doin', mate?" he said.

"Doin' as well as I can. Just under two years to go. How about you?"

"Just starting a nickel," he replied. "Might get out a bit earlier if I behave me-self."

I asked what he was in for.

"Ahh, I got pinched nicking birds knickers, you know, underthings. It's the third time. Bloody ol' blighter of a judge gave me five years. Funny thing is he don't know the half of it."

I couldn't help but laugh. This little dwarf of a man stole woman's panties and filleted one of the toughest cons in the joint. He was an enigma; one I would spend much time trying to figure out.

"No offense, Arnie, but what possessed you to do that? And get caught three times?"

He grinned and said, "Some chaps collect stamps. Other lads fancy a collection of coins. I wanted to be different. Wanted a collection like no one else had."

He lit another smoke. "Funny thing is knickers are the only thing I've ever been caught lifting."

Arnie then told me about some amazing scores he'd gotten away with: jewels, art galleries, rare books and more. He worked alone and because of his size he could slip into places most other thieves couldn't. He had made a fortune.

"But you're locked up for stealing panties? Helluva deal." All I could do was shake my head.

"Mate, I try to stop, I really do. But I get more of a thrill sneakin' into some bird's bedroom and stealing a pair of black lace bloomers than I do liftin' a bag full of diamonds. I can't explain it."

"What about you?" He asked. "What did you do to deserve an extended stay in these luxurious surroundings?"

"I was the wheelman for a series of bank heists. I worked with a gang who had successfully pulled off half a dozen robberies. But one idiot started throwing money around and got picked up. He sang like Sinatra and we all got taken down."

"There's always some git, isn't there?" Arnie said, shaking his head.

I really started enjoying the little Brit's company and decided to give him some advice. "Don't get comfortable," I said. "New cons won't know what you did to Bugs."

"Mate, as you chaps say over here, this ain't my first rodeo. Thanks for the concern but I'll be okay."

Danny McCoy was trying to make his way into the AB hierarchy. He was in for second degree murder. He had beaten a farm laborer to death in a bar brawl outside of Modesto. He liked picking on those smaller and those, at least in his mind, weaker than him. He saw Arnie as in easy target. He started taunting him, making fun of his accent and mannerisms. He decided Arnie must be queer. Arnie ignored him.

McCoy spent his time in the yard with other members of the AB pushing iron. He wasn't well-liked. He was a braggart who tried too hard to fit in. One afternoon he spotted Arnie across the yard.

"Watch this," he said. "I'm gonna have a little fun with that limey runt."

He walked up to Arnie who tried to go the other way. McCoy stepped in front of him.

"Hey, you little shit, I hear you're a panty thief. You like wearin' woman's panties? I bet you like it in the ass."

"Piss off, ya bloody wanker," Arnie said.

McCoy threw a slow, looping overhand right that Arnie easily ducked under. The small man then sprung from the ground and planted both feet in McCoy's face. The crack of his nose breaking echoed like a shot across the yard, and the force of the kick knocked him on his ass where Arnie promptly stomped on his nuts.

The AB crew laughed their asses off. They gave McCoy the boot and adopted Arnie who had no further issues during his stay at Pleasant Valley.

—

Arnie and me stacked our time. And we grew tighter. He had a job lined up for as soon as he got out and he told me he couldn't carry all the loot himself.

I did my jolt and got paroled. Arnie had been earning good time and was supposed to get out six months later.

"Stay out of trouble, mate," he told me. "Good things come to those who wait."

I got a job in a warehouse in Riverside, east of LA. Got home to the studio apartment I was renting one night to find Arnie sitting on the couch sipping a gin and tonic and smoking a cigarette.

"All right, mate."

"How the hell …" I started. Then laughed. Arnie could get in anywhere.

He got up and mixed me a proper drink.

"It's been yonks, mate"

I had learned British slang from Arnie. We could have conversations with no one knowing what the hell we were talking about.

"This place is grotty, and your job is shite. We have plans to make and filthy lucre to nick, so let's blow this bog."

I grabbed the few things I had, and we left. Out on the street, Arnie led me to a beautifully restored '63 MG Midget. He tossed me the keys.

Get a feel for her, mate. You'll be doing most of the driving."

"Look, Arnie," I said. "She's gorgeous but there's two problems. She ain't fast enough for a getaway car and she's conspicuous as hell."

He laughed. "She's just for running around in. We have just

the thing when we need to make a run for it. Now take us to Laguna Beach."

I took back roads over the coastal hills. The top was down, and the wind teased Arnie's hair. He wore a big smile. British Pub Rock from the mid-seventies blasted from the stereo. It was good to be free.

"Wait until you see what we have in store. Like taking candy from a baby."

Laguna Beach was halfway between LA and San Diego. It contained some of the country's priciest real estate, multimillion-dollar homes with commanding ocean views. The place was full of millionaires and old hippie artists. Highway 1 was the main street through town and was lined with trendy restaurants and chic boutiques.

Arnie directed me into a neighborhood called The Canyon. There were more shops and restaurants.

"There," he said. He pointed to a weathered building with cedar shingles. Very beachy looking. A simple sign spelled out "Jewelry" in scrolled letters that looked like they were left over from the seventies.

It wasn't what I was expecting until Arnie filled me in.

"It's a jeweler's collective," he informed me. "Studio space is expensive as all hell. So, all these chaps make and sell their wares right here. Seven different jewelers. All high-end stuff for all the snooty rich birds. The alarm system is shite and there's four screws holding a vent in the back of the building. I can squeeze right through. I have good intel one of the blokes is finishing a three-carat wedding band. There's easily a million or more worth of high-quality material in there."

Arnie had a fence in San Francisco who would give him two-thirds of the take, which we were going to split fifty-fifty. After the heist, we'd have a casual drive up the coast. After that, I planned to walk away from the life for good. Maybe I'd invest a bit and move to Mexico—a beach, beer and a senorita. Just what I had always dreamed of, retiring at a young age.

We planned the job for Monday night, seventy-two hours away. After casing the jewelry store Arnie had me drive a bit further down the coast to San Clemente. He had rented a condo for a week that had sweeping views of the Pacific. After dropping our things, Arnie suggested we grab a bite and a pint or two.

A beautiful brunette served us, and Arnie couldn't take his eyes off her. At the time, I thought nothing of it. After we ate and polished off a couple of beers, we headed back to the condo. Arnie took me through the garage and pointed out a brand new dark blue Camaro.

"Fancy that for a getaway car?"

"That'll work," I said with a grin.

Arnie explained he had financed everything with the proceeds from previous jobs—paid cash for everything.

Back in the condo, Arnie grabbed us some beers and turned on the tube. *Get Carter* played on a movie channel. Not long after, I fell asleep. A couple of hours later I woke up to find no sign of Arnie. At first, I thought he'd gotten cold feet, but he came through the side door a few minutes later.

"Wasn't ready to call it a night, mate, took a stroll. The scent of sea air reminds me of Brighton where I grew up. I used to rob the tourists when they went for a swim."

The same thing happened the next night only Arnie didn't return. I should have known something was up, but I was having too much fun being free and back on the job. I later found out that on the first night, he'd followed that brunette waitress home from the restaurant. Then on the second, he'd picked a lock and entered her apartment. But it was a slow night and the restaurant closed early. She'd come home with her boyfriend, a stout So-Cal surfer dude who tackled Arnie when he found him in the bedroom with his arms full of lingerie. Arnie was back in the slam and I was out three hundred and fifty thousand or so. My retirement dream surrendered for silk and lace from Victoria's Secret.

Arnie got sent back to Pleasant Valley, this time for a ten-year stretch. The sentencing judge called him a danger to society. I heard he killed two inmates who tried to make him their bitch.

I sold the MG and took the Camaro. I went back to Riverside and my warehouse gig vowing to stay straight because I was afraid of what I would do to Arnie if I went back to Pleasant Valley.

Maybe in thirty-five years I might be able to retire to Mexico. Now, all I can do is dream about it. And dream about kicking the shit out of that crazy little English bastard.

That would have to do.

BRAIN DAMAGE

BY TOM LEINS

HMP Channings Wood, Newton Abbot, Devon

Monday morning. A cold day in hell.

I sit in the prison visitor's suite, drinking a scalding vending machine tea, staring at the blinking red eye of the CCTV camera. Governor Diggs takes a keen interest in the rehabilitation of his former inmates, and I have no interest in doing a third stretch in this hell-hole.

Barrett laughs when he sees me. His big belly undulating beneath his grey prison sweatshirt as he swaggers across the linoleum.

"Man, I can't believe you came."

His face is so bruised it looks black. I fist-bump his plaster cast.

"What the fuck happened?"

He shrugs and his gut wobbles again.

"I tripped, man. You know how it is. Making enemies, making money—it comes with the territory."

The beginning of his sentence overlapped with the end of mine, and during the three weeks we shared a cell he flooded the facility

70

with enough Spice to trigger a zombie outbreak. Synthetic cannabinoids. The devil's weed.

"Nice to be back in the Big House, Rey?"

I glance up at the CCTV camera again.

"As long as I'm on this side of the fucking table I'm fine, mate. How've you been?"

He taps his battered face with a forefinger.

"They're not exactly feeding me breakfast and giving me a sponge-bath. Last week they woke me up with a fucking cattle-prod, man."

The cattle-prod is a new touch. I was beaten with table legs, batteries in football socks, the usual stuff. That shit barely registered in the grand scheme of things.

He leans forward, pleasantries over. I owe Barrett, and this is him cashing in his chit.

After an altercation with a pair of Aryans in the exercise yard I was forced to smoke a joint laced with Spice by a man with a rotting skull tattooed over his face and a toothbrush shiv pointed at my windpipe. I was about to take a leap off the stairwell onto the threadbare safety netting when Barrett wrestled me back from the brink and hauled me back to my cell to sleep it off.

I got off lightly. I saw motherfuckers drinking their own sick, their own blood, even toilet water. Men with pillowcases over their heads being used as punchbags. Anything to get another taste. And that's without the tremors, seizures, fits. The white supremacists even had a few skinny boys smeared in cellblock cosmetics who were nicknamed the "Spice Girls" and pimped out for suck 'n' fuck duties.

I lean in to listen to what he has to say.

"I need a favour, Rey. You down with that?"

I nod.

"Of course."

"My wife's sister is missing."

"Okay."

"She's fuckin' brain-damaged, Rey."

"What, like in a coma?"

I picture a girl's unresponsive body being dragged out of Torbay Hospital, loaded into the back of a transit van and sold to local perverts. I know that Barrett is into some dark shit, but this is fucking raw.

He chuckles indulgently.

"No, man. She was thrown down the stairs by an ex-boyfriend. Subdural hematoma. In a coma for nine days and pronounced dead at one point. The doctors expected her to be in a fuckin' vegetative state, but she recovered, man. Had to relearn how to speak, how to control her bodily functions, but she's okay – just a little…"

He taps his bruised skull.

"Just a little soft in the head. Her decision-making process isn't too good. My wife is worried about her, which means I'm worried about her."

"The ex-boyfriend? Is he good for this?"

Barrett shakes his head.

"Nah, man. He won't be hurting anyone again in a hurry. I can't tell you what I did to him, as these motherfuckers have probably got this whole conversation taped and I don't want to extend my stay in this little holiday camp any longer than necessary."

He raises his middle finger towards the surveillance camera.

"Anything I can get you while I'm here, Barrett? Crisps? Ciggies? Can of Fanta?"

He laughs.

"No one trades cigarettes any more, Rey. Toiletries and tinned tuna are where it's at. Anyway, I've got the best paid job in prison—biohazard team—cleaning up the blood, puke, shit and spunk."

He brushes imaginary dirt of the immaculate shoulders of his prison-issue sweatshirt.

"I'm livin' the fuckin' dream, man."

Four Hours Later.
Hele Village, Torquay

Monday afternoon. A cold day in Hele.

I'm standing outside Barrett's pebble-dashed ex-council house, shivering, waiting for his wife, Emily, to open the door.

Next door, a kid, no older than ten, stands in the doorway of a warped lean-to with a corrugated Perspex roof. He's drinking a can of Stella.

The rain sounds louder than gunfire on the Perspex, and he shouts to make himself heard:

"What the fuck do you want, bruv? Fuck off, or I'll tell Barrett you've been sniffing around his missus."

"Barrett fucking sent me. Why aren't you at school?"

"Been excluded, bruv."

I shake my head and press the doorbell again.

Barrett told me that Emily was an ex-Miss Teen Paignton, but the sun-damaged woman who opens the door seems more likely to win 'Best in Show' at the Devon County Fair … small but imperfectly formed. The word 'shapely' barely covers it.

She has a tattoo of a handgun on her collar bone and a pair of enormous, silicone-inflated breasts, with the words 'JUICY' and 'FRUIT' inked across the swollen flesh. Barrett told me he bought the boob-job for her 40th birthday. The gaping leopard-print bathrobe leaves nothing to the imagination.

"Are you Rey?"

"Yeah."

"If I catch you staring at my tits again, I'll ram one of these spike heels through your eyeball so hard you'll wish you were back in the prison showers with the fucking Aryans."

She doesn't invite me in, but leaves the door wide open, so I follow her into the house, as the boy next door ogles her arse from the garden path.

She slumps onto a battered leather sofa, next to an ashtray full of lipsticked cigarette butts.

The room is pretty fucking bare. No pictures. No television. No fucking décor. Apart from the sofa, all I can see are a laptop and a carrier bag full of well-worn sex toys. Since Barrett went inside and his 'liquid assets' dried up, he told me that his wife has covered the rent money by doing a webcam show called 'See Emily Play'.

"Tea? Coffee? Beer?"

"Whatever you're having is fine."

She disappears into the kitchenette and comes back with two cans of orange Tango.

I pop the ring-pull and take a glug to be polite. It tastes like shit. Emily glares at me.

"Barrett told me you had a couple of people you wanted me to look into. People who might know where your sister is."

She doesn't answer, continues to stare.

"Her name is Matilda," she spits. "Why the fuck are you doing this? You don't look like the kind of man who does things out of the goodness of your heart?"

"I owe Barrett. Simple as that."

She grunts, unimpressed. I'm sure a lot of men owe her husband all manner of queasy debts – some real, some imagined.

"Do you drive?"

I shake my head.

She finishes her can of Tango and retrieves her car keys from the sideboard.

"Let's go."

"Where are we going?"

"You'll see."

Hookhills, Paignton

Emily is only four-foot-eleven, and has to sit on a heart-shaped cushion to drive.

On the way to Paignton, she tells me that she was one of a dozen girls who used to attend parties at the house of a mob lawyer named Thorgerson. The girls were always picked up in a minivan at Paignton bus station and blindfolded. Thorgerson used to let Emily's sister, Matilda, watch TV in his study, while Emily worked the crowd. He always seemed to have a soft spot for the girl, and that made Emily nervous enough to stop attending the parties.

Emily has no way of contacting Thorgerson, so we need to coax the details out of the middleman. Or rather, I need to coax the details out of him.

"You not coming?"

She shakes her head.

"Don't let him know you are looking for Matilda. You'll spook the old bastard, and I might need him for work in the future."

I nod.

"Fuck this up, and I'll cut off your dick and sell your body to medical science."

I nod again.

If I fuck this job up, Barrett will do far worse to me than that.

—

The maisonette she points me towards looks half rotted, but the front door has recently been painted a vicious shade of spree-killer red.

The name next to the downstairs doorbell is "Layne, Arnold."

I ring the doorbell, and slip my right hand into the brass-knuckles in my jacket pocket.

A minute later, a cadaverous man in a crumpled, ash-streaked suit opens the door. His skin looks the same color as the bottom of a well-used ashtray, and his features are warped like those of a burn victim.

"Come in, Mr. Rey. I've been expecting you."

I glance back at Emily and then I slip inside.

The man lights a cigarette, only to stub it out immediately. Instead he retrieves a piece of nicotine gum from his jacket pocket and starts chewing aggressively.

"I'm desperate for a cigarette, but doctors say that, since the accident, my lungs can barely process Paignton air—let alone one of these bastard coffin nails."

"What happened?"

He chuckles bitterly.

"Whatever you do, don't try and light a cigarette and apply deodorant at the same time…"

"Shit. Seriously?"

"Don't be daft, son. Crackhead housebreaker with a blowtorch."

"Jesus."

He nods solemnly.

"Come with me, Mr. Rey."

How does this freakshow even know my name?

"You know who I am?"

He nods and I clench my fist around the weapon.

"Then you know what will happen to you if you hold anything back."

"I assure you, Mr. Rey. My acquiescence will not be a problem."

He leads me into a small, barely furnished lounge area. Behind him, three dead tropical fish are floating in the brown water. There is a novelty condom machine bolted to the wall, and a stack of *Tailgunner* back issues balanced precariously on the rickety coffee table.

"What's the matter, Mr. Rey? Never been in a suburban brothel before?"

Never one this downmarket…

"Secrets are a valuable commodity in Paignton. Would you like to know a good one?"

"Sure. Try me."

He runs a hand through his rat-grey hair and scratches his lumpy, ravaged face.

"I received a collect call from HMP Channings Wood this morning. Mr. Barrett told me that you and his wife would be paying me a visit."

"How did he…?"

"Mr. Barrett has fingers in a number of pies—including mine. Trust me, his wife would not do jobs for me if Mr. Barrett hadn't approved them in advance. Mr. Rey, would you mind removing your hand from your pocket? Your manner is making me nervous."

I remove the hand—without letting go of the knuckle-duster.

A tall, heavily tattooed girl limps into the room in her underwear, transparent heels in one hand, crumpled dress in another. She smiles at me with glossy lips. I see a pubic hair pressed against the lip gloss.

"This is Linda. My wife. She runs the place now—on account of my appearance. Men tend to lose their erections when they look me in the eye."

Linda circles me, the way an animal circles its prey, and then leans in – nice and close.

"You won't need to use your knuckle-duster on my husband, Mr. Rey. He's more scared of Mr. Barrett, than he is of Mr. Thorgerson."

"I feel like the only person in this town who doesn't know Mr. fucking Thorgerson. Anyone care to fill me in?"

Layne retrieves a *Herald Express* from the coffee table and points to the photo on the front page.

It depicts a slim, prematurely gray-haired man outside Torquay Magistrates Court. He is unsuccessfully attempting to shield his face with his briefcase. The article name checks a series of increasingly vicious career criminals who I would rather not come into contact with.

"This Thorgerson fucker: does he have the girl? Matilda?"

Layne pauses and scratches his deformed jaw.

"If I say 'yes' do I implicate myself in Thorgerson's scheme?"

"Look, mate. I have no idea who Thorgerson is, or what kind of scheme he is cooking up, but I assure you that Barrett will send worse people than me after you if he suspects that you are actually involved in this shit."

He takes a deep, wheezy breath.

"Very well. It is my understanding that Matilda is indeed in the company of my associate, Mr. Thorgerson. He became enchanted by the girl at one of his soirees, and invited her to… live with him."

"What the fuck? Did you tell Barrett this?"

He holds his hands up, in a pacifying gesture.

"I'm telling *you*, Mr. Rey."

"I'm going to need that address. Right now."

He shakes his misshapen head sadly.

"I'm driving a minibus full of girls to his house on Friday. You are welcome to join us, but I will have to blindfold you. It's for your own protection—in case a disgruntled client of Mr. Thorgerson tortures you at a later date."

I remove my hand from my jacket pocket and Layne flinches.

I shake his hand.

"Smart men thrive during tough times."

"Very true, but idiots will always suffer."

Four Days Later.

I waited in the shadows, next to the greasy bus station brickwork, while Arnold Layne blindfolded the six girls and helped them into the minivan. Emily was the last one onboard. Despite the blindfold, she turned around and blew me a kiss, before Layne bundled her into the van.

I drift across the uneven paving slabs towards the van and Layne offers me a piece of nicotine gum. I shake my head and he pops it in his own mouth instead.

He waves vaguely at the van full of girls.

"Soon ripe, soon rotten."

I shrug and Layne removes an extra blindfold from the pocket of his sports jacket.

"Do you mind?"

I shake my head. It's only then that I realise: he isn't holding a blindfold. He's holding a chloroform-soaked rag.

I attempt to throw a wild punch at his ravaged face—and then my world goes black.

———

I feel like I'm floating downstream on a river of ambient noise – but it might just be tinnitus.

A thin gray-haired man with a designer tan—Thorgerson, I assume—tosses a glass of champagne in my face. I attempt to wipe my face, but realise that I have been handcuffed. Police-issue cuffs, by the look of it, Not the kind of cheap sex-shop knock-offs you can pick with a paperclip.

I lick my lips. The champagne tastes expensive.

"I would have preferred a beer, Thorgerson…"

He snorts.

"A comedian, huh? Every party needs a funny man. It's a shame you won't be making it out of this room alive, Mr. Rey."

I glance around the room. It's a garage of some kind. Two cars sit under tarpaulin.

Emily is a few feet away from me, her face bloodied, also handcuffed. She scowls at me and I offer her a wink.

"Where's Matilda?"

He rests his empty champagne flute on top of one of the cars and pouts. He's wearing a pink polo shirt, chinos and tasselled loafers. A handgun is casually tucked down the front of his trousers.

"She's safe. Under this very roof. I can assure you: she will enjoy all the trappings of my success. This house used to belong to a ruddy rockstar."

Emily's eyes burn with fury: "She was fine where she was."

He chuckles indulgently.

"Hardly. I've seen that grotty little shit-hole you live in with your fat jailbird husband. Matilda deserves better. I will never forget the sacrifice she has made for my wife and I."

"Hold up. What fucking sacrifice?"

Thorgerson laughs guiltily.

"My wife is an ex-catalogue model, Rey. Years of fad diets have ruined her reproductive system. She's too skinny to menstruate. Too skinny to conceive. Luckily for us, we found a perfectly accommodating surrogate! Surprisingly open-minded in the bedroom too!"

Emily glares at him.

"Fuck you, creepshow! She's fucking brain damaged!"

She tries to spit at him, but she's too far away, and her bloody phlegm lands on the knee of his chinos.

"You fucking bitch!"

Thorgerson steps forward and raises his foot, to stomp her.

I seize my chance and kick out at his standing leg, slamming my boot-heel into kneecap, which dislodges with a sick crunch. He hits the concrete floor like a sack of shit. My second kick breaks his jaw. My third kick sends the gun sliding under one of the cars.

I clamber to my feet.

Emily is on Thorgerson's back, knee on his spine, clawing at his eyes. The chain from her handcuffs tight against his windpipe.

"Emily! Let's go!"

Arnold Layne steps inside the garage, a look of pure horror

etched across his scarred horror show of a face. He grabs a pristine claw hammer from the nearest shelf, but before he can use it, I lunge forward and rupture his rotten face with a head-butt. He groans as I frisk him for the keys to the minivan. I skid them across the concrete towards Emily.

She looks up and smiles nastily at me, not letting go of Thorgerson's throat.

"I said, let's fucking go!"

—

It was eighteen months before I found out the truth.

Barrett was pushing a pram along Paignton sea-front, making no effort to conceal the bulky offender monitoring tag strapped to his ankle. He grinned broadly at me, saying nothing. I nodded and carried on walking. Emily and Matilda trailed behind him, arm-in-arm, in matching sun-dresses. Emily winked at me, while her sister just gazed blankly at me—a vacant, lopsided smile plastered across her pretty face.

Emily didn't choke out Thorgerson long enough to kill him that night. She just choked him out long enough to give the sick motherfucker brain damage.

CAREFUL WITH THAT AXE, EUGENE

BY MARK SLADE

"Oh shut up," Eugene said. "You never stop talking."

"Come on," Cedric said. "You love to hear my opinions."

"Leave me alone," Eugene kept his gaze tight on the woman and the man at the table across from him. The pub was crowded now, as opposed to an hour ago when it was just Eugene and Cedric. Eugene saw her on the street and followed her to the pub. She was beautiful, very tall, and that flowery dress clung to her body nicely. "You can keep your awful ideas to yourself."

"You've been staring at that woman for the past hour," Cedric said.

"I can't help it if I like redheads," Eugene told him, drained the rest of the beer in his glass.

"Oh, I know that," Cedric chuckled. "I've known you all your life. I know a lot about you, Eugene."

"Too damn much," Eugene said. "God, look at the legs on her. Why isn't she with me having a drink? Damn."

"Hmph!" Cedric sipped his beer. Set his glass down hard,

splashing liquid on the table. He pointed his finger at Eugene. "Maybe you should shut your mind off, then!"

"That's rather difficult, wouldn't you say?"

"Not at all Eugene. Not at all," Cedric smiled, the lines on his face lengthened. "I had a friend who did it. Now no one knows what he thinks."

"Oh, God," Eugene rolled his eyes. "You're talking about that twerp who was in the rock and roll band before he lost his mind because of all the acid he ate."

"Yes," Cedric said. This irritated Cedric. Eugene's damned jealousy of his former friend. "Yes. That's who exactly who I am talking about. You are such a sourpuss. Get happy, why don't you? Stop being such an asshole."

"Language," Eugene said. "I don't like that kind of talk." He sighed. Eugene never took his eyes off the woman, who flirted heavily with her date, sharing a slice of pizza, kissing, and licking cheese from each other's chin. "I could have so much fun with her."

"That's your problem," Cedric finally finished his glass of beer. "You give up too easily."

"What do you mean?" Eugene said.

"Look at the way your dressed to begin with."

"What do you mean?" Eugene repeated, this time the fluctuation in his voice hit decibels that could only annoy dogs.

"Look at you! In a T-shirt and pajama bottoms!"

"This is the way I dress when I'm hunting," Eugene said. "How else could I hide my axe?"

Cedric laughed. "Now you're talking right, Eugene. We have to collect energy for the Reckoning."

—

Eugene caught up with the man and woman at the end of Second Street behind the old Chevrolet place. Only a few cars remained on the lot of the dealership that went out of business a few months ago. Eugene watched the man and woman first. The man unlocked one of the cars. He helped the woman inside the cab of the pickup, placing a hand under her dress, caressing her ass. The man smiled, looked around to make sure no one was watching.

He had a dirty leer on his face.

This angered Eugene.

The man climbed into the cab. He didn't even have the decency to close the door. He unzipped his fly, pulled out his thing, pushed her dress up to reveal she had no panties on. He pulled her legs apart and…

By that time Eugene was already behind him, axe lifted high. The blade came down hard across the man's back. The man screamed. The woman screamed. The man turned to see who was assaulting him. Eugene removed the blade and swung again, catching him in the neck and shoulder. Blood spurted and dashed the woman's face and dress. The man gurgled, intuitively felt his would once the blade was removed. The man swayed and fell backwards out the truck onto the hard pavement.

Eugene giggled.

The way he fell reminded Eugene of a scene from *Gilligan's Island* when a crate of coconuts fell to the ground and rolled across skipper's foot.

The woman must've been in shock. She squealed so loud Eugene had ringing in his ears. She tried to climb out of the truck but Eugene prevented this action. He smiled at her, showed her the axe.

"Look up, dear-heart," Eugene pointed to the dark sky. The woman's large, concerned eyes followed his long jagged index finger. "The stars sparkle and call out a prayer to the lord of your soul…."

———

The meeting was at the Grand Central Hotel and Eugene had no time to change out of the blood-splattered T-shirt and pajama bottoms. He walked six blocks, barefoot to get to the hotel. He walked past the desk clerk, leaving bloody footprints on the shag carpet in the lobby. The desk clerk tried to flag Eugene down, but quickly realized the hotel belonged to the Gervais crime family and men and women running through the hotel with bloodstains on their clothing was a normal thing.

Eugene stepped inside the elevator with a young couple. They eyed him carefully, looked away whenever Eugene glanced at them. The glances turned into glares, especially at the blonde haired woman in a business suit and heels. The man next to her was very nervous. He kept touching his tie and clearing his voice.

The elevator came to a stop and the doors opened. The man hurried out, but the woman stood there and locked eyes with Eugene. She gave him an icy stare, kept her hands on her hips. A showdown.

"Umm, Mrs. Thomas," the man called out. "I need to get you to your room."

"I'm just trying to find out what this creep's problem is," she said.

"Mrs. Thomas," the man pleaded. "You need to get some sleep before the meeting with Sony tomorrow. You want to be fresh."

"Yeah," she relaxed her hands, walked out of the elevator. "This hotel is getting worse every year I come back to this one-horse town."

"Yeah," Eugene said, tapping the top of the small axe poking out of his pajama bottoms. "I don't have time to for you anyway."

The woman gasped. "Did he just threaten us?"

The elevator doors closed and it continued its journey to Mr. Molly's suite. Eugene walked past Molly's bodyguards. Their suspicious eyes followed him as he trekked bloody footprints all over the hallway. Eugene opened the door and saw Mr. Molly's lieutenants.

Atrocious Gravers sat in the antique Chippendale, drinking his scotch and orange peel. Bunny Pudd and Horus Kade sat on the white sofa having beer with whiskey and tabasco shots. Standing just a few feet away from the door was Malcolm Green. He wasn't drinking anything.

Malcom never drank, never did drugs, never cheated on his wife. He just liked to steal. Not just an old friend, former cellmate and current champion—as well as explainer of Eugene's hijinks—Malcolm was also married to Eugene's sister, crazy Kelley, so called because she once stabbed a woman in the face with an icepick and was cleared of attempted murder using the defense that the woman had pissed on her dead mothers grave. None of which was the truth. Crazy Kelly didn't like the nervous blinking habit the woman had. The judge and jury in the case had been bought off.

Mr. Molly was lying in his beach chair, suntanned by a mirror wrapped in tinfoil held by Jhansi, a teenage Pakistani boy. All eyes moved to Eugene as he stepped inside the suite and shut the door quietly.

"What the fuck is this?" Mr. Molly mumbled in a gravelly voice.

Mr. Molly was an import from East London. The Gervais family brought him in to help bring two warring families together, and he ended up taking over the business. That was twenty-five years ago.

"What?" Eugene stood against the door.

Mr. Molly waved Jhansi away and yanked his sunglasses from his face. "Malcolm, why is your crazy-ass brother-in-law covered in blood?"

"I don't know, Mr. Molly, but I'm about to find out." Malcolm grabbed Eugene by the elbow and led him to the kitchen.

They stood there for a bit, glaring at each other.

"What?" Eugene shrugged.

"You're covered in fucking blood!"

"So what."

"And you came here?! To Mr. Molly's residency?!"

"What?"

"What if you brought the cops, you dumb fuck!?"

Eugene shrugged, waved a dismissive hand. "Nahhhh."

"You have an axe in your pajamas," Malcolm said. "That's wonderful. The murder weapon, I assume."

"Yeah," Eugene chuckled. He pulled the axe from the waistband of his Pajama bottoms, examined the blade. "This thing is handy. Even though it's small. Sure does some damage to the human being. Cedric was right. This would be fun."

"Oh shit." Concern entered into Malcolm's voice. "Cedric is back?"

"I didn't think he ever left," Eugene said.

"Oh, he did, Eugene. When you were in Cedars," Malcolm said. "You stopped taking your medicine."

"I don't need it. Besides, I have to prepare for the Reckoning."

"For fuck sake!"

"Language, Malcolm," Eugene wagged a finger. "You know I don't like that word. God knows I've heard it enough from my sister growing up."

"Eugene, there is no Reckoning. You've been talking about that since we were a teenager—"

"Oh, Malc, you're silly," Eugene interrupted. "Those things don't happen overnight! They take time. Sometimes years. So, when the Others come down to earth in the vessels they'll take the chosen ones to their world, along with the chosen ones' families and friends. All the chosen has to do is collect energy from disposable humans. And off we go! To a much grander, better world!"

"Fuck, Eugene. When we go back in there, please don't talk about the Reckoning. I need to stay in good with Mr. Molly. Okay?"

"Why?"

"He already thinks you're crazy as it is! Don't talk about it!"

"He's protected! Just like you and Kelly ... the Others ... when they come to collect, the unprotected will be hooked up to all kinds of machines, and subjected to all kinds of horrible—"

"Shut up," Malcolm snarled.

"I can protect you guys!"

"Shut up, Eugene!" Malcolm stepped closer, held his open hand up, ready to strike Eugene, then thought better of it. He didn't want a scene in front of Mr. Molly. He didn't want to screw up his chances to get back into Mr. Molly's good graces.

"My loved ones—you, Malcolm—don't have to suffer to get to their world," Eugene said.

They locked eyes and Malcolm shook his head.

"Look," Malcolm inhaled and exhaled sharply. "Just ... when we go in there, shut your mouth, and listen to the plan, okay?"

Eugene thought about it. He was tired. Hungry. He needed a beer. He didn't want to argue anymore.

"Yeah," he nodded. "Okay. I'll just sit in a corner and ... listen."

"Good," Malcolm smiled. "Let's be good soldiers."

They went back into the living room. Mr. Molly had gone back to having Jhansi sun tanning him. Gravers, Kade and Pudd were laughing, sipping their drinks. Eugene wasn't sure if they were laughing at a joke or laughing at him. Either way, he was annoyed. Eugene did as he said he would. He went off to the bar that separated the living and the kitchen, sat on a stool, picking at the nuts in a saucer and lining them up according to size and shape.

"Now that we're all together," Mr. Molly said. "Why don't we go over the job with Malc and Eugene."

"Sure thing, Mr. Molly," Gravers set his glass down on the table. He liberated a folded piece of paper from his jacket pocket, stood and handed it to Malcolm.

Malcolm unfolded the paper. It was a photograph of the United Farmers bank. "This is on Beaker Street?"

"That's right," Pudd said. "The nearest police station is Wielder. That's twelve blocks, four red lights. Traffic is always jammed."

"Interesting," Malcolm said. He looked at Eugene and offered the photo. "Wanna look?"

Eugene shook his head.

"There's an ice cream shop right across the street," Kade said. "You'd be interested in that, wouldn't ya, Eugene?"

The room erupted into laughter. Only Mr. Molly, Malcolm, and of course Eugene, didn't laugh.

"What's that supposed to mean?" Eugene said with venom in his voice.

"Oh nothing," Kade said. "After we rob the bank, maybe you wanna hustle over to the ice cream shop for a nutty buddy."

More laughter. Eugene fiddled the axe handle in his pajama bottoms. He was contemplating burying the axe into Kade's forehead. Oh, that would be bliss! But Malcolm would be very upset with him. More than likely that incident would ruin Malcolm's chance to receive more work or even move up in Mr. Molly's crew.

For a brief second, Cedric appeared. He reared his head back and laughed. Then he disappeared.

So Eugene faked a laugh. He slapped his knee.

"Oh, Kade, you're such a card!" Eugene said.

I just want to bury my axe in your face as you rear your head back and laugh, Eugene thought.

"Okay, okay," Mr. Molly shooed Jhansi away, sat up in his beach chair. "Enough kiddin' around! Get on with the plan!"

The laughter vacated the room immediately. Mr. Molly pointed a crooked finger at Gravers and he continued with the instructions.

"I got a guy on the inside," Pudd said. "He's a security guard. He shuts down the alarms. So the backdoor will be unlocked."

—

"Everybody on the floor!" Pudd screamed.

Suddenly, four men in dark suits wearing stocking masks appeared. They waved sawed-off shotguns and pillow cases. The bank hadn't even opened yet and the cashiers had just placed the money in their tills. The bank manager and his assistant manager were hanging around the door of his office. The assistant manager was someone Eugene definitely took notice of. She was tall, dyed strawberry blonde in a business suit, no heels on her stockinged feet.

Everyone complied with Pudd's demands. They laid down, pressing their faces on the cold tile floor. Even the security guard, who was in on the plan, did so, and offered up his gun when Pudd ordered. The security guard's younger partner questioned this act.

"Just do as they say, son," the security guard said. "You don't want to end up in a coffin, boy."

His partner removed his .45 and slid it toward Kade.

"You take the three tills on the left," Pudd told Malcolm. "I'll take the three on the right."

Malcolm screamed at the one old lady to open all the cashiers' boxes, drowning out Pudd's orders to a chunky, middle aged woman. The women did as they were told. They filled Pudd and Malcolm's pillow cases, then went back to lying face down on the floor.

"Get the bank manager," Pudd told Eugene. "Have him open the vault."

"I've got a better idea," Eugene said. He ambled over to the Assistant manager.

"What the fuck is he doing!?" Pudd asked Malcolm.

"Shit," Malcolm said. "I don't know. Hey!"

Eugene turned on his heels. "What?"

"Get the Manager," Malcolm said.

Eugene smiled lasciviously at the woman. "Can you open the vault?"

Frightened, the woman nodded, the strands of hair whipped her cheeks as her head bobbed up and down quickly. "Y-yes ...."

"See," Eugene kept his eyes on the woman, still smiling. "She can open the safe."

"Jesus!" Pudd said. "What the fuck—fine! Just fucking do it!"

Eugene helped the nervous woman to her feet, helped steady her by keeping a hand on her waist. He offered a gentlemanly hand and the assistant manager accepted as they headed toward the backroom behind the cashiers.

—

The meeting was over. Everyone was laughing and talking as they went out the door.

"Oi!" Mr. Molly called out to Malcolm.

Malcolm let the others walk ahead of him. Eugene tried to hang around to hear what was said. Malcolm waved him on. Eugene shrugged, went out the door.

"Is he all right, then?" Mr. Molly asked.

Malcolm laughed. 'Yeah, Mr. Molly. Of course."

Mr. Molly gazed at him. Those steely blue eyes were looking right through Malcolm. Malcolm looked away, cleared his throat.

"He better be," Mr. Molly pointed a finger. "If he's not, you'll be the one to pay for it, my son."

—

Blue lights flashed outside the window of the main entrance of the bank. Sirens could be heard, muffled voices.

"Fuck," Kade said. "The cops are out there."

"This isn't going as planned!" Pudd cried out. He leaned in and whispered, "Gravers is probably gone."

"That's what he's supposed to do, according to the plan. Any signs of trouble, peel out, don't look back."

A single gunshot could be heard. The hostages stifled gasps

and quieted whispers of concerns when Pudd struck the bank president with stock of his shotgun. Pudd looked at the cashier's area, then at Malcolm.

"What was that?" Kade asked. "Oh, shit ..."

"Sounded like Eugene's smith and Wesson Revolver," Malcolm said.

"He's still carrying that? We're all supposed to be carrying these!" Pudd showed his sawed off to Malcolm.

"I know, I know," Malcolm said.

"Jesus," Pudd sighed. "What's taking him so long?"

"I don't know," Malcolm walked toward the cashiers.

"Where are you going?!"Pudd called out..

"I'm going to find out what he's doing!" Malcolm yelled back.

"Son of bitch!" Pudd stomped his feet.

Malcolm ambled to the back of the bank. The hallway was jammed with empty cardboard boxes and boxes filled with files. Someone was standing at the end of the hallway. A shadowy figure. Malcolm struggled to make out who the figure was. He took a step closer, saw someone lying on tile floor.

"Son of a bitch," Malcolm picked up his stride toward the shadow. "Eugene, what did you do? Did you kill that woman?"

Sunlight streaked momentarily through a distant window in the hallway, revealing a man standing there. He wasn't Eugene. The closer Malcolm came to the vault, the more he could see the person on the floor was Eugene, dead, with gunshot to the head.

"Eugene!" Malcolm's voice cracked. He swallowed back emotion. He always knew he'd find Eugene like this and wondered how he would handle it. Not as well as he thought. Eugene was the kid brother Malcolm always wanted.

The man had to be a cop. But how'd he get in the bank? The security guard armed the doors after he let them in.

I watched him, Malcolm thought.

He couldn't be a cop. He didn't identify himself as one. Maybe it was another employee? But Pudd checked out the bank. There were only ten employees in the whole building, including the managers.

The man stepped forward. Malcolm cocked his gun. Sunlight streaked the wall of the hallway. The man was Cedric. Malcom pointed the sawed off shotgun. Cedric phased in and out. The assistant bank manager appeared. Malcolm gasped.

"Stop!" She screamed. "Or I'll shoot—"

Malcolm fired, both barrels. The first bullet struck the woman in her collar bone, the second in her chest. She flew back and fell hard on the floor. The sawed off hit the floor and slid away.

"Fuck,' Malcolm declared.

Suddenly, a bright light ascended to his eyes, blinding Malcolm. He felt weak, no control of his limbs. He couldn't even speak. Thinking was difficult, but he managed: What ... the ... fuck . . . .

Machines whirred, beeped. Loud humming and whooshing sounds droned in his ears. Malcolm realized he was lying on a white table, in a white room, with strange white beings with faces from his past. Others he knew were laid out on slabs, with wires from the machines hooked to every port in their body. Malcolm's parents, school teachers, old girlfriends, friends, enemies, Mr. Molly, Gravers, Kade, Pudd, the woman he just shot . . . .

Everyone from Malcolm's life was on a slab. Except Eugene. He was nowhere to be found.

All the white beings with no genitals stood over the ones on the slabs, slicing into their bodies with scalpels. There was one being with a face he didn't recognize. Cedric. He held his scalpel to Malcolm's face, smiling.

It was at that moment, Malcolm realized Eugene wasn't crazy.

The Reckoning did come.

HEART BEAT, PIG MEAT

BY KENNETH W. CAIN

Layne Arnold had a pig heart.

Everyone said so, referring to the procedure he'd undergone known as xenotransplantation, where they give someone an organ transplant from a different species. And while it was still illegal in the United States, Layne had been so far down on the list for transplants that, because of his health, he'd been forced to seek out alternate methods. He'd frequented various black markets outside the United States, taking long trips to remote locations in South America and China. On some of those trips, it was even rumored that he'd employed medicine men to use black magic to cure his ailments.

Regardless of the outcome of those ceremonies, he kept searching, until eventually he found someone who would perform the surgery he'd been seeking. He hadn't been the same since, what some believed to be the direct result of a unique viral strain taking hold in the man, somehow transforming him.

As far as Sam Hargrove was concerned, it was all nonsense. But those were the things he'd learned about the man so far, even if it was mainly gossip. Most people wouldn't know that much, but Sam had been paid to follow the guy because of some potential shady deal. So he'd dug up all the usual trivial bull that accompanied most cases like this while trailing the guy these last few days.

Layne actually spent most of his time on the go. It was a wonder he slept at all, which meant Sam hadn't gotten a good night's sleep since taking on the assignment. And truth told, although the guy had proved difficult to keep up with at times, Sam hadn't seen anything the least bit suspicious about the man's dealings. Not yet, anyway. Mostly, Layne kept to the local food markets, picking up orders to prepare dinner. Not much else.

Was he deformed? Sam couldn't rightly say yet. Whenever he did show his face in public, he wore hoodies, his face well hidden. But, from what Sam had seen, he looked like any other man. Did he have some ability to transform into something else? Who knew? But as far as Sam could tell, he was just an ordinary man leading a rather unextraordinary life. What that meant was that this would be an easy paycheck, other than losing a few winks of sleep.

Throughout the night, the guy could be seen in the kitchen of his massive home, endlessly cooking. The house sat on fifteen acres of sparsely wooded land. There wasn't much else to it. And Sam needed the money. He'd lost at the tracks all too often in the three weeks leading up to this case, so he needed to get square with the bookies before they came looking for him. All in all, it was a pretty boring job, so it was no wonder Sam drifted off in his car, after dragging ass all day. That he would wake to an unfamiliar setting with strange drums playing, he hadn't expected one bit, so he was instantly on guard.

Where the hell am I?

A quick survey of his surroundings revealed little more than the fact he was in a cave system of some sort. Rough earthen walls surrounded the chair he was bound to on all sides. Various sized openings led off in five directions, none of which offered the slightest hint at what he could expect beyond. Not that he needed to worry about that just yet, given his situation. First, he would have to escape these bindings.

Observing his restraints, they weren't all that taut. Mainly because they'd used cheap rope. He doubted they'd even secured it from a hardware store, as it seemed to him more indicative of what you might find at a flea market. That said, the rope wasn't what he focused on. It was the chair he was bound to, sitting precariously on three legs, the fourth a good inch shorter, his shifting balance causing it to rock forward unstably.

This was one of those old maple chairs from the seventies, the kind that ended up in everyone's garbage sooner or later. Often, only to be discovered by some trash picker who would sell it to some restorer's warehouse, where it would be stripped down and resurfaced, then sold to some hipster. But not this one, thankfully, with its spindly legs.

Sam rocked back and forth, side to side, again and again until the chair went up on two legs. Time almost seemed to come to a standstill, him balanced precariously, trying to throw his weight forward. Finally, the chair toppled. Sam tucked his head as his body collided against the earthen floor. To his surprise, both the chair and the bindings held. Things never quite worked out how they did in movies, did they? He knew that, which was why he was glad to have prepared for such a dilemma.

Wriggling in the chair, Sam forced his left boot off. Once he succeeded in freeing the boot, he used his feet to turn it upside down and out slid a switchblade. Now that it was out in the open, he wriggled the chair around until his hands could secure the blade, which he quickly released, and with which he then went to work on his bindings. Unfortunately, the only part of the rope he could reach with the blade was a huge knot, so he had a lot of work ahead of him. But keeping himself focused, sawing and sawing, after some time he severed enough for the rest of the rope to loosen on its own. Whoever had tied him up should've paid better attention while in the Scouts. Quickly, he began to free himself. Upon succeeding, he retrieved the knife and tried to get a better understanding of the five paths.

Nothing looked so dissimilar about any of them other than the slight curvatures or the overall size of the openings, all of which could be traversed by walking hunchbacked. The constant loud drumming seemed to match his heartbeat, making it hard to focus on anything for long. Realizing this, Sam ducked into the opening before him for no particular reason, and hurried along through the tunnel. He followed the twists and turns, always remaining mindful of where he'd started. Before long he saw a room, but as he approached, he could see the fallen chair and rope on the floor.

A complete circle?

Back in the room where he'd started, he tried to discern which path he had headed down but couldn't be sure. He wanted to kick himself in the ass for not paying better attention. This time, he took time to bust up the chair. The longest section, one of the back legs that remained nearly intact, he retained to use as a weapon. He placed a smaller shard by the opening he chose, the one he thought he'd gone down the first time, and headed down it again. After several minutes, when he found himself back in the room, it surprised him to find the shard wasn't where he'd left it.

Someone or something had moved it.

What the hell is with all that drumming? Has it gotten louder?

Sam grabbed the rope and carefully began to unwind some of it. Once he had a good length separated, he cut it away and then used it to bind his knife to the end of the chair leg. This transformed the leg into a rudimentary spear, which he felt he needed now. If whoever moved that wood had a gun, he would need every advantage available to him to survive. He swiped the weapon through the air to practice before deciding which path to head down next. He tried to gauge which he'd chosen last by the position of the chair, but even that seemed to have been displaced. Whoever was doing this to him, they were trying their best to either delay him or piss him off. He couldn't be sure which, but he didn't plan on sticking around long enough to find out, either.

This time, before heading down a path, he tried to judge the slight differences he'd noticed before. He deduced the path he'd taken the last two times by a small dimple in the wall on the left side of the opening. To be sure, he marked the opening with his weapon, using it to scratch a single slash into the rock wall. This time, he chose the next path over, quickly ducked in, and began hurrying along. He wasn't all too surprised to find himself once more returning to that central room, so he quickly marked that path with two slashes to indicate it was connected to the first.

After the third and fourth paths proved unsuccessful, he marked them respectively with three slashes and then four, just to be sure, in case he somehow ended up back here again. Then he ducked into the fifth opening, certain this path would lead to freedom. With little care, he rounded each turn, anxious to get back to his office and have a snifter of scotch before bed, but he was starting to notice something about this path—it was getting tighter the farther along he travelled. Worse yet, he thought he was getting closer to the source of that drumming. It was so loud now that he couldn't tell it apart from the beat of his own heart. It made for one heck of a headache too, something far worse than any hangover he'd experienced since his twenties.

Sam sighed, got on his hands and knees, and proceeded forward. Even as he crawled, the passageway seemed to close in on him from all sides. He could feel the walls scraping against his body, an indication of just how tight it was becoming. It got to a point where he'd been going at this for a few minutes and the path had narrowed so much that it made him feel claustrophobic. If this kept up—

Something caught his eye up ahead. The path appeared to open up to complete darkness, but if nothing else, at least he would be able to stand.

He scurried along, struggling to squeeze through those last few dozen feet. For a brief moment, he was certain he'd end up stuck, unable to go forward or back, fated to die there trapped in the embrace of those earthen walls like a boa constricting its prey. He tried to force the images of that reality away, which proved difficult given his predicament, which seemed to worsen by the moment. The feeling persisted until he freed himself of the passageway and finally stood in the darkness. After a second of catching his breath, he took in his surroundings, instantly noticing how much louder the drums were here. The beats were almost deafening, precise strikes so loud he had to cup his free hand over one ear to try to reduce the pain. That helped some.

The cavern, although dark, revealed much. Whatever this place was, it must have been used to feed animals. The smell was horrific, what Sam believed to be the stench of manure and perhaps rotten food, likely slop. That meant pigs. Go figure, given who he'd been following. Did that mean Layne had somehow found him out and brought him here, to an underground pig farm? Then another realization dawned on him. Not only was it probable that these were Layne's pigs, but if he'd been captured by the man, it was likely he would feed Sam to them, as he had seen in many movies. What man in his right mind would do that?

Something moved to his right. Sam stood there, the one hand still cupped over his ear, the makeshift spear in his other, focused on that area. He was certain he would see a pig charging him, but surely he'd have time to—

A face emerged from the darkness. Not a pig face, but that of a man. That of Layne. Only it wasn't Layne, not completely. Whatever transformation the guy had undergone, it was significant. Somehow, someway, the naked man Sam saw charging him, either by virus or black magic or otherwise, was half-man, half-pig. The rumors, for what it was worth, were true, though he'd had no idea to what degree until now. That alone was so unnerving, so terrifying, all he could do was stand there in shock as the man came at him. By the time Sam shook out of his daze, it was too late to even try to fight back. Layne collided with him, an instant deep stabbing pain in Sam's side as he flew backward into the shadows.

Still stunned, Sam got to all fours and felt the searing agony in his side. What the hell had he gotten him with, a knife? Or was it a claw? Whatever the case, Sam felt something within the wound burning. With some difficulty, he got back to his feet and only then realized he'd lost his weapon. He scanned the immediate area but saw nothing, so he expanded his search to the right as he heard feet plodding against the earth. Spinning on his heels, he turned and tried to locate his assailant, but couldn't see him. Then he felt it again, this strange being slamming into him, literally tossing him deeper into the darkness, and once again that horrible pain in his abdomen.

This time Sam stayed down, pressing a hand into his stomach and feeling the wetness of blood there. With his other hand, he crawled about on the ground, searching for his weapon, a rock, anything he could use to fend off Layne. He hadn't gotten very far when he heard the man bounding for him yet again, but he felt safer being this close to the ground, where Layne couldn't see him or reach him with any accuracy. Yet, when the man appeared before him and leaped into the air, passing overhead, Sam saw the flicker of a hand reach down and slash a long gash right above his left shoulder blade. Whatever Layne was, he was efficient.

Sam abandoned any hope of drowning out those drums. Whatever cannibalistic ritual Layne was subjecting him to, those drums were part of it. If nothing else, they were a psychological tactic, a distraction, and right now Sam needed to focus. He imagined most people who ended up in this predicament likely couldn't focus, and that meant Layne had made short work of them. That wasn't Sam. Screw the pay. He was determined to bring this man down once and for all.

On all fours, Sam scrambled about on the ground, swiping his hands out in every direction as fast as he could manage. Already he could hear Layne trotting back for him again, and he steadied himself for the blow. If he could, he would roll out of the way right before contact, so he prepared himself for that. As Layne neared, he leaned to his right and collapsed, quickly rolling away into the darkness. Layne skidded to a stop, and Sam could hear him changing directions in the darkness and charging again. How long could Sam keep this dodging up?

As Layne approached, once more Sam dove right. To his surprise, Layne seemed to anticipate this. Their bodies collided, Layne trampling over him, once more tearing a deep gash, this time in his left arm. Sam instantly went to lift himself, hearing Layne quickly spinning and running for him again. Then his hand bumped something familiar. He identified it with his fingers, grasped it in his right hand, and thrust it out as Layne bounded upon him.

His hand slid down the shaft as the knife made contact, driving a splinter deep into his palm, forcing him to release his hold. Layne wailed, some distorted cry that sounded not only animalistic, but monstrous. And although Sam couldn't see Layne, couldn't locate him in the darkness to finish the job, he'd succeeded in wounding the man if nothing else. That was enough to create an opportunity, and that was all he wanted right now.

Sam dragged himself up to a standing position and headed deeper into the darkness. He hobbled along, both hands out in front of him, hoping to run into something recognizable. When he finally crashed into the wall, he slid along to his left, feeling for an exit, any opening. By the time he found one, Layne had stopped wailing. He couldn't be sure if the man was dead or alive or just biding his time. Whatever the case, Sam wasn't about to stick around to find out. He ducked into the opening and quickly hurried through the passageway, relieved to find that the path didn't narrow so much, which he surmised meant he wasn't heading back to that room.

After several minutes of fleeing, the passageway angled upward and eventually opened up to the night, the stars like salt in the sky. But he didn't stop to appreciate them. He kept running for as long as he could, all the way to a gas station where he called the police.

By the time the cops arrived, he'd cleaned up some. The attendant offered him some spare clothes, which helped. To his surprise, those burning wounds weren't actually that bad, mere scratches mostly, which was odd. He'd thought them much deeper gashes, some so deep he worried he would need stitches. But that burning sensation had subsided, so he ignored them as he gave his report.

They found Layne in the cave system, dead. So, while Sam would likely not get paid, at least he didn't have to worry about the guy tracking him down. But something else kept nagging away at Sam's insides. A feeling. Something he wasn't used to. He tried to ignore it throughout the rest of the night and over the next few days as he immersed himself back into his work. It wasn't until a full week later, once he was starting to feel like his old self again, that something unusual happened.

Sam was out with a friend, having some Italian food at a dingy little restaurant in the city, when he had to burp. Only, what came out wasn't a belch. It was a grunt. Not only that, but it was a pig's grunt, plain and simple.

ONE OF THESE DAYS

JIM SHAFFER

An ill wind blew north off the Gulf. Breathed in bayou swamp heat, delta gas. Revived, picked up speed. Swooped over burning fields. Whistled and rattled through sugar cane blades. Fanned the flames. Lifted sparks and embers. Sailed them over my head. Across the garden. Toward the plantation's big house.

—

They hanged my mama, a black woman named Beatrice Brown-Smith, from a high enough branch of an ancient Southern live oak in the garden of a Louisiana plantation not far from the main house. Cut up her white husband Simon Herndon Smith, my daddy. Tied him to the trunk of the tree. Made him watch. Beat her, stripped her, raped her, strung her up still breathing. Hooded men. Vacant-eyed, drunk, sweat-stinking, rough-handed men. Dancing wild in the pulsing yellow light of a burning cross. Not the same men maybe, but the same kind of hate-filled men who bombed black churches, killed black children, murdered civil rights workers, chewed Red Man tobacco, and jeered defiantly for court cameras at their acquittal. Mocking justice as if it had been served.

Lying on a bed in Our Lady of the Lake hospital in Baton Rouge, wrapped in white cotton sheets, taped and sutured to within an inch of his life, my daddy faded in and out, floated between grief and loss, relived what he saw.

"They killed your mama, Frank." He gripped my hand. "I'm sorry." Rocked his head on the pillow.

"Not your fault."

"Thought we were safe. Now. Today. In our corner. No bother to nobody."

"You bothered somebody."

When I got the news about my parents, I was up north in a small town outside Philadelphia on the tail-end of a case: the murder of an old college friend made convincingly to look like suicide. With more questions than answers, I left the case unsolved. But what happened to my mama and daddy was no mystery.

My daddy squeezed his eyes shut. Grimaced at some raw, open thought. "Going up north. Taking your mama's ashes. That church. Where we married. Bury her there."

Simon and Beatrice, my parents, met in college. Both participated in civil rights protests on campus. Discovered they shared similar beliefs, ideals. Fell in love. Courted. Loved some more. Got married after graduation. Mama's parents were pleased. Welcomed Simon to the family. But Daddy's wealthy parents protested the marriage. Called my daddy in. Bought him off. Gave him only half his inheritance. But a large lump sum. With a codicil-like warning, "Don't ever bring her into this house." So my daddy never saw his parents again. Wisely invested his inheritance. And when he retired from his one-shingle law practice, used the interest alone to purchase Gardenia plantation in St. Charles Parish, Louisiana. A gift for my mother who'd been his secretary and paralegal all those years. Symbolic maybe. A black woman, queen of her own plantation. No slaves. No chains. No suffering. Freedom. Hope for a new age. The gift, the gesture, could have been perceived as white man's guilt. Or homage to one race's suffering at the hands of the white man. Or. could have been just plain love. Hard to fault a man for doing a righteous thing even if you may think it's for the wrong reason.

"Reach in the drawer there, Frank." Daddy turned his head toward the night stand. "Signed the plantation over to you. All there. Legal." I pulled the paperwork and deed out of the drawer.

"Just what I need."

He closed his eyes. Smiled. "One of these days. You'll figure it out. Sell it. Whatever. I'm done."

I stared across the bed at the white wall where a lone, walnut-stained crucifix hung, the dead body of Christ a light, silvery shape against the crossed, dark wood. A still and silent reminder of what happens to those who rock the boat, step out of line, speak truth to lies, or worse, for the right here, right now, have the wrong color skin.

My daddy's eyes popped open. "Just don't sell it to that damn bigot."

"Which one?"

"Preacher been skulkin' 'round. Name's Clay. Slick white man in a white suit. Made an offer to buy. Told him no. Didn't like I told him no. Walked 'round like he already owned the place. You know the type."

"I got the picture."

"Wants to turn the plantation into some kind of retreat for his parishioners. I checked him out. Preaches hate from the pulpit. 'Course he loves God, too."

"He behind this?"

"Could be ... Reverend Clay. Man of God. Shit."

—

Driving hard, I followed the half-mile driveway under an eerie canopy of bald cypresses hung with fine strands of Spanish moss.

Their spread of branches dimmed the harsh noonday light. From the open window, slightly cooled air hit my face as the car ploughed through a thin layer of ground mist. Glanced in the rear view mirror. Ghostly swirls of mist and dust obscured the ground's vile, bloody past.

When the cypress tunnel ended, I slowed the car. Full light returned and illuminated the Greek revival façade of the antebellum Gardenia plantation house. My maternal ancestors would have called the impressive white pile the "big house." I steered my Mustang around the circular drive and parked at the foot of a set of wide steps leading up to its massive oak doors. Guarded from floor to ceiling by four Doric columns, a spacious double gallery stretched across the front of the house. Ample space for a genteel and leisurely diet of mint juleps and cigars. And safely positioned out of sight of the chains and whips and bloody open wounds that would never completely heal or be forgotten. An unlit cigarette dangled from one corner of my mouth. Trying to quit by pretending, I tossed the dead cigarette out the car window. Killed the motor. A swell of seets from a flitting flock of swamp sparrows accompanied the steady ticks from the cooling engine. Mocking pretence, I lit a fresh smoke. No one came out to greet me or rushed down the steps to collect my bags. Those days gone with the wind. I pushed the car door open all the way, placed one foot on the ground, propped the other on the rocker panel. Enjoyed a slug from a half pint of Jack I pulled from my inner suit coat pocket while I contemplated the vista of some long dead white southern gentleman's warped vision of paradise regained.

In its heyday in the mid-1800s, the Gardenia plantation boasted six hundred acres of cane fields and two hundred slaves. The sugar cane crop went to the refineries further south eventually finding its way into rum, whiskey and fine liquors Louisiana prided itself in producing. Overheads at a minimum. Pay for a small troop of overseers and free slave labor, the inflated profits stuffing the pockets of the plantation owner. Sounded like paradise. For some, anyway.

I pushed off the car and stood. The heavy air smelled of dank earth, decay, and the scent of magnolias. I turned and spied a large, full-blossomed magnolia tree sitting on a grassy patch in the circle of the drive. The dead sweet air smelled like the end of everything. I shrugged out of my damp suit coat. Pulled my .45 from a side coat pocket. Tossed the coat on the front seat of the car. Tucked the gun in my waistband at the back.

Trying to move some air, I plucked my sweaty t-shirt from my chest. Held the cigarette between my teeth as I stepped away from the car, intending to mount the steps, key in hand, and take a look inside. But the whine of what sounded like a power saw stopped me. Turning toward the sound, I spit out the bitter, soggy cigarette. Crunched across the oyster shell drive, heading around the corner of the house toward the sound.

I strode along the broad side of the house, shuffled down a gentle incline, and edged up next to the back corner. With my back pressed against the dusty brick wall, I felt for my gun. Glanced around the corner.

A moderately-sized swimming pool filled part of the back yard. Seemed an out-of-time addition to a Southern plantation house, but given the heat and humidity, tradition be damned. Surrounding the pool, a flagstone patio led all the way up to the back of the house. Next to the house's far corner a battered old-model red pickup sat silent in full sunlight. FORD stamped across the tailgate. Two bumper stickers mounted on either side of a Confederate flag license plate issued the commandments: HEAR THE TRUTH! and GO TO CHURCH! Visible in the back window of the truck's cab, a gun rack complete with rifle. Posing on a corner of the patio nearest me, a white, wrought iron patio table corralled by three matching wrought iron chairs.

Decorated with a copy of the Confederate flag, a bath towel hung askew from the back of one of the chairs, as if tossed there in hasty retreat.

The saw screamed again as I crept around the corner and scooted along the back wall to a set of open sliding glass doors. The house was supposed to be empty. I peeked around the edge of the doors. Gardening and landscaping tools leaned against the near corner of the low-ceilinged room. A lawn mower and two large gas cans sat next to neat rows of plastic buckets of chlorine powder and tile detergent. A long-handled pool skimmer hung horizontally on the back wall. From the tools mounted on the far wall above a crowded work bench, I figured the rest of the room my daddy's workshop. And planted in the middle of the room, a man bent over a table saw, guiding a plank of wood through the saw's hungry blade. His back to me.

I stepped inside the room. Waited for the saw to finish. The man was making crosses. Latin crosses. From the stack laid flat on the floor against the window wall that gave on the patio, they looked about eight feet tall. The longer base stem on each one cut to a point, making for easy insertion into the soft, rich delta soil. The man switched off the table saw and removed his safety goggles. The spinning blade slowed, then stopped, bits of hard wood caught in its steel teeth.

"So tell me." The startled man spun on his heels. "Do you treat the wood with gasoline *before* you plant it in someone's yard? Or you douse it on the night?" I asked.

In a scratchy voice, "Who are you?" When he spoke, sawdust shook from his trembling jowls like dry, flaky skin.

I stepped toward him. "Frank Smith. Son of Simon. You?"

He stepped back. "Clay. Sam Clay. Rev. Sam Clay."

"What you doin' here, Rev. Sam Clay? Besides makin' crosses. I mean. Ain't your house."

"Heard the Smiths gone. Abandoned this fine plantation."

Gaining a little confidence, his arm swept the fine space as if it encompassed the whole world.

"Abandoned? Where'd you hear that?"

"Let me see." His face displayed the disarming, toothy smile of a fine southern gentleman, hoping his charm alone could mask the deeds and intent of the good ol' boy he was. "Can't likely recall."

"Let me help. Maybe one of your bigot friends. One of your church members."

"How dare you. I'm a man of God." He clenched his fists. Stiffened his body defiantly, shaking more dust free, revealing his true nature.

"My daddy told me all about you. A hate preacher. And making pointy crosses."

"Jesus died on the cross."

"Execution."

"Sacrifice. A symbol."

"A cross just like yours burned under that tree out there where my mama was beat, raped, and hung. You calling that sacrifice?"

"And atonement. God sees all our sins. You can't mix light with darkness. God's word. Not mine."

"Even yours."

I pulled out my gun. Took one step closer. Pointed at the head of the snake. His eyes locked on the gun's black hole. Like a supplicant, he knelt, pressed his hands together, began to pray.

"Our father, who art in—"

"Who killed my mama?"

"I am the way, the truth—"

"Who killed my mama?"

"Christ is the answer."

"What are the questions? Who killed my mama?"

He peered up at me. "I'm a good and faithful servant. Trust and obey." He cowered. "I just carried out God's will. Don't shoot me."

I'd heard enough. I slammed the butt of the gun against his temple. He toppled. Out cold. I lifted his body and slumped it over the table saw's circular blade. We'd had sacrifice, atonement, obedience to God's will. Missed out justice. Thus ending the lesson for the day, I switched on the table saw.

Covered in blood, I carried one of the late Rev. Clay's crosses over my shoulder much like Jesus is depicted on his path to Golgotha. Planted the cross under the old oak where my mama had hung and died. A fitting memorial.

I retrieved the pint of Jack from my car. Sat at the patio table. Grieved and smoked and drank and pondered the final step. I hadn't even fired a shot.

By the time I finished the pint, the sun had dipped below the horizon. The sparks and embers from the burning cane field at the edge of the garden floated on a light breeze toward the house. I stood, a little unsteady but focused. Stuffed the empty pint in one pocket my cigarette butts in the other. Wiped down the table and chair.

Then I entered my daddy's workshop. Donned a pair of garden gloves I found on a shelf. Grabbed the two gasoline cans. Splashed their contents around the shop, laying a trail out the door where I poured a small pool of accelerant on the patio. Replaced the now empty gas cans where I found them. Exited the shop. Pulled the property deed from my pocket. Set it alight. Dropped the burning deed in the patio pool of gasoline. Whoosh. I retreated to the far side of the swimming pool as the pressure and heat blew out the shop windows. When the flames appeared in the windows of the first floor above the shop, I knelt on the edge of the pool, removed the gloves, and rinsed the blood off my hands. I waited a few minutes, but there was nothing more to see.

I hopped in my car and headed around the circular drive. The now cloying scent of magnolias hung in the air.

As the fire exploded through the windows on the second floor of the big house, I entered the time tunnel of bald cypress and Spanish moss, now glowing orange from the flames. I checked the rear view mirror and observed the end of one vile and bloody past. But I saw another thing. I saw the fire, this time.

JUGBAND BLUES

BY C.W. BLACKWELL

The kid had teeth like a busted comb and eyes that went both ways at once.

He'd been following me with that sorry-ass six string for five blocks. I just couldn't shake him. He slowed when I slowed, hustled when I picked up the pace. I told him to quit a few blocks back, but the kid wouldn't leave me alone. Like some damn stray dog. I was halfway down East Broad when I finally spun around and walked straight to him.

"You really got it coming, kid." I gave him my best mad dog and scuffed my feet on the blacktop to make a little noise. "Only way that guitar could be any sorrier is if it was halfway up your hind end. *Now get!*"

The kid peddled back and lost his balance, feet sliding on the loose asphalt. He fell flat on his skinny ass, guitar clanging and jangling over the ground. I watched him for a beat, sweat rolling down his temples. It was a hot summer day in Spartanburg, maybe the hottest day of the year. The kind of day you don't want to be sitting ass-down on a hot road.

"I just want to buy a song from you, Mr. Anderson," said the kid. He got to his feet and held out a greasy dollar bill. It looked like he'd dredged it from the bottom of a backyard shithouse.

"What do you mean, *buy a song?*"

"I want you to teach me 'Jugband Blues'. Just play it slow enough and I'll pick out a lick or two." He pushed that filthy buck in my face, too close for comfort. "You're Pink Anderson, ain't you? I seen you play that song at Mama Jean's and I just had to learn it. I got another dollar if that's what it would take."

"You're too young for Mama Jean's."

"I seen you there just the same."

"Snuck in the back, I bet. You got a name, son?"

"They call me Dipper Boy."

The poor kid was uglier than a mud fence, and from the smell of it a long dip in the creek would do everyone some good.

"Dipper Boy, huh? That's your blues name?"

"Yessir."

"Tell you what, Dipper Boy. You come by Mama Jean's tomorrow night and I'll play that song slow as molasses. If you want to throw a buck in the jar, well I sure wouldn't stop you."

Dipper Boy's lips rolled up over those crooked teeth in some sort of crazy grin. "Well I'd like that just fine, Mr. Anderson."

—

The next night I arrived at Mama Jean's early so I could have a cold beer or two before the set. I elbowed through the crowd toward the back of the bar, the early drunks eyeballing me as I passed. The heat wouldn't quit, and it made everyone a little crazy. There'd already been a nasty fight out back and the winner came inside with bloody lips and hands and sat on the stool beside me. He gave me a long speculative look like maybe I'd be next. I always thought alcohol kicked a little harder on the hot days. Then, maybe Spartanburg was just getting meaner.

I drank the first beer fast, and nearly finished a second one when someone flicked my arm from behind. I spun around with the bottle in my hand—I've been around long enough to know that a beer bottle makes a decent weapon in a pinch.

"Pink, we gotta talk." It was Bernadette. We'd been seeing each other every now and then since I played a gospel set at the church cook-off a few months ago. We kept it on the sly, of course. It wasn't just that she was a preacher's daughter and I was a blues man. There was also a little issue of Bernadette's engagement to the youth minister, a skinny kid named Josiah Harris.

I guzzled what remained in the bottle and she led me out the back door. The alley smelled like stale beer and kitchen trash. A filthy porch light spilled over the brick walls and a young man lay slouched against a trash bin, drunk and bloody. Probably the one who lost the fight earlier. We stepped around him and edged down the alley, just out of earshot.

Bernadette pressed into me, head against my chest.

She started to cry.

"Baby, what is it now?" Her dress plunged in the back and I ran my fingertips along her bare shoulder blades. Tiny beads of sweat weeping from the pores. "You can tell ol' Pink."

"It's Josiah," she said.

"What about him? Did he hurt you, baby?" The thought of it got me hotter than I cared to be on a night like this. Sure, Bernadette and I were just having fun—just a summer fling. It didn't mean much. But I'd be damned if that skinny church boy ever laid a hand on her.

"No. Not yet."

"He'd better not. They'd stop calling me Pink and start calling me Cherry Red."

"I saw him, Pink. Saw his Ford parked on the street when I left your place Saturday night. I think he knows about us."

"Lots of old Fords in this town. You sure it was his?" A Ford coupe trundled down Church Street beyond the alleyway as if to prove my point, downshifting as it picked up speed and faded into the city.

"I'm sure of it," she said. "He's been so cold to me ever since that night. I'm not worried what he'd do to me, but if daddy found out, well." She shuddered, and more tears came.

I took her up in my arms, kissed both sides of her face where the tears had left little glossy trails. "It'll be just fine, baby. We'll cool it for a while, that's all. You can trust ol' Pink. It'll blow over if we just cool off."

She gave a reassured smile, but it faded fast.

One look in my eyes and she knew I was worried too.

—

Showtime.

I perched on a stool along the back wall and thumbed the steel guitar one string at a time, tuning to an open 'G' as I went. I wasn't thinking too hard about getting the tuning right. I was thinking about Bernadette's father, Reverend Banks. Most knew him as a man of the cloth, but others—the types like me that hung out in juke joints and drank bootleg liquor—knew he had a devil on his shoulder bigger than any angel could grow. He had an icy touch when he shook your hand like he was taking something from you that you didn't know you could give up. A little ragged corner of your soul, maybe.

I gave the crowd a quick smile and started off with "Meet Me in the Bottom," a song I learned from Bumble Bee Slim way out in Indianapolis a few years back. Some danced in the shadows while others just bobbed their heads over glasses of booze and smoldering ashtrays. I imagined Reverend Banks in the back of the crowd, beady eyes simmering in the darkness, a pistol hidden in his coat pocket and a bullet with my name on it.

The paranoia just wouldn't quit.

I played for an hour without much in the can to show for it. Sweat stung my eyeballs and I mostly played with my eyes shut. I didn't always see when someone tossed a nickel or dime into the can, and by the sound of it, there'd be a dollar or two at most. When I finished the set, I noticed a glass of whiskey on the stool beside me. I looked around to see if someone had just set it down, but it didn't look like it belonged to anybody. Sometimes folks bought me drinks as a tip, but they usually let me know first. I took the glass and poked my nose over the rim, gave it a whiff. It smelled good enough to drink, and I'd worked up a thirst.

"Don't drink that stuff, Mr. Anderson."

Dipper Boy appeared at my elbow, mugging me with those bulgy eyeballs. He looked as serious as a dead man on judgement day.

I tossed him a glance, then studied the whiskey.

"Why not?" I said. "You're too young for whiskey anyhow."

"I'm plenty old enough," he said, even though he clearly wasn't. "I saw a guy stirring it with his finger, like he was mixing something up in it."

"Bullshit." I smelled the glass and held it to the light, paranoia creeping back. I wanted to take a sip just to prove to the kid how foolish he was.

He grabbed my wrist. "Please don't."

"You best let go of me, son," I said.

"I'll give you five dollars not to drink that stuff, Pink. It's all the money I got in the world." He pulled out a few ratty bills and a handful of change. "You can buy yourself a whole ass-pocket of whiskey for that price. Just leave it."

I waved him off and set the glass on the stool.

He had me half-convinced.

"What did he look like, the man you saw stirring the drink?"

Dipper Boy looked around the room but came up empty. "Kind of skinny. Big ol' ears. I don't see him now."

I emptied the tip can into the palm of my hand. Maybe a buck-fifty inside. "Look, son. I don't know what you saw or didn't see. But I'm sure it's nothing a couple of cold beers couldn't sort out."

I put my hand on the kid's back and led him to the bar. I didn't mind having an extra pair of eyes looking out for me, but I had a feeling the kid was just trying to get me to teach him songs. It happened like that all the time. There's a kid outside every juke joint wanting to learn the blues, and some of them will tag along from place to place, nagging you for a riff or two. I was nice about it this time, but I told him that I wasn't a good teacher and he ought to find someone else. He nodded quietly and sipped his beer, told me a little about where he came from. Some scrappy little neighborhood up in Chapel Hill. He'd run away from a mean daddy and that was something we both had in common.

I was about to tilt the beer all the way back and send Dipper Boy on his way when I heard a commotion in the room. Not a fight this time, but something else. Somebody groaning and retching. A circle formed around an old drunkard with crazy white hair. He stood doubled over, foam building up into his beard like a sick dog. He spilled his guts onto the floor and collapsed on his side, body shaking and twisting in white hot agony.

I looked for the glass of whiskey.

It sat just where I left it, but empty.

"Hey, Pink." The kid hung at my elbow again, pointing across the room. "It was that guy. He done it."

Standing near the back door was Bernadette's fiance, Josiah Harris. Big floppy ears, body swimming in his too-big clothes. He watched bug-eyed as the old man twisted up and died on the juke joint floor.

I knew damn well it was supposed to be me.

—

Josiah ran like hell.

He might have gotten away if he hadn't stopped to look over his shoulder so many times. I chased him down Church Street, soles clapping out against the old brick buildings, echoes repeating down the lighted avenue. I followed as he cut across the park on South Liberty, bursting through the bushes onto Main. He ran another block or two before I finally caught up to him in the parking lot of a little white Baptist church, hunched over and heaving. I didn't slow when I reached him, just shouldered into him like a linebacker and knocked him in the dirt. I picked him up by the collar and buried my fist in his face. Blood whipsawed into the streetlights and he softened a little. Another blow and he went completely limp. I lifted him to his feet and he teetered side to side like a helpless drunk.

"Try a gun next time, Josiah," I said. "Rat poison is for cowards."

He spit blood on the asphalt, eyes swimming. I'd rung his bell good.

"It's not too late to kill you," he mumbled.

"You crazy? One more hit and you'll be the devil's problem."

A silver Buick roared into the lot, headlights blaring. The car door opened and a fat man squeezed out wearing a brown suit and a frock coat. A double-barrel shotgun slung over his shoulder. He waddled toward me, whistling some old gospel hymn. Bald head gleaming in the headlights.

"Get in the car, Pink," he said. His voice sounded dark and deep and had every bit the quality of a Baptist preacher.

I held up my hands. "No offense, Reverend Banks. But I think I'll walk."

"If I tell you again it'll be my shotgun doing the talking."

"Just shoot him," said Josiah. He spit out a tooth and folded his arms like a sad little boy. "Do it for Bernadette, for the shame he brought us. Besides, ain't no way he's gonna get in that car after we tried to kill him."

Banks looked Josiah up and down like a bad deal. "If I tried to kill him, he'd already be dead." The shotgun swung level and the hammers rocked back. "Last chance, Pinky."

I was cooked. Reverend Banks might kill me now or kill me later.

Either way, I knew I'd strummed my last tune.

I heard the Buick's chassis groan. The headlights dipped slightly as if someone had crawled into the front seat. No one noticed but me.

The transmission dropped into gear, engine roaring.

I leaped out of the way.

The car launched forward, lifting Banks and Josiah off their feet and onto the hood. When the car stopped, they spilled over the fenders and onto the asphalt, howling. The headlights went dark and I saw Dipper Boy in the front seat, that goofy ear-to-ear grin. I scooped up the shotgun and cracked the butt-end over the reverend's bald head just as he got to his knees, then fired a round at Josiah—knocking his legs out from under him.

Next time he wouldn't run so fast.

I slid into the driver seat and shooed the kid over, slamming the stick shift into reverse. We screamed out of the parking lot in a billow of white smoke.

"That wasn't very smart of you," I said. "Now we're both in hot water."

Dipper Boy shrugged, tapped a finger on the dash. "Got enough gas to get us to Charlotte," he said.

"What's in Charlotte?"

"Only the best juke joints and roadhouses in the state. We'll be famous there."

"I just can't shake you can I, Dipper Boy?"

"Long as we're starting an act together, you can call me Floyd. That's my real name. Floyd Council."

"All right, Floyd," I said. I flicked on the headlights and put my foot into the pedal, gunning down Union Street toward East Hampton. "Thing is, I never even heard you play. You any good?"

"Getting better every day. Soon they'll be asking us which one's Pink."

"Like hell they will. Why don't we take it one gig at a time?"

I pulled up to an old clapboard house with a white-painted brick porch and laid on the horn. A light came on in the kitchen, curtains sweeping and falling over the barred window. Bernadette came out the front door and ran to the driver side, still wearing the dress she had on earlier.

"Why are you driving daddy's car?"

"He tried to kill me, Bernie. Twice. He and Josiah."

"Where is he? You didn't kill him did you, Pink?"

"No baby, he'll be alright. Josiah might walk a little funny from now on."

"Are you okay?"

"I will be once we get out of town. Hop in."

She glanced at the house and back again, eying the kid.

"Who's this?"

"This is Floyd. We're starting an act together in Charlotte."

The kid gave a friendly nod and climbed into the backseat. Bernadette went back inside and when she came out again, she had a suitcase in one hand and a small duffle in the other. She slid next to me and laid her head on my shoulder. "I was hoping you'd come for me, Pink. I'd already packed and everything."

"A few minutes with Josiah and I can see why," I said.

I wheeled the Buick down the road and onto I-29 toward Charlotte. A Son House tune came on the radio and we sang along, watching the highway reel by, hot and dark and desolate. Headlights heavy on the road.

"Pink and Floyd," said Bernadette. "Sounds like an act you'd hear on the radio someday."

The kid perked up. "Maybe someday sooner than you think," he said.

Julia Dream

by Morgan Sylvia

The prison is cold and gray, as is the world outside it. The guard leads me past rows of empty cells. Cracked paint forms spiderweb patterns on cement walls. Our footprints leave marks on the dusty floor. I struggle with the box and the bag, which barely conceals the pickaxe. Not long ago, I'd never have gotten these things inside. But no one cares anymore.

You sit framed in sallow daylight, as drab and colorless as the walls, your face turned to a grimy window. You look thin. Weak. Sick. I can almost see the metamorphosis that brought you from then to now, the age layered over youth.

How long have you waited for me in your cage, with your empty eyes and your empty smile?

I put the box and bag down and pay the guard. He turns and walks away, disappearing back into the shadows.

"Hello, Albert," I say quietly.

You don't move. Your face is empty and lifeless, as are your hours.

I kick the box. "I've brought these back to you. All your scribbled ramblings."

121

No reaction. We're only feet apart, but there is a river between us. A river of years, that has swept lives and light along with it. A river we can never cross.

I'm not surprised by your silence. The guard said you wouldn't speak. Not aloud, anyway. They took your pen and paper away once, but you only wrote in blood.

A fly lands on your nose. You don't notice.

I rustle through the box. Your spidery handwriting crawls across hundreds of loose papers. These have sat in my attic for years, gathering dust below stars that have forgotten you. "Why do you still send me poems, Albert?"

Silence. Is there anything left behind your lifeless eyes?

I look around, taking in your world. Echoes. Shadows. The bars on the window cut black lines through drab, pale skies. Outside, pigeons roost on the windowsill. Factory smoke curls up towards colorless clouds. A siren wails in the distance. It is discordant, eerie and beautiful at once.

It's peaceful here, in a strange way.

You don't deserve peace.

I glance at the dog-eared paperbacks on your shelf. "What are you reading? Benjamin Franklin? Vonnegut? Shakespeare? Have you grasped something of their wisdom, there, in your cage?"

Nothing. I am talking to a ghost.

I sigh. "It wouldn't matter if you did. Any understanding you have has come too late."

I stare at you, looking for the person you once were. The golden boy who led us from sneaking cigarettes under the bleachers to starting fights at punk rock shows is gone. You're a shell, a husk, faded and lifeless.

A rat scurries across the floor. It occurs to me that, of all the souls in this place, only it and I have come here deliberately.

You knew I would visit eventually, didn't you?

I crumple a page up, toss it through the bars. It bounces off your head.

—

I wish I could say it was all your doing. You did brainstorm the whole thing. You were always the reckless one. In middle school, you stole candy from the corner store, let the Welch's cows out, burned the Jones' shed down. In high school, we snuck out, drove Ken's brother's car too fast, stole cassettes. We all ran wild and stupid back then. We were all angry. Some of us had more reason to be than others, but we hadn't realized that yet. We smoked our first cigarettes behind a wall of rock, huddled together against salty ocean wind. We drank our first cheap wine together in an emerald green field as black thunderheads rolled in. Spent hours and days and weeks in our clubhouse, smoking and drinking and talking about girls and guitars and all the things we would do. Things we knew even then would never happen. The 'clubhouse' was really just an old shed, but it was ours, a perfectly imperfect refuge against the world that was waiting to swallow us whole.

I can still feel those days, even now, smoldering in my soul. At the time, I thought you were brave. Now, I see it very differently. At least, when the kaleidoscope clears.

You never see the choices you make, until you look back at them later.

We had already been molded by then. Broken down in an endless, drab hell of uniforms and gray walls, by a colorless world of barked commands and shiny boots marching in lockstep. You couldn't bear it, could you? To be one of them, the line of uniformed drudges that went before us, faceless numbers passing into cold steel buildings. Workers filing into factories. Accountants plodding into offices. Soldiers trudging into war. We knew what was waiting for us. The crushing weight of debt. The pain of stagnancy. The bitterness of boredom. We sought to escape these terrors by any means necessary.

There's a slicing pain to the moment you realize you're nothing.

We were still within range of normal life. We could have sprouted into bankers, factory workers, or counselors, had we realized we were at a crossroads. But the light inside us was fading, even then. We were young enough to appreciate youth, but old enough to understand regret. I saw that hubris in you that night, when you turned your face and your rage to the dark mansion on the hill and started ranting about revenge. You filled the gloaming with beautiful madness, and we lapped it up like dogs. We went along, as always, too dumb, too numb, too empty to do otherwise.

Funny thing is, you did end up a nameless, faceless number in a cold steel building.

There was never any way back for us from that night, was there? The one that split our lives.

The one that turned you, Albert, into inmate 4B364.

—

I pull a yellowed paper out of the box. *"A prism breaks through darkness. Dissolve into numbers, my dear worms. Drown all unauthorized thoughts in disinfectant."* I let my hand drop. "What are you trying to tell me?"

At last, you turn your head. Your voice is cracked and cobwebby. You've forgotten how to use it. "Echoes," you say. "The thoughts have flown away."

My throat seems dry, suddenly. "So you are in there."

"Hello, Roger."

Words are thick and heavy on my tongue. "Do you know what's happening out there?"

Your voice is empty, as are your days. "Everything. Nothing."

I feel nauseous again. The painkillers are wearing off, and the ache is returning. "You knew this was coming, didn't you? Why else would you write pages upon pages about famines and storms and *disinfectant?*" I pick a letter at random. *"The fading, rotted wisdom of pallid kings who never wore crowns."*

Your words weave past dust particles hanging in the stale air. *"Run, run after the wind, as cities fall silent. Run before the axe falls."*

I look down. You've just quoted the last line. I'm stunned. "You sent this decades ago. How do you remember?"

You tap your forehead. "Mirrors. Magnets. Miracles."

And then I see it. A spark of that red-gold fire that once burned behind your glassy eyes.

There you are, Albert.

You tilt your head. "Why did you come here? For answers? Is that what's important now, aside from those numbers your world succumbed to?"

I swallow. "It's your world, too. Even if it has forgotten you."

"As you did?"

I never forgot. But you know that, don't you?

"Maybe," you say, "you're not asking the right questions."

Maybe you're right.

Maybe I'm not.

You face the window again. "Doesn't matter. We're all just cogs in the machine."

I look at the snippet in my hand. *We're all just cogs in the machine.*

My hair stands on end.

Your yellowed teeth move against dry lips. "It's quieter than I thought it would be, the end of things. What's it like out there?"

"It's been chaos and order all at once, somehow. Mostly chaos."

"And yet the farmer's bones still creak in the damp cold morning. The swine still scream."

Dribble glistens on your dry lips. My voice twists in disgust. "You're drooling."

You stand and walk to the bars, curl thin, dirty fingers around them. Your voice seems stronger now. I glimpse a trace of who you were. Who you could have been. "The world we grew up in is dying. There's a new one being born out there, amidst all the slime and screaming. Of course, I won't live to see it." You pause, surveying me. "Nor will you, I think. You're pale. Weak. Sick. You don't look so well, Roger."

Your words strike me hard, just as you meant them to. You were always good at that. Even caged, you're as wild and cunning as the rat scratching at the end of the hall.

You're right, of course. There's nothing I can do but wait. The hospitals are empty. I cannot get my prescriptions filled anymore, even at exorbitant rates. It's a matter of time.

The smile that splits your face chills my soul.

"But who knows?" You continue. "If you're lucky, one day a child will look up at you and ask where you were when the skies emptied."

You point at the box. Your eyes shine bright and mad. "I remember that one. '*You wanted sun and emerald seas. But the clock never waited. Now flowers bloom in your dreams and curses.*'"

Rage darkens my eyes. I know who this one is about.

Julia.

Every night, in my dreams, she walks through a blue forest filled with silver streams, the orange cat trailing behind her. Pink roses blossom in her footsteps. And then I am seventeen again, looking out my old bedroom window, waiting to spot the beam of her flashlight in the forest. When she reaches the garden, I pull the yellow moon from the sky and offer it to her. But then the light fades and she is gone.

—

We were growing, changing, by the time Julia came into my life. Julia, with her spells and paintings and tarot cards, her fat orange cat, her poetry. Alone among us, she saw nothing of this realm. She lived in dreams and stories, even then. On summer nights, we sat together in the thick branches of a weeping willow, planning a lifetime of adventures. We would take a steamboat up the Mississippi, swim with dolphins in the Caribbean, teach emerald spiders to spell. Silly, shiny dreams. She always had her nose buried in a notebook. She wrote as though she was trying to capture words and phrases before they slipped away, as though they would fly off like the seagulls we watched by the cut.

My memories of that night start with Julia writing on the cabin wall in black sharpie. *Pyramids hold their secrets as the lights die around them.* She had to hunt for an empty spot among the posters and lyrics and art plastered on the walls. She found one beside that stupid taxidermized armadillo she called the Armored Texas Rat. "Is it dark enough yet?"

"Not yet," Ken said. "We have time for a beach fire."

We walked down to the shore, lost soul strapped in clouds of sweet smoke. The bottle flashed in the light as we passed it around. We watched endless waves racing out to endless skies, growing and dying at once.

I was uneasy. "Are you sure about this?"

Campfire flames flickered in your eyes. "They're all off on their yacht for the summer. Even the brats. It'll be easy."

"What if we get caught?" Ken asked.

"We won't." You dragged on a joint, passed it along. "I've been watching. I know the security code. And I already have a buyer for the jewels. We'll make millions each. Enough to leave this place forever *and* pay them back for what they did to my mom."

Julia smiled, her eyes reflecting golden sparks from the fire. "They deserve it."

She was wearing velvet that night. My ring shone on her finger.

You held out the little squares. We took the tiny suns eagerly, waiting for the world to melt around us and show us its secrets.

How many hits did you take, Albert?

We cut through the woods, howling like madmen as we crashed through branches and bramble, headed for the dark mansion that should have been yours. Leather-clad gods, punk angels raging into a world we thought we could take on.

We thought we were diamonds, but we were only glass.

I didn't expect the code to work, but it did. We walked right in. You immediately took the pickaxe from its display box and began smashing mahogany bookshelves, shattering glass, destroying priceless artifacts.

"Be careful," I remember telling you. The acid was kicking in. The words floated slowly through the air, gold and green.

"Can you?" You screamed at me. "Can you live up to their standards and still live?"

"Hey man," Ken said, when one swing got uncomfortably close to him.

"Fuck him," you sobbed. Then you started really tearing into everything. You shattered Lladro and Waterford heirlooms, hacked the fine furniture into splinters, slashed paintings that cost more than our parents' houses combined. Destroyed the family photos of the man you would never call father.

And then Julia came back down the stairs, laughing, draped in diamonds and jewels, looking not at me, but at you.

Why did you swing without looking? Where would she be today, if you hadn't? Would she be standing beside me, not reduced to dust and dreams? Why was she looking at you, Albert?

Why did you take her from me?

That scream. Was it yours or mine? I'm not sure. I only know it was a sound ripped from the blackest abyss of the human soul.

Then the sick thud as she fell, the words and dreams draining from her eyes. Red liquid spilled onto marble tiles, filled with poems and magic. You stared at each other. Something passed between you. Something that makes my stomach churn.

Her eyes were ice in that final moment.

I vaguely recall Ken shouting and running after you. Minutes later, I found him lying on the manicured lawn, bloody and torn, his eyes lifeless.

When the police finished questioning me, I burned the cabin

to the ground. Julia's poems floated over green black pines in tendrils of smoke, mingling with the words of Johnny Rotten and Sid Vicious. Sometimes when it storms, I feel like those poems are returning to me as raindrops. I try to capture them, but they always slip through my fingers.

As have the years.

Time takes everything, and moves on without us.

—

I kick the box towards you.

"Leaving already?" You ask. "That's just as well. I'm very busy. I've walls to stare at and nightmares to dream. And I didn't tell the maid to set an extra place."

I don't answer. I'm dizzy. It's an effort to open the bag and take out the pickaxe. I paid handsomely to retrieve it from the evidence locker. It won't be missed, any more than you will.

I leave it in plain view, but out of reach. It won't stay there long. I've paid well to ensure that. You'll know what's coming, but you won't know when.

"Is this revenge," you ask, "or forgiveness? Freedom, or just another prison?"

Fever melts my thoughts. "You choose."

You sit down, turn back to the window. "Take the box. Maybe there is truth in there, after all."

"Goodbye, Albert," I say, through ragged breaths.

You don't answer. You've gone back into your shell, a ghost again.

I walk away and leave you there to die.

—

My driver is waiting to take me home. We glide past empty fields and factories, where great machines are falling silent beneath empty blue skies. Fog hovers over emerald grass that looks soft, but is filled with sharp seeds.

We roll to a stop at the mansion's front entrance. Getting

out is incredibly taxing. With what feels like the last of my breath, I tell the driver to take the Tesla. I won't be needing it again.

I don't watch him drive off.

By the time I reach the top of the stairs, I am dizzy and out of breath. The shadows inside are long and empty. I've sent the help home rich and frightened. The fire I light in the hearth doesn't warm either my body or my soul. I sit huddled in a blanket as the mansion fills with ghosts and memories. I drown them in fine scotch.

Minutes become monsters.

I read your poems again. Your glimpses of wisdom are useless against a disease that steals breath. I should take the box to the sacred place, the place where cold pale ghosts whisper against green black pines and salt air. The place where we once laughed and passed joints around while the Violent Femmes and David Bowie played on our boom box.

But I am weak, and there are only timbers there now.

In the morning, I walk down to the beach one last time. Every step requires Herculean effort. My breaths jab my lungs like needles. My limbs feel leaden and useless. But eventually I make it to the ice-cold sands. Waves grey and cold pound the black rocks. I stand there, watching endless waves racing towards endless skies, growing and dying at once.

I throw the poems into the sea.

You stand at my side suddenly, young again. Julia is there beside you, straight red hair shining in golden sunlight.

What a trio we make. The demon in his cell, the angel in her grave, the fool in his castle.

"Want to know something, Roger?" You ask. "Something not pretty?"

"Truth is never pretty," Julia says. "Even when it's draped in diamonds."

You open your mouth and scream, and it is *that* scream again, the one I can never forget.

Sharp pains pierce my chest. Beneath the distant peal of the harbor bell, I stagger back to the house. The bloody pickaxe sits on my porch. It takes a ridiculous amount of energy to pick it up. To walk inside. To collapse on the couch, where I gasp for air like a fish. The world blurs at the edges.

Julia turns to me across the years, her eyes filled with stars.

—

I suppose I should fill in the gaps, like a proper bard.

There's something I forgot to tell you.

Those diamonds, once I rinsed the blood off, were worth billions. It wasn't hard to figure out who your buyer was. Your buddy John, the ex-con.

My bones are cold, but they still remember.

One day, not long after I bought this place, I ran into Julia's younger brother at the causeway where we used to meet. I wanted to tell him what happened, but the words stuck in my throat. I just turned and walked away.

Years later, I anonymously paid his college tuition.

I wonder who we would have been, had we chosen differently. In the end, it doesn't matter, does it? I faded in a mansion, and you faded in a cell.

Julia waits for me, wrapped in words and diamonds, beneath emerald grass that looks soft but is filled with sharp seeds. Tonight, I will burn this mansion and all its shadows and memories and go to her. We will dream ourselves into oblivion, where an orange cat waits for us in a blue forest filled with pink roses and silver streams.

KEEP YOUR HANDS OFF OF MY STACK

BY RENEE ASHER PICKUP

When I met Jack, he was every woman's dream—the kind of muscular that comes from hard labor and calloused hands, not hours at the gym. He had that just messy enough look, like he'd always shaved three days before, hair that was always combed but fell in his face just right—so he looked cute and approachable, not like he didn't give a shit. He had beautiful brown eyes and dark, thick lashes, a smile that could melt Antarctica. He came home from work dirty, but cleaned up and managed to wear a plain tee shirt and loose jeans like a goddamn GQ model. He liked simple things, cheap beer, football.

And he liked me.

He liked that I worked a "respectable" job and called my work clothes my "sexy librarian" look. He liked that it took me over an hour to get ready even if we were just going to the bar. He liked the way his friends would joke about how he landed himself a sugar momma, even though he never seemed to let me pay for anything when we were out. He moved into my place within a few months, took over mowing the lawn, fixing clogged sinks, and anything else I'd normally have to pay someone to come in to do.

He even cooked for me three nights a week.

The problem, the way I saw it after it was too late, was I got used to it. Jack was charming. Jack was helpful. Jack loved me. Jack was great in bed. These were all facts, and after awhile I stopped questioning them. About six months in, work got crazy, and I was tired all the time. I would stumble through the door after eight every night, trying to kick off my heels before I even made it to the couch. And there was Jack, a glass of wine at the ready, "Dinner's almost done, baby." He'd feed me, listen to me talk about my shitty coworkers and my demanding boss, then he'd put me to bed and if I was up to it, he'd show me a good time before letting me pass out. He was always gone in the morning before I got up. Construction work is all early hours, but he was always home when I got there. Always ready to be my right hand.

It took me a while to realize he hadn't been working. He started parking his work truck in the garage, claiming it was easier to not have to unload all his tools every day. It made sense. He talked me into getting his cell phone on my family plan, and it saved us both a bunch of money, so it made sense. When he stopped leaving me cash to pay his share, I didn't notice. Everything was on autopay, and I was just so busy.

When I woke up on a Saturday morning to a tow truck pulling his truck out of my driveway, I had questions, of course. Jack had an explanation. Something wrong at the bank. His stuff was all on autopay as well. He didn't change his address, so he didn't realize the payments weren't going through. It seemed odd to me that he wouldn't notice an extra few hundred dollars in his account every month, but I reasoned it away. Jack was never too concerned about money, anyway.

When one of my girlfriends at work suggested we play hooky and take a long lunch, get away from the boss, have a drink or two, I didn't think it was going to change my life. We went to a bar across town, hoping not to get spotted, and just as a plate full of onion rings landed on the table between us, I looked up to see my boyfriend coming out of the bathroom and taking a seat at the bar. Mary saw my face, and before I could compose myself, she followed my gaze and saw Jack sitting there, not a care in the world.

"Look who decided to play hooky today, too!" She yelled and waved him over.

He took her lie and ran with it, but I could see it in his face. This wasn't a one-time thing. We fought for the first time that night. He had more reasons, more excuses. Losing his job was so embarrassing. He had leads on new jobs. He didn't want to worry me when I was under so much stress already. It was hard enough being a man with a girlfriend who paid the rent and made all the money without being *emasculated* by losing his job, too.

It all made sense. Except, it didn't. But when he said he just didn't want to depend on me, didn't want to be a burden, and came in for a hug, I accepted it. I went to bed. I was too fucking tired.

The next day at work I couldn't help but wonder how long he'd been out of work, how he'd managed to hide it from me. It hit me then that he'd been hiding his truck in the garage because he knew it was going to be repossessed. But he had money to drink at the bar all day long. He had cash to keep his hair cut fresh and surprise me by doing the grocery shopping before I got home. He'd just bought me a little gold necklace with a tiny heart charm on it. I was rubbing the pendant between my fingers as I thought about it.

I pulled up my bank account and everything looked in order. I checked my wallet, surely, I would have noticed if he was stealing cash. Everything was where it should be—My bank card, my credit card, a hundred bucks or so in case of emergency. So how did he buy me jewelry? How did he pay his bar tab?

When I got home that night, he wasn't there. For the first time in months, he was out. A note on the fridge said he was out with a buddy who could get him on a job site soon. I don't know what came over me, but I found myself frantically rifling through his drawers, looking for something, anything, that could confirm my suspicion that he was ripping me off somehow. Once I saw the mess I made and had to go through all the trouble of carefully folding his things back up and placing them back to cover my tracks, I felt humiliated. What kind of person does that? What kind of person doesn't just talk to their partner?

But then, I saw his laptop on the nightstand. It was open, and logged in.

The laptop was new, too. It didn't seem like a big deal when he brought it home, it wasn't anything fancy, and I thought he had a job. Now it seemed to be taunting me with the knowledge that he couldn't have bought a laptop two months ago if his fucking truck had to be hidden in the garage, so it didn't get towed by the repo man. I found myself rubbing the heart pendant with my fingers again and got so angry at myself for seeking comfort from a gift Jack gave me that I wrapped my hand around the dainty chain and yanked as hard as I could. The chain broke, leaving a little red line of irritation at the back of my neck and across the pads of my fingers.

I sat down at the computer and opened every file on it, clicked through his entire browser history—of course, this corn-fed construction worker with his "aw, shucks" attitude about technology was smart enough to delete his browser history. Another wave of rage hit me. I opened up the mail program on his desktop, not smart enough to logout of that, apparently. I scrolled with the bedroom door open, listening for his keys in the door so I could close the window and toss his computer back on the nightstand at a second's notice. The emails addressed to me started three months ago: notices that my paperless bank statements were now available, and my credit card was on the way, FedEx. I kept scrolling and saw that before me, there was an Allison. Before Allison there was a Madeline. I'd scrolled back a year and a half before I noticed. I wasn't the first, and I wouldn't be the last.

My fingers trembled over the keyboard. I could feel my chest tighten around my pounding heart and if I hadn't heard the keys in the lock at that very moment, I'm pretty sure I would have blacked out in rage. But the door opening snapped me into action. I closed out of the email, hit the sleep button and placed his computer as it was when I found it. I laid back on the bed and scooted to my side, pretending that I had come home and just flung myself there to relax, and fell asleep. My heart was still pounding in my chest, sweat collected in my armpits and under my breasts, but I did my best to act startled awake when he came in the bedroom.

"Great news, baby! Bill can get me on the job site Monday. It's all gonna be fine."

"That's great," I smiled, feigning exhaustion. "I knew you'd figure it out."

I stripped off my clothes and put on a baggy shirt and tried like hell to fall asleep as I wondered if the new job was a new credit card in my name or a new woman he could swindle. I stared at the closet door, where I kept things like my social security card, birth certificate, and everything else Jack needed to steal my identity. Obviously, I thought, tomorrow I was going to call in sick to work, get my credit report and go to the police. Then I'd contact one of those credit recovery programs and figure out how much it would cost me to get all the shit he'd charged challenged. I almost rolled over and screamed in his face when I realized I didn't even know how far in debt he'd plunged me. Somehow, I found the strength to lay next to him all night, fists clenched so hard my nails cut into my palms, and just breathe until my alarm went off.

He didn't have a lie to carry on anymore, so he wasn't gone when my phone started chiming. He was all smiles, offering to make me breakfast, telling me to go ahead and be late for once. I didn't know what I'd do if I had to confront him, tell him everything I knew, so I smiled and agreed. I sat at the kitchen table in my pajamas while he fried bacon and eggs, singing to himself. Like the perfect boyfriend he'd been from day one. I felt like I was going to vomit all over the table one second, and like I would explode if I didn't scream the next.

"You should just call in sick today," he said. "Let's celebrate the good news."

I choked down coffee and nodded. Managed to force out, "What's the new job?"

His smile faltered for a second as he served the eggs onto the two plates already heaped with bacon, but he recovered quickly. I wondered how many times he'd lied to me just like this and I didn't know. "Ah, you know. It's a remodel. Private residence, real rich folks. It's not prevailing wage. But it'll keep me working, get me in good with Bill's brother, who runs a contracting company."

"So, it's a pay cut?"

He bent and kissed my forehead and I fought every instinct in my body not to recoil.

"It's only money, baby," he said.

That's when it happened. I blacked out. I didn't ever believe that was a thing that happened to people. No one "sees red," no one gets so fucking angry they "black out." That's bullshit. That's an excuse people make to excuse themselves from their actions. But I did. I blacked out and when I realized what was happening I had managed to push him up against the stove, where he'd put his hand down on the still hot burner that burnt him so bad it brought him to his knees. I guess the element of surprise worked in my favor first, the fact that electric burners don't cool down when you turn them off. The cast iron pan he just had to have for his goddamned fried chicken was still hot when I picked it up, the handle burning in my hand.

"What the fuck! What the fuck!" Jack screamed, trying to get to his feet, holding his wrist in his hand staring at the pink, muddled flesh where the stove had marked him. He looked up and locked eyes with me just as I brought the pan down on his head. It was heavy, but it didn't knock him out. He was dazed at best, but the pain in his hand kept him sharp. I saw his confusion turn to anger I knew in that moment that if I let him stand up, he'd kill me.

What I'm saying is, it was self-defense.

I brought the pan down again and again, a primal and ugly scream coming up from deep in my guts and spewing out of my mouth. I realized; I couldn't stop if I wanted to. Because fuck Jack for making me think I was special while he leeched off me. Fuck Jack for doing the same to a half a dozen women before me. Fuck him for making me think I loved him when I didn't even know him. I brought the pan down again and again until the thunking noise turned wet and I was so exhausted from the emotional outburst that I couldn't hold the pan anymore. When it dropped to the floor, I thought, maybe there's a chance I didn't kill him. I clearly hurt him really, really bad. His face was red, swollen, and bleeding, but surely it took a bigger, stronger person than me to beat a grown man to death.

Surely.

His chest didn't rise and fall. The blood running down his face, over his nostrils didn't seem disturbed by air.

"Oh, fuck. Oh, fuck oh fuck oh fuck," I said, the words rushing from my mouth as my guts tightened and I realized I was in big trouble. I'd just attacked Jack in our shared kitchen over nothing. I could tell the police about the credit cards, but there's no law that says you can kill a man for swindling you. There's no law that says that if you beat a man over the head once, and you're sure he's going to hurt you after that, that it's okay to keep beating him until he's dead.

It was nine am on a Friday. My neighbors must have heard me scream. They might have already called the police. My breath was coming in quick, shallow gulps, turning from breathing to sobbing to hyperventilating. I put my hand on the stove to steady myself and burnt my pinky and ring finger so badly I wailed in pain, giving the neighbors another reason to call 911. But much like the pain in Jack's hand kept him sharp a little longer, it sliced through the panic. He'd never turned the burner off. It was still just as hot as when he fell against it.

I sniffled and wiped my nose, looked at the terrible scene in front of me, and decided that whatever happened if I threw myself backward on the hot stove was a fuck of a lot better than prison, and closed my eyes.

I almost couldn't do it. I stepped back once and caught myself with my back foot. Then I looked down and saw how fucking pathetic Jack was on the floor—all his lies exposed, all his weakness. He was a sad excuse for the kind of man he wore as a disguise, all "yes ma'am" and pulling out chairs, pretending to give a shit. There was no fucking way this lump of meat on the floor was sending me to prison. I bent my elbows and made two fists, trying to imagine how I'd stand if he had me by the shoulders and threw myself back as hard as I could. My left arm hit the hot burner and my head hit the back burner, thankfully cold. The smell of my own burning flesh took my focus from the pain in my head and sent all my attention to my upper arm, burnt much worse than Jack's hand had been. I bit into my lip to keep from screaming and held my teeth there, tears stinging my eyes. Soon, blood ran down my chin.

I thought, maybe, I could just sit down for a minute. Just sit down and rest for a minute. Then I'd make up a story about confronting him about stealing my identity, the way he raged at me. I'd tell them I reached blindly for anything to defend myself and grabbed the pan, I'd show them the light burn on my hand that proved I hadn't been planning this. I'd say he was just too big, too strong, and he wouldn't stop coming for me no matter how many times I hit him. I'd say I must have been in shock, or the adrenaline high hit me after the burn, so it made me stronger, more out of control. The adrenaline part was partly true. I could feel it leaving my body after nearly twelve hours of pumping through every part of me. I could feel the energy and emotion leave me like it was running down an open drain.

So, I leaned back and let it drain.

Leaned back and went to sleep next to Jack one last time.

LUCIFER SAM

BY K. A. LAITY

"We're nearly there." Keith stroked her long golden hair, but it did not soothe her. "I can feel it. She's ready to give it all to us."

Maisie frowned. "I don't feel right."

"Opel has so much and we have so little," he said, his hands resting on her shoulders now, as if he were considering whether to shake some sense into her. She shuddered a little. "Are you cold?" He was all solicitousness now that he wanted something from her.

"No, it was just … just a feeling."

"Your feelings are important," Keith said, but he wasn't thinking of her feelings right now. "Your feelings can bring us a great deal of money if you would only stop worrying about the petty things."

"It seems wrong—"

Keith sighed. He could sigh for Britain. "We've been over this before. It's not wrong. If she chooses to give us her money—"

"But is she choosing?" Maisie kept coming back to that point as if it were a scab she had to itch. Opel Lang was such a sweetheart but so sad, missing her late husband.

Keith sat down on the chair opposite her at the little oak kitchen table. *He was so handsome!* How she could have pulled such a guy, her being so mousy and completely happy alone with her cat in this bedsit. What had he seen in her, this tall fellow who looked like a poet and talked like a newsreader?

He put on his Reasonable Guy face. He took one of her hands and squeezed it. Their hands rested on the gingham table cloth that had belonged to her mum. It was looking a bit worn in the afternoon light, but she loved having a touch of her mum with her every day.

"You bring her comfort." Keith smiled at her. Maisie smiled back. She had read an article in some magazine that said people in love mirrored one another's expressions. She always worried that she didn't seem normal enough to him, though Keith never seemed to notice how hard she was working at it. Normal wasn't natural for her.

"I … guess."

His face lit up at once. It was the right thing to say. "You do! You bring her comfort. You make her feel better. That's what you should do. It's a gift."

"Even if it's not real?" That was the thought that haunted her.

"But it is! I'm sure it is. You know it is." As usual Keith became more persuasive as he talked. "You are *sensitive*." He squeezed her hand in his again. "You pick up on things that are … ineffable."

It was a good word. The sound of it was like floating, the double ffs like a breath of air. "I suppose."

Sam leapt up on the table and sniffed her face. Without thinking about it, Maisie leaned in to him, smelling his cat's breath. It was the way he said hello.

"It's really not hygienic," Keith grumbled, dropping her hand and pulling away from the cat. They didn't get along too well.

Another magazine had said that pets and boyfriends often were competitive with one another. The best thing to do was to get them to be matey with each other.

That had not gone well so far.

"He's very clean," Maisie said.

"I just don't feel comfortable with cats. I can't explain," Keith said, shaking his head as usual. He got up and walked through the glass doors that let on to the little balcony. The old house had been broken into flats long ago. As if to make up for the tiny amount of space in the bedsit, it had a glorious balcony, at least in spring and summer. The absolute best was when the fog rolled in from the coast. It was like they were flying over clouds.

"Sam's really all right, you know. He'll warm up to you soon." Maisie stepped out on the balcony with Keith. The light was a bit strong at this time of day and there was far too much traffic noise, yet it lifted her spirits. "Look, I put some fairy lights around the railings." She slipped her arm into his and nodded toward the new addition.

Keith gave her a half smile. "They're nice." He leaned down to kiss her and Maisie felt the familiar flush of pleasure, but then he suddenly pulled away.

"Ow! That bloody cat!" Sam looked smug.

"He's just trying to play. He does that to me all the time. It just means he wants picking up. Maybe if you tried—"

"Look, can you concentrate on what's important?"

The whiplash change of subject made her feel wrong-footed again. *I'll get them to like each other.* "I know ... what's important."

"Remember the script. We have to get her to sign a check. Get that checkbook out."

"I know."

He rubbed her arm and she managed not to flinch. "Opel has so much. She's not even using it. And we're not asking for it all."

"I know."

"We've sunk the hook. Now we need to tug on the line." Keith frowned. "The screen isn't out."

Maisie winced. "I thought I would wait until just before she came so we don't have to worry about knocking into it." For the hundredth time, she wished the flat could be rejiggered; if the bed were by the balcony end instead of the bathroom end by the door everything would be different. Full size, the bed took up a lot of room, but Keith had insisted on it when she wouldn't agree to move in with him.

But she adored the screen. It had been her final project for her painting course the previous term. She had decided on a motif of celestial magic which fit well when they started the readings. Maisie had only been dabbling. It was Keith's idea to turn it into a thing—a money-making thing.

They had their tea and then it was time to get things ready for Ms. Lang's visit. Keith wrestled the screen into place. Maisie replaced the tablecloth with the reading cloth. It was velvety black. The old brass candleholder went in the center of the table. She had found it in a charity shop and thought it looked like a genuine antique, like people carried in old books. In front of her own seat, she placed the black mirror.

"Empty your mind," Keith said, one hand on either side of her head. Irritation flared for a moment, but Maisie quashed it. Why was she so out of sorts today? She took a few deep breaths and calmed herself. Whether real or imagined, she found these sessions so energizing, getting all the daily detritus out of her mind.

A soft knock. Keith greeted Ms. Lang and led her into the flat. "Can I get you a cuppa, Opel?"

"Oh no, dearie. I've had half a pot with my sandwich. I'm nearly swimming." Opel Lang was a sweet white-haired woman with a gentle demeanour. Her clothes were always a bit posh, though they showed signs of mending and wear. She was smaller even than Maisie, barely coming up to the younger woman's chin. Her eyes were bright, however, and her step sure. "Hello, Maisie."

Maisie smiled and took her hands. "Hello, Opel."

She had insisted on first names right away. "None of this formality just because I'm decrepit," waving away their protests that she was nothing of the sort. Then as now, she had removed her hat and coat, and settled into a seat right away with a sort of briskness that Maisie associated with tidy secretaries.

"Shall we begin right away?" Maisie asked. "It's a bit bright yet, but I think we'll be fine."

"Almost midsummer. My Silas, he used to tell me about the bonfires they had in Wales when he was a boy." Thoughts of him lit her eyes.

Keith lit the candle flame. "I'll just turn out the other lights." He flipped the switch by the cooker and then walked to the other end of the flat to get the other light. It was more than bright enough to see everything. Keith picked up Opel's hat and coat from the chair and threw them onto the bed behind the screen.

"Oh, don't!" Opel gasped.

"What?" Maisie said, twitching in her seat.

"Sorry?" Keith picked up the hat and coat again uncertainly.

"Sorry, love. You're too young to know that. Never put a hat on a bed." Opel smiled but it was easy to see she was disturbed. "It's bad luck."

"Oh." Keith put the hat and coat gently on the chair, then leaned against the bookshelf.

Opel turned to Maisie. "I know it's not rational," she put an emphasis on the word, "but you must understand … when you've always done a thing …"

Maisie nodded. In the flickering candle light Opel looked like the grandmother she always imagined, just a step away from a fairy godmother. "It's all right. I've always thought superstitions were there for a reason." Keith rolled his eyes behind Opel's head.

"Shall we try to quiet our minds now?"

"Oh yes, but I have to say I love the fairy lights on your balcony! What a charming touch."

Maisie smiled. "Thank you. They're so pretty in the evening light. Now let's take a nice deep breath—"

"Oh!" Opel pulled back. "I didn't know you had a kitty. How lovely he is!" Sam jumped up on her lap and she began to rub his ears with pleasure. "What his name?"

"Lucifer," Keith said.

"Sam," Maisie said, shooting him a look.

"Lucifer Sam," Opel said, smiling broadly as she chucked him under the chin. "A devilish charmer."

"Though a distraction," Keith said, walking over to shoo the cat away. Sam's ears went back.

"He can hop down—"

Sam hissed and jumped away from Keith, toward the balcony. Opel tutted. "Oh, he doesn't seem to like you very much. My gran always used to say a man who doesn't like cats would never bide by the hearth."

With an effort, Keith smiled. "I like cats. Just this one doesn't like me."

"Okay, let's try those deep breaths again. Ready?" Maisie took Opel's hands in hers on either side of the brass candlestick. "Slowly in . . . And . . . slowly out again . . ." The repeated pattern was soothing. Holding Opel's gentle hands was soothing, too.

She cleared her mind. Maisie found it easy to do. She had spent most of her childhood making her mind blank so as not to have to deal with what was right in front of her. She pressed her feet into the floor, imagining that they had roots that grew through the floorboards all the way to the actual ground and deep into the earth. "Silas, we call to you. Do you hear us?"

A string of words: no sense. *Goat, gold, kitchen, mirror, tin, straw, loom* ... "There you are! I can see you!" Maisie could feel

Opel's fingers tighten a little on her own as she pictured the man Opel had showed them in the old photograph. His jaunty naval cap, the unsmiling mouth, but the eyes that danced with humor.

"Is he near?" Opel whispered.

"On a shore, far away, through mists," Maisie said, unaware of the change in her voice. "Pebbles, driftwood, cockles. Trying to find you, trying to find you. Opel, are you there?"

"I'm here!"

"Opel, you're a dream …"

"No, no, I'm here, Silas."

Keith behind her now, hands on her shoulders, whispering, "You must stay calm, Opel. Don't break the connection."

"Can you hear the waves, Opel? Do you see the reeds?"

"I can't see any of it, Silas. Where are you?" Her hands tightened on Maisie's again and she sat up very straight in her chair. "Tell me!"

"Wouldn't you miss me, my eyes, my heart …"

"Yes, Silas, yes. I miss you. Where are you?"

"Pussy willow—" Opel leapt to her feet. Maisie's eyes popped open. "Opel, are you all right?"

Opel sobbed. "That's what he always called me. When it was just us two. When we were—"

She put her head in her hands and let the tears fall. Maisie stood dazed. Keith put his arm around Opel's shoulders. "It's okay, it's all right."

Maisie blinked. She could still hear the waves, smell the sand, see the reeds. There was something she was meant to do but at the moment she could not remember it. She looked to Keith for a hint, but he was concentrating on Opel.

"There, there." Keith patted her shoulder. "We are so close." He coaxed Opel back to her chair and Maisie returned to hers as well. "I don't know if Maisie feels up to another try. Yet we were so close."

Opel looked up and smiled. She opened her little handbag and took out an embroidered handkerchief and dabbed at her eyes. "I'm so sorry! I just—it startled me when you said that. His name for me. But I would love … more."

"I—I guess so." She wasn't acting. Something was definitely weird about this session. Maisie shivered. Keith had laughed at her signing up for the hypnotherapy course—well, he had until he saw a way to make money from it. That's all he had talked about since Opel's last visit.

"I don't want to overtire you, dearie." Yet Maisie could feel her eagerness.

"Maisie has a real gift," Keith said, his hand still on Opel's shoulder. "She can probably do a bit more. But it means she wouldn't be able to work later, which is a shame. You know rent is due soon."

Maisie froze. He was too naked in his demands. Her mother would disapprove. "Poor people talk about money. It's vulgar." They were poor themselves, Maisie learned once her mother died. But she didn't want to be vulgar.

Opel had her checkbook out at once. "I think you need a little more this time. You were so kind before. And rent in this city is outrageous, I know. Not like in my day. Some of my friends, they still expect prices from the last century." She tore off the check and handed it to Keith.

"You're very kind, Opel. This makes a real difference." He smiled, though his eyes told Maisie it wasn't enough yet.

Opel leaned forward to Maisie. "And I want you to have this." She thrust something glittery into her hand. "It's just a little tortoise. Not worth much, but my Silas give it to me."

"Oh that's really lovely," Maisie said, turning the brooch over in her hands. It sparkled. Green shell, diamond head and legs, with eyes of crystal blue. "Thank you, Opel. It will always be very special for me. Thank you."

Opel grinned. "I want to pass along the things I've loved to people who can love them, too. Before I'm gone."

"I'm sure you'll be with us for a long time yet," Maisie said, ignoring the way Keith's eyes were sparkling.

"Maisie, why don't you try again?" Keith smiled like a scary clown. "I'm sure we can do better."

Maisie felt a pressure against her leg and reached down to pat Sam. He always knew when she was stressed. Sam was a strange grey color, his hair soft as angora. Two big green eyes that could look totally innocent one minute and cold as a killer the next.

Fortunately, the killer instinct was mostly aimed at his catnip mouse or the occasional beetle.

Opel smiled. "Cats are such a comfort."

"Yes." Maisie emptied her mind. The sun had begun its descent. Soon the lights on the little balcony would shine brighter as the sun turned golden. It was the best time of day.

She reached for Opel's hands. "Let's try again." Maisie tried to ignore Keith's steps as he paced around the flat. Deeper: feet flat, letting her roots grow down into the earth, sending her mind out, back to the smell of the ocean, the whistling of the reeds.

"There you are, there. Let me hold your hand. There."

"Silas?" Opel spoke his name like an enchantment. Their hands tightened again. Maisie felt as if she were floating, not floating, swirling waters, golden sun, the call of the curlews sweeping over the marshes. How long did it go on? Perhaps a lifetime. Perhaps five minutes. The lovers were reunited, that much she knew.

"You goddamned cat!"

Maisie and Opel both gasped. Their hands parted and at once the vision dissolved. "What are you doing to Sam?"

"Why not ask what the bloody cat is doing to me!" Keith demanded, then returned to sucking on the new red stripes on the back of his hand.

"What?" Opel asked, trembling from the break.

"You provoked him," Maisie said, her ears ringing for some reason. She shook her head.

"He's crazy." Keith was approaching that point she knew too well. Drops of sweat stood out on his too tall forehead. Sam had disappeared.

"Let me get something to put on those scratches." She stood up, swaying for a moment.

"Are you all right?" Opel asked at once, half rising from her own chair. Maisie could have cried at the kindness on her face.

"I'm fine. Just a little dizzy." Maisie stumbled to the bath, willing herself not to look for Sam under the bed. It would only annoy Keith.

She found the little bottle of peroxide, some antibacterial gel and grabbed the half-empty box of plasters too. That should do.

She stepped out of the bath and gasped. "Oh, Keith. What have you done?"

Keith looked up at her. Belligerent, scared—and more belligerent because she saw that he was scared. "She had a … turn. Something. Not my fault." Opel lay limply on the lino.

Maisie was at her side in a flash. "Is she—?" The word would not come. She slipped a hand behind her neck to lift the poor woman's head. Maisie felt a pulse. Not dead! "Call emergency services!"

He didn't move. Maisie looked up. He was angry, belligerent—scared, too, but gaining confidence. "Look, Maisie …"

"Keith, no." Her mind was blank. Her gaze dropped. *He couldn't have …*

"We have her signature. We have her checkbook. We don't need—" Even he couldn't bring himself to say it out loud.

"Keith, no." Just a whisper this time but not because she feared him—though she did. Always had. Even from that first moment in the café when he had smiled at her.

"It is obvious: we can do it. Together. Just keep quiet about—"

"No, Keith." She struggled to get Opel to lean against the cooker. "I'm calling emergency services now." Maisie darted for the phone before he could stop her.

Keith sprinted around the table. "It was just bad luck. She slipped, hit her head and if we just let her sit, I'm sure she'll be—" He wormed the phone out of her grasp. For the first time, she was angry. Furious on behalf of Opel who was so kind, who did not deserve this, who loved Silas. How could he be so cruel? Anger made her brave.

"I hate you!" She screamed in his face.

Keith slapped her so hard her ears sang. Maisie saw black, staggered, then rose up as angry as before. She bared her teeth at him. All at once a blur flew past.

Sam had launched himself at Keith's face. Keith screamed.

"Stop it, stop it!" Maisie yelled, not even sure which one she meant. She tried to grab Keith's hands. Sam was a spitting, snarling velvet-gray blur. Her phone clattered to the floor. Keith growled or maybe Sam growled as they all twisted, stepped and feinted, no one willing to let go.

Sam got around the back of Keith's neck, scrabbling and hissing. Maisie saw the possibility of grabbing the furious cat. She shouted but Keith paid her no mind, spinning around, grabbing in vain at the elusive cat. His errant arm punched her on the other cheek. She flailed back against the table, legs furiously churning.

Keith had hold of the cat's tail and yanked it until the animal screamed. A furious Sam sank his teeth into Keith's forehead. He screamed. With a mighty effort he pulled the cat off his face and staggered back, blinded by the blood.

Maisie cried out. Sam landed on his feet and ran for the darkness under the bed. Keith hit the balcony handrail, jogging the fairy lights loose and staring at her through blood-eyes as the momentum of his crashing force flipped him back over the railings. Maisie had the absurd image of his feet stumbling loosely, his worn Docs shooting up as far too slowly he went over and down.

Over and down.

And then there was just the empty air and the first few stars of twilight like chalk marks against the grey. She didn't hear it. The air was full of chattering sparrows, and the cars below. Then the horns. And voices.

And then a voice nearby. "What happened?"

Maisie sat down hard. Her phone lay a foot away. She picked it up and dialed. "Something terrible has happened." Maisie scootched over to Opel, where she sat looking very pale. She put an arm around her frail shoulders.

Sam trotted under the table, winding himself around one of its legs. He looked at her and sniffed. Maisie put her face on Opel's shoulder and they both cried.

Nobody Home

by Joseph S. Walker

They gave Levin the clothes he'd been wearing seven years ago, which is how he found out how much weight he'd lost.

They gave him a pamphlet from a local church with lists of local homeless shelters, food banks, twelve-step programs and employment agencies, which is how he found out he was a social outcast.

They gave him fifty dollars in cash and a bus token that would take him anywhere in the city, which is how he found out nobody had come to pick him up.

The trustee who gave Levin this bounty said that, due to a lawsuit from the local board of health, they'd had to stop including a pack of cigarettes. Levin said it was all right. He'd never been a smoker.

Then they let him go.

—

The house Levin and Shayna had lived in was a couple of miles from the nearest bus stop. He had no problem with the walk. For seven years he'd walked the prison yard for two hours every day, never earning the status with any crew that would have given him a place on a bench, or even on the ground in a shaded corner. The only thing strange about walking was being able to go in a straight line for thirty yards without hitting a wall.

He was afraid he would have forgotten how to get to the house, but it turned out he remembered fine. It looked just like the last time he'd seen it, a little white two-story with red shutters and trim. It was dusk by the time he arrived, and even in the fading light the place looked like it could use some fresh paint.

Levin thought about being out here, in the sunlight, his shirt off, putting a new coat of paint on his house. He thought about Shayla bringing him a beer and the two of them stepping back to look at his work.

Anyway, he tried to think about those things. What he really thought about was the fact that Shayla hadn't visited him in four years.

The mailbox was brown metal, not the white plastic he remembered. The junk mail inside was all addressed to Shayla Atwater. At least she hadn't moved. But there were no lights on, and there was no car in the driveway.

Had she gone to get him after all? Had they just missed each other?

The keys that had been in the pocket of his jeans seven years ago were still there.

The one to the front door still fit.

———

Muscle memory found the switch just inside as he closed the door with his foot. The room flooded with light, showing him some things familiar, some things new. The big things were mostly the same. The couch, the recliner. He didn't remember the colorful painting of a fish over the couch, or a lot of the little things scattered around. He let his eyes move slowly across the room, focusing on what he could see because he was so rattled by what he heard.

Nothing. Silence.

The little hooks by the front door where they kept keys were still there. Levin looked at the hooks, then put the keys back in his pocket and began to move through the house. The same table in the kitchen, the same chairs with the worn places where the backs rubbed against the edge of the table.

The refrigerator was well stocked. The date on the milk was the middle of next week. He turned on the overhead light and saw the ceiling. He'd almost forgotten about it, Shayla's pet project. She wanted the kitchen ceiling to look like a big stained-glass window. So the two of them had stood on stools and ladders, alternately laughing and cursing, putting up a random pattern of painter's tape and then filling the squares and triangles and parallelograms they'd created with a dozen of the brightest, most vivid paints she could find. Levin's shoulders had ached for days, but when they peeled the tape off the result was just what Shayla had wanted, a rainbow scattered and broken across the ceiling.

Eight years later it was still up there. The colors had faded a bit in places, maybe.

Levin turned off the light and headed for the stairs.

In the bedroom he found the changes he'd been expecting to find everywhere. The bedspread was new, an abstract purple and white design, matching the new lilac tint on the walls. None of his clothes were in the closet, and the drawers that had been his in the bureau were empty. At least everything he did find was obviously Shayla's. There was no other man living here.

They'd called the room across the hall the guest room, though it held an old fold-out couch instead of a regular bed. The couch was still there. Levin opened the closet and found a stack of U-Haul cardboard boxes with his name printed on them in big black letters. He opened the top box and found it stuffed with his old shirts, neatly folded.

She hadn't thrown his things away.

But she had put them out of sight. He closed the box back up and went back to the main bedroom and sat on the bed, thinking about that.

The emptiness of the house still pressed on him. Prison was never this silent. At any time of the night you could listen to men snoring or screaming or singing or crying, and others yelling at them to keep it down. You could listen to the steady metronome pacing of the guards, bursts of unaccountable laughter, flushing toilets, distant clangs as doors opened and closed.

Levin let himself fall back onto the bed, his head on the softest pillow he'd felt in years. Shayla still lived here. Sooner or later she'd come back, and then he would find out what his life was now. Prison made you capable of waiting, whether you wanted to be or not.

One of Levin's cellmates, Hendricks, could wait better than anybody Levin ever met, sinking into absolute stillness until he needed to move. Hendricks had been a physics professor before some mysterious incident knocked him sideways. All he would ever say about why he was there was that he'd had one very, very bad night. He told Levin that what made him good at waiting was his knowledge of physics. He said that every moment in time existed forever, so there was no reason to ever be upset or impatient or angry about the particular moment you were in. You were in all the other moments, too, if you only knew it.

Thinking about Hendricks, waiting to be in another moment, Levin closed his eyes and let the silence take him.

—

He didn't know how much later it was when a door closing downstairs woke him. He jerked upright, baffled for a moment by his surroundings, his first thought that he'd escaped and they were hunting him. But no. He remembered: Shayla's house.

Our house.

Someone was walking around downstairs. He heard one of the chairs at the kitchen table move. He called out before he realized he was going to.

"Shayla?"

No answer.

Levin swung his feet to the floor and headed for the stairs. He could tell from the shadow of the banister on the wall that the lights in the kitchen were on again. He went down the stairs and turned the corner and Grayson Atwater, Shayla's father, was sitting at the kitchen table, wearing his deputy's uniform and holding a bottle of beer.

There was a gun on the table in front of him.

Gray nodded at the chair across from him. "Sit down."

"Where's Shayla?" Levin said.

"We're gonna talk," Gray said. "But not until you're sitting down." He drank from the bottle.

Levin stepped forward, his feet leaden. He pulled out the chair and perched on the edge. "You don't need the gun," he said.

"We'll see."

"So I'm sitting. Where's Shayla?"

"She's at our house. And before you jump up with any cute ideas, Linda and I have moved since you went away."

"And you won't tell me where."

Gray shrugged. "I could tell you. But it's going to be a moot point pretty soon."

Levin realized he was breathing very shallowly. He licked his lips. "I know I've got mistakes to make up for, Mr. Atwater."

"Officer."

"Officer, sure. Officer Atwater. I've screwed up. But I don't think Shayla sent you to kill me in our kitchen."

"No," Gray said. "But you'll notice she's not here to roll out the red carpet, either. She sent me to see how you are, so she could decide what to do."

"How I am," Levin said. "I'm good. I'm clean. Three years. My hand to God. You can check my records, Gray."

"Officer."

"Officer. Check the records. I've been going to the prison NA meetings like clockwork for three and a half years. I got three months and relapsed. I'm telling you that to be honest. Then I got clean again and it stuck. Three years."

"Impressive," Gray said.

"Tell Shayla that," Levin said. "Tell her I'm ready to work. I'll keep up the meetings. I'll do whatever she wants."

Gray finished his beer. He put the bottle on the table and rolled it between his hands. "You got any idea what you did to my little girl, Levin? Do you even remember?"

Levin swallowed. He opened his mouth and Gray lifted a finger and shook his head.

"I don't really give a fuck if you remember. I remember. She remembers. The lies, the missing money, the bruises. Even after you went away she wanted to give you a chance, until she realized you were using even inside that place."

"That was before NA," Levin said. "Before I got clean. I wrote her about it. I tried to call but she changed her number and she never wrote me back."

"Yeah," Gray said. "Because she listened to me. I saw what you really are." He reached into his pocket and pulled out a little brown plastic bottle and put it on the table next to the gun.

Levin stopped breathing. The little bottle swelled up. Filled his vision. "What's that?" he managed.

"That," Gray said, "is what I'm going to find in your pocket after I shoot you."

"No."

"Oh, yeah. It was your first stop when you got out. A little something-something to celebrate your freedom. Then you came over here and when you didn't find Shayla you went a little wild. Busting up the place, breaking things. Even tried to attack me when I showed up. Gave me no choice."

"Officer," Levin said. "You don't have to do this."

"I'm not a hard guy, Levin," Gray said. "I'm even going to do you a last favor." He picked up the gun and used the barrel to nudge the bottle halfway across the table. "You can have a little taste before you go. I'll even wait a few minutes to let it kick in." Gray leveled the gun, pointing it at Levin's chest. "This is a limited time offer."

Levin's hand came up, starting for the bottle before he'd even really thought about it. He bit his lip hard and jerked the hand back. "That would be good for you," he said. "To have it in my blood."

Gray laughed. "You think anybody's going to be looking at your blood? This isn't *CSI*. There isn't going to be any mystery here. You're just going to be another junkie who had to be put down."

"No!"

With all the force he could muster, Levin braced his hands against the edge of the table and lunged upward, shoving the other end into Gray's gut. He was spinning for the back door when he heard the loud slap of the gun and he was sure Gray had missed until his feet stopped moving and tangled underneath him and as he hit the floor he felt the wet stickiness spreading across his chest. He didn't feel the pain until he was on the floor and then it was like a giant vice on him, squeezing everything out of him.

He couldn't move. He heard his own breath, bubbly and uneven. He became aware that Gray was beside him, grunting as he knelt and rolled Levin onto his side. He was putting the little bottle into Levin's hand. *Sure*, Levin thought. Fingerprints. Good thinking, Gray.

He tried to say it out loud and just spasmed.

"It's okay," Gray said. "You can let go. It'll be over soon."

Levin wasn't listening. He was looking over Gray's shoulder at the rainbow ceiling. Every moment existed forever. He saw himself and Shayla up there, perched on ladders, the colors spreading. He willed the painting Levin to look down, to catch his eye, to leap between the years and let him start again. He could wait. He could wait for that Levin to look down and see him.

On The Run

BY S.W. LAUDEN

Roger stopped breathing when the timer unexpectedly blinked to life. The clock's ticking bounced off the marble walls, multiplying all around him. His heart raced as the echoes reflected back toward him like a swarm of murderous bees, an endless cacophonous loop that made it impossible to concentrate. Sweat slithered down his cheeks, dripping onto trembling hands. *Holy shit,* he thought, *They must have armed the bomb from out in the van.* From what Drago told him, he had three minutes to get across the plaza before the thing went off.

Roger was the last person inside the bank. The two tellers and an ancient security guard all fled the second he set the device on the counter. He grabbed the stuffed messenger bag, pulling the strap tight across his chest. The banded stacks of Euros were heavy, but he couldn't let anything slow him down. Not if he wanted to save the girl.

Alarms wailed as he pushed through the front doors, his thin frame bounding down the concrete steps. Pigeons erupted in a blur of feathers and slapping wings when his feet hit the cobblestones. He pulled the ski mask from his head, afternoon sun beating down on his shaggy hair. The blue sky overhead fractured like shattering glass as he tried to adjust his eyes. Clusters of people flooded the plaza, late arrivals to some kind of festival.

He dodged right and a mother cut him off with a stroller, her potato-faced toddler a drooling demon. A middle-aged couple to his left inspected a swirling oil painting on a rubbery wooden easel. Mimes twisted long balloons into monstrous shapes up ahead. Umbrella-wielding tour guides shepherded hordes of zombie tourists from every direction.

A sea of peaked booths rolled like waves into the distance. The air reeked of cologne, cigarette smoke and charred meat as he jogged toward a burbling fountain. That's where he first met the blue-eyed brunette who set this nightmare in motion, like the gritty gears of a medieval clock. She sat down beside him on the lip of the pool the previous afternoon, easily exchanging a shy smile for a cigarette.

"You're American." It was part observation, part accusation.

"Yep. Name's Roger. I'm from Chicago."

She took a long drag, eying him over the cherry. Thin wisps of smoke escaped from between red lips. "Are you alone, Roger?"

He'd been warned not tell strangers he was travelling solo, but couldn't help himself. Probably because of how she pronounced his name, a soft "gee" delivered in a delicious accent.

"Yep. Big post-college backpacking trip."

"Was Rome your first destination?"

"I spent a week in London but needed to get the hell out of there."

Her shy smile was back. "Was it a girl?"

"No, nothing like that. Just way too expensive. I got on the first flight out of Heathrow and ended up here. I'll probably hit Cairo next. Maybe Lagos after that. Trying to leave room for unexpected adventures. What's your name?"

"Francesca." She stood, twisting her boot on the cigarette. "Let me show you my Rome."

———

A fast-approaching helicopter brought Roger crashing back to the moment. It was a small white dot on the horizon one moment, a giant metallic bug buzzing overhead seconds later. Vibrating blue stripes arced along both sides of the chopper, the word "Polizia" emblazoned in bold letters. The entire crowd looked up in unison. Roger made a beeline for the fountain.

A snaking white gusher erupted as he arrived, sending a welcome mist across his flushed cheeks. His skin drank it in, every pore a parched mouth. Kissing couples sat holding hands all around him. Roger hurried past them, throat tightening with jealousy. He strained to get a clear view of the narrow alley on the far side of the plaza. That's where Drago parked the van, waiting for the money. Roger had to deliver the messenger bag before they hurt Francesca.

Her beautiful, tear-streaked face haunted his thoughts as he ran. She'd shown him the Colosseum, the Pantheon and the Sistine Chapel, skillfully skipping the lines like locals wherever they went. Night brought fragrant food and sweet wine at darkened *ristorantes*. Midnight found them dancing to hypnotic music at a club inside an abandoned church. It was close to dawn when he escorted her through a maze of streets to a weathered yellow building. Her flat was on the second floor, right above a flower shop.

It all felt like an impossible dream as she hugged him goodbye. Roger never wanted it to end. "Aren't you going to invite me up?"

"I don't want you to get the wrong idea about Italian women."

"Your secret's safe with me."

She woke him with a kiss a little before noon the next day. It took a moment to realize there was something on her tongue. He tried to pull away, but she kept her lips pressed to his. The small squares of paper passed between their hungry mouths.

"What the hell was that?"

"Just a little LSD. Let's take the train to Pompeii this morning. We can spend the day among the lost souls who wander the ancient streets."

Roger had never tripped before. "Seriously?"

Francesca rolled over to straddle him. It didn't put his mind at ease, but it was a pretty good start. She kissed his neck, softly whispering into his ear. "Don't worry. I'll be with you."

"But what if I freak out?!"

"It will be our 'unexpected adventure.'"

He was just starting to calm down when the door crashed open with a spray of splinters. Three men wearing matching denim vests stormed toward them. Francesca wailed as two of the men dragged Roger to the floor, the tips of their boots delivering vicious blows to his ribs and legs. He kept his arms wrapped tight around his head until the beating stopped.

Roger was a quivering mess when the third man knelt down beside him. He had a lined face and a shaved head. "My name is Drago. I'm the leader of the Roman Legions."

Roger's skin began to crawl, either from fear or the drugs kicking in. "Is that like the mafia or something?"

Francesca shot up in the bed. "They're a filthy fascist biker gang!"

She was silenced with a backhand. Drago kept his sunken eyes on Roger. "We need your help sending a message, or things will get much worse for your girlfriend."

"A message? To who?"

"The prime minister."

———

The memories felt like weights around Roger's neck as he struggled across the crowded plaza. He knocked a young girl to the pavement, a red balloon slipping from her tiny fist. Roger watched the orb slowly wobble upward, the ribbon wriggling behind it like an eel. It was swallowed up by the afternoon sun as a second helicopter flashed by overhead.

The ticking of the bomb rose up like a ghostly whisper in his ears. Time was running out. He almost jumped out of his skin when somebody tapped him on the shoulder. It was a young blonde tourist who shouted something in a guttural gibberish. Roger drove his fist into the intruder's pointed chin before taking off at a sprint.

A motorcycle roared by on the roundabout. Roger lost his footing as he leapt from the curb, sneakers slipping on the tire-slick stones. His knees hit the ground first, followed by his palms—electric waves of pain rippling through his bones. Roger skidded to a stop, landing on his stomach. The tall delivery van was parked a hundred yards away, a steady beacon in an undulating landscape.

The rear doors swung open. Drago's men jumped down to the ground like castle sentries. Francesca sat cross-legged in the middle of the cargo hold, shoulders slouched and arms tied behind her back. She looked up at him with terrified eyes.

Roger sprang, pushing off like a sprinter from the blocks. He'd covered several yards before noticing Drago seated behind her. His body was twisted in the driver's seat, head craned to watch Roger's approach. He gave a thumbs-up before turning to start the engine. The rear brake lights blinked to life, the glowing eyes of Satan himself.

Fifty yards. Twenty-five. Ten. The van lurched forward a few feet as he closed in. Roger panicked. He pulled the messenger bag over his head, flinging it into the gaping maw. *They can have the money. I only want Francesca back.*

An explosion erupted in the plaza behind Roger. The ground beneath his feet jumped and buckled. He looked over his shoulder as fiery chunks of the bank building slammed into the crowd. People screamed and scattered in every direction as one of the police helicopters shot upward, quickly bursting into flames.

Drago's maniacal laughter drew Roger's attention back to the van. Francesca brought her arms from behind her back to snatch up the bag of money. There was no sign of restraints on her wrists as she waved to Roger. The shy smile was back, only mocking now. He watched her climb into the passenger seat, taking Drago's hand in hers. The two sentries jumped inside, closing the doors before the van sped off.

Roger lunged feebly to catch the bumper, but it was no use. The van receded into the distance before vanishing completely. Tears filled his eyes as reality momentarily crept into his altered consciousness. Francesca, if that was even her name, had double-crossed him.

Footsteps thundered toward him, followed by sirens. He let his forehead drop to the ground. There was nowhere left to run.

—

"Are you awake?"

Roger forced his eyes open. The only thing he wanted to see was the inside of Francesca's flat. He looked through the bars of a jail cell instead. A middle-aged man in a suit sat on a wooden chair across from him, file folder open in his lap. They seemed to be alone.

The man's American accent came as a surprise. "Sounds like you had one hell of an adventure yesterday. Mind telling me what happened?"

Roger sat up, elbows on his knees and head in his hands. "I need water."

"I bet. The American Embassy sent me to represent you."

Roger's head throbbed. "You're a lawyer?"

"Name's David Mason. Tell me about this girl, the one you call 'Francesca.'"

Roger leapt up involuntarily. "How do you know about her?"

"According to these notes, she's all you talked about when they arrested you. Says here you told them she lives in 'a yellow building above a flower shop.' They have people out looking for her to corroborate your version of events."

Roger's shoulders slumped. He felt sick. "She's not there."

"Don't be so hard on yourself. You certainly aren't the first backpacker to overdo it in Italy." Mason stifled a laugh. "Although I doubt you'll be allowed back into that museum."

"What museum?"

"The one where you handed the security guard your smartphone and a postcard addressed to the prime minister." Mason glanced at his notes. "According to witnesses, you then ran out into the plaza where you stole a red balloon from a little girl. You allegedly punched her father when we tried to get it back. Any of this ring a bell?"

"But the bomb…The helicopters …"

Mason crossed his legs. He almost seemed amused. "That was an air show for the *Natale di Roma* festival, Rome's birthday. Those helicopters were relics. The 'bombs' you heard were firecrackers."

"But…"

"The police found you in the middle of the street a few blocks from the museum. You apparently tried to steal a delivery van, but the driver fought you off. Do you remember what kind of drugs you took?"

Roger's response was barely audible. "LSD. Francesca gave it to me."

"Sticking to your story, huh? In that case, I think I have everything I need."

Mason stood, heading for the door. Roger called after him. "Where are you going?"

"To get this all sorted out before the press gets wind of it. I'll have you out in an hour or two, but you'll have to pay a fine and apologize to the Italian government."

"I don't have much money left."

"Don't worry. They take credit cards."

A cautious smile formed on Roger's lips. "Are you saying I didn't rob that bank?"

"Christ no, son. Sounds to me like you just had a really bad trip."

Panic set in as Mason slipped from view. "Will you tell me when they find Francesca?!"

Her name echoed off the walls, multiplying all around him. Roger slid to the ground, fighting off unwanted thoughts. *What if all of this—the jail, Mason—was just more hallucinations?* He squeezed his eyes shut tight, wishing himself back into Francesca's bed.

REMEMBER A DAY

BY KURT REICHENBAUGH

Dwayne finally made the big time. And for a day, everyone who watched it on the local news would know his name. Within a week, they'd forgotten him.

I remembered the last time I'd seen him. He'd slipped some then, but was still the same character I'd known all my life—no time for memories, nostalgia was for suckers, life was a buffet and get yours before the rest of the fuckers arrive.

Best friends since we were four years old. We were both born in November to mothers who should have been debutants. Descendants from old southern bloodlines. We raced our bikes along wet sidewalks. Dwayne would often win. He was faster than I was and he had no qualms about kicking your front tire if he needed that edge.

Growing up, we spent every day together. Our town was smaller then. Miles of undeveloped land to explore; Florida pines and oaks draped in Spanish moss. We'd pack Shasta colas, Slim Jims and Doritos and get on our bikes and go. Places to fish, build forts, hide from our parents, plot vengeance on our teachers.

My mother used to tell me I was her brightest boy. Her beautiful bright boy, she'd say. I felt weird when she said things like that. None of my heroes were bright boys. They were outlaws, rebels, and they lived and died in far-away lands with no strip malls or suburbs.

My grandmother said Dwayne was full of the devil. "He'll go to hell with his boots on if he doesn't get right with the Lord," she'd say. We'd laugh about that.

Dwayne looked up to his grandfather. He called the old man 'Grandaddy' like a proper southern boy should. I remember his grandfather as a white-haired old gentleman with hard-knuckled hands, phlegmy laughter, and a face battered and dented from early years of boxing. The old man drank whiskey, cursed blue streaks, whistled at women and drove his cars too fast. Usually around Christmastime we'd hear that Granddaddy had wrecked his car again.

Dwayne began stealing cars in high school. He had the knack for it. He loved cars almost more than he loved girls and was good at stealing both. Once, he tried showing me in the parking lot of the Hillsboro movie theater. You knew when the picture (he called movies "pictures" like his granddaddy did) had started and ended, and you knew that the owner was occupied inside the theater, providing you more than enough time to steal the car. A theater parking lot was like a candy store.

He never did anything serious with the cars he stole. Joy-riding down Hillsborough or Dale Mabry, or raising hell with the hookers on Nebraska. I'd go with him on those jaunts. It was all just for shits and giggles anyway—stolen car, a six pack of beer, a girl next to you and that was heaven. He'd abandon the car in a strip mall afterward. It was pure merry hell and no one ever got hurt. The owner would get the car back in the end and no one was worse for it.

Still, I didn't take to stealing cars the way Dwayne did. Same with girls. He could tag a girl at a party or a dance and have her. Boyfriend or not, it didn't matter any to Dwayne. More than a few guys wanted to kick Dwayne's ass for screwing their girls. My grandmother always told us that no nice girls would like us as long as we went around raising hell. "Nice girls," Dwayne laughed. "A nice girl is one who puts it in for you."

I had no luck with girls. "It's not luck, it's attitude," Dwayne would say. "You see a girl you like, you let her know it. You tell her, 'you're going with me' and you follow through."

I had plenty of girls I liked but none reciprocated the honor.

That's how life rolled through high school and graduation. Then Dwayne and I drifted apart that last year. I got a part-time job at the Winn Dixie while Dwayne ran errands for a guy named Marco who had various business interests. Dwayne's errands involved runs between Tampa and Miami. You can guess what for. Obviously the money was good. Better than anything I was making stocking shelves. The days of riding bikes into the Odessa wilderness armed with Shastas and Slim Jims were long gone.

My grades sucked. Dwayne rarely bothered attending school anymore. I graduated with a forgettable GPA and no prospects but a fifty cent raise at Winn Dixie. I didn't like to think about what became of Mom's beautiful bright boy.

Dwayne shared an apartment with this dancer named Melinda he'd met at the Kitten Tail Club north of Mission Bell. They tried fixing me up with one of her friends, another dancer, named Tammy. We spent the night at Dwayne's apartment smoking pot and listening to Pink Floyd. Then Dwayne and Melinda took their party into the bedroom. "Don't do anything I wouldn't do," Melinda said before closing their bedroom door. Tammy fixed another bowl and we shared it before having awkward sex on the sofa. It was my first time and Tammy knew it. Later that night she asked me to give her a ride back to her apartment. I dropped her off outside her building and she didn't invite me inside. "Give me a call sometime," she said. I was almost home before realizing I didn't have her number.

A few days later I went to the Air Force recruitment office and signed up.

Dwayne and Melinda threw me a going away party.

Tammy didn't show.

Melinda called her a bitch and said I could do better.

Dwayne had to make a run to Miami early the next morning and wished me luck.

"I think you're crazy for doing this, man," he said. "Why don't you let me fix you up with Marco? He's always looking for good help."

"I don't think so. This is something I just need to do for myself."

"Sorry things didn't work out with Tammy."

"Forget it. Not a big deal."

I volunteered to go anywhere in the world, and the Air Force sent me to the Mohave Desert in California.

In the military you find no shortage of guys who are into guns. I met a guy named Steve who was a gun enthusiast. I had an open invitation to go shooting with him. He stored his guns at the armory and kept a few in a lock box at a buddy's apartment. He even made a little extra money on the side, dealing and trading in firearms.

I had no idea why I bought a gun. It was a spur of the moment thing. One minute a guy is showing you a gun, the next you're offering to buy it from him.

"You can keep it here instead of registering it on base," Steve said. "It's up to you."

"I think I'll keep it here then," I told him.

We were in Torrence's apartment at the time. Torrence was a sketchy dude who didn't seem to have any apparent means of income, but he had a hot girlfriend from Eastern Europe we liked to look at. He reminded me a lot of Dwayne.

Edina, Torrence's girlfriend, was a hair stylist. She would cut our hair for cheap. We all liked Edina. Edina seemed to take a particular concern with regards to me. She was one of those people who can read others with a remarkable sense of accuracy. She must have sensed the rootlessness in my life. Edina set me up with a friend of hers named Marcie. Marcie was another hairstylist. She was short and cute, like a living cartoon, and we got along fine.

I could spend afternoons with Marcie smoking pot in her apartment, going to the movies with her in the evenings, spending nights in her bed. She was my girl for a short time and I never thought about Dwayne or Melinda or anyone else when I was with her. So, for a time, things were good. I had a girlfriend, a job, and a gun.

Life had a way of running on autopilot. I moved off base into Marcie's apartment. We kept lawn chairs on her back patio where we had a view of Joshua trees in the high desert beyond the pool. We drank beer on weekends, listening to the radio and the jets from the base taking off and landing. Marcie and I slipped into a comfortable relationship. I'd cash checks and buy groceries. She'd buy pot. I should have worried more about the pot. At any point I could have been pulled in for a random drug test.

A few months later we heard Torrence got busted robbing a liquor store down in San Bernardino. Edina moved to L.A. Then Marcie let a friend of hers use her car to drive down to the valley for the weekend. Instead, her friend used it to drive to Mexico where she and a boyfriend were busted bringing marijuana back from the border. Marcie lost her car because of that little stunt. She said you couldn't trust friends.

We lived out my enlistment in that apartment in the desert. I guess I loved her, but Marcie didn't live for anything but getting high, good sex, and the next paycheck. There was no talk of getting married after my enlistment was up. So it wasn't a surprise when she told me she decided to move to Seattle and stay with some friends there. She said it would be nice if I wanted to come with her, but I didn't have to.

I left the Air Force and moved back to my hometown with a little savings, some books, a few letters, pictures of Marcie, and a gun.

Finding work wasn't easy. I went on a lot of interviews but didn't have any luck. Finally, I took a gig hopping bells at a new resort north of town. Graveyard shift to start. I kidded myself that working nights would allow me to attend classes at the community college during the days. One semester disabused me of that notion. Working shifts at night and trying to study by day while nodding off in a lecture hall. Life was sleepwalking through work and classes and driving between the two and always late for both. I dropped out before flunking out.

I took an apartment near the resort. I was able to catch more lucrative shifts—tagging golf bags, hoofing luggage and flirting with the girls at the front desk. If a guest needed anything I saw to it that they got it, whether it was a bottle of whiskey from the liquor storeroom or female companionship for the night.

Still, everything had begun an interminable collapse around me.

I finally met up with Dwayne months later. He'd gotten thinner. He fidgeted and cleared his throat a lot, checked his phone frequently as we drank our beers. I asked about Marco.

"I'm no longer working with Marco. We had a mutual understanding and agreed to part ways. I'm branching out on my own. Things are really moving for me, brother," he told me. "What do you say? I can always use an extra man. More money for you than you're pulling down at the hotel."

"I'm doing okay, but thanks anyway," I told him. "I'm in line for a management slot there. But I'll keep your offer in mind." That was a lie, of course. Management was for the college kids.

I asked about Melinda. "Old wounds, buddy. We don't talk about Melinda anymore. She's made some choices that don't jibe with my plans. So I cut her loose." He looked down at his beer. "Let's forget about her."

He told me Grandaddy had passed two years back, succumbing to a life of too much whiskey, fast cars and red meat, just the way it ought to be.

"I miss him," Dwayne said. "Remember how he used to try and teach us to box, out in the back yard? Jesus we were hopeless."

"I remember him laughing every time one of us had a bloody nose or a busted lip. And how your mom would scream at him for it."

We both shared stories of childhood, laughing about the failures and the fights and the girls who hated us. "I think about those days a lot, Dwayne. I miss them. All of them, all of it."

Remembering those days in the golden summers of youth.

"Speak for yourself, brother," he said.

That was the last time I saw him.

His last night on Earth started at a house in one of those rich asshole estates in Wesley Chapel. Police were called out to a disturbance there. By the time they got there Dwayne had split, taking off in Marco's Escalade, leaving behind one dead Marco Santos and a hysterical woman who turned out to be Melinda. Dwayne made it to Temple Terrace where he dumped Marco's Escalade in a Publix parking lot and stole a Honda Civic from a terrified woman who'd stopped there to pick up medicine for her husband. By then the police were on his ass. They tried stop sticks on him just before he got to the 275, but Dwayne was too good a wheelman for that. Still, he needed to change cars again. He attempted another carjacking outside a bar on Bearss that didn't pan out for him. The Honda got him as far as Fletcher, near the university, where he had to bail out. His life ended in a storm of bullets when he pointed his gun at the police in a Walmart parking lot. The cops don't fuck around with armed desperadoes.

I heard the story on the news the next morning, after getting home from a long shift.

I wondered where he was trying to escape to.

I wondered if he thought of me for a second in that final desperate chase.

I'm still at the resort, workings as many hours as I'm physically able to work. I tried to find Melinda once, since Dwayne's grand departure, but was unsuccessful. My attempts at asking around just made me look foolish.

In my worst hours, I take my gun out if its lockbox and think about the life of an outlaw and remember a day in the golden sun full of promise for both of us.

What would they think of their brightest boy now?

OBSCURED BY CLOUDS

BY ALLAN ROZINSKI

As he drove the Winnebago down the highway, Rayland Cone watched the storm clouds roll in, heavy and thick, the sun gone into hiding. He turned the radio on and surfed through the channels, trying to find something to distract him, but neither music nor the talk shows muted the unwelcome thoughts stirring inside his head.

In the semi behind Cone was Champ, transporting the Tilt-A-Whirl and the Ferris wheel on the back of his flatbed. Bo followed Champ in the other rig, hauling the Rocket Ride and the Moonwalker. They were all headed to the next carnival site just down the road in Wilkes-Barre.

It wasn't the nine-to-five world. No union, no health care, no pension plan. You went by the schedule for carnivals that were held roughly the same the time every year, adjusting as needed to the few new jobs that came in. They set up, maintained, and ran the rides, pulling everything together in a pressured rush so the carnival could open on time. And when it ended, they would tear it down, pack it up, and head on out to the next engagement.

Between gigs, they went back to the home base on a lot near Nay Aug Park in Scranton, the neon sign that read *Fortune Brothers Carnival* greeting them at the entrance. They'd set up the rides next to the game and food stands the Fortunes rented out to local vendors, resuming the intermittent, ongoing carnival on site until it was time to close again to hit the road for the next scheduled carnival on their calendar.

—

Cone had served a stretch for third degree felony forgery. His grandfather, Desmond Bennett, had gone from bad to worse after being admitted to the hospital, moved to critical care, the doctor informing the family that they should prepare for the worst.

Except Desmond Bennett made an unexpected recovery.

Cone's counsel was a public defender. He showed up shortly before Cone's trial was held, his tie too short, his suit looking like a hand-me-down, baggy and threadbare. His manner irritable and unfocused, he seeming hopelessly overmatched for any challenge, let alone the upcoming trial.

Desmond Bennett sat in the witness stand, the prosecuting attorney, Abel Thompson, standing in front of him before the court. Visible to those in attendance was the image of two documents, side by side, displayed on a screen from an overhead projector.

"Mr. Bennett, on the screen we've had set up before the court, there are two wills that you are alleged to have written. The will on the left indicates that your daughter, Rachel Cone, is the sole beneficiary of your estate. Did you sign that will?"

"Yes. My lawyer prepared it years ago at my request and I signed it."

"The other will names your daughter, Rachel Cone, and your grandson, Rayland Cone, as co-beneficiaries of your estate. Did you sign that will?"

"No, I did not."

"Hmm. You did not sign that will," Thompson said, nodding. "Have you had your attorney or have you yourself prepared a will since the will we see here on the screen that named your daughter as the sole beneficiary of your estate?"

"Absolutely not. It's a fake," Desmond Bennett said, throwing darts at Cone with his eyes.

—

Upon Rayland Cone's arrival at the State Correctional Institute at Coal Township, he was deposited into a cell with Bo Badman, a short-timer nearing the end of his sentence. They'd clicked with each other from the start, Bo using his connections to smooth the way for Cone and insulate him from targeting by jailhouse predators and grifters.

After his prison term ended, Cone got a job at Paper King, a factory located in a nearby industrial park. Paper King's employees shared in the misery that was the daily bread of the defeated, hope and meaning giving way to the mindless repetition that ruled the lives of the damned. They'd signed on to become slaves to machines ceaselessly pumping out paper and cardboard products, mechanical monsters that never stopped shitting junk, everything from advertising displays and holiday decorations to cardboard containers and doggy diapers ... they breathing in the fouled air heavy with dust that made their lungs rebel in protest, coughing and wheezing their way through the work day and awakening in the dead of night to hack up gobs of phlegm mingled with blood. To Cone, it felt as though he'd just left one jail to be trapped in another.

In the last postcard Cone had received from Bo when he was still inside, Bo informed Cone that he'd gotten a job with Fortune Brothers. After Cone did his time, he bought a track phone and sent Bo a letter that included his phone number. They'd called each other a few times after that, seeming to find less and less to talk about before they stopped calling.

Until Cone's phone rang one day and he answered it.

"Ray?"

"Bo! How you doing?"

"You know. Trying to stay one step ahead of disaster. Hey, I have good news for you. You think you might want to come work for Fortune Brothers?"

"Doing what?"

"What I'm doing, for the most part. They want you to come in for an interview. I already put the good word in for you, though. Once they look you over to make sure you don't have any "Hail Satan" or swastika tattoos on your face or somewhere else on your body you can't hide, you ought to be good to go."

"Sounds righteous," Cone said. "So, what do I need to do?"

"Give me your address and I'll send you an application. They'll call you for the interview. Don't worry, be chill. They're not hardass."

—

Cone drove to the Fortune Brothers Carnival Services home site. He walked past the various stands that offered food, games, and novelty items. Bo was running the Ferris wheel; Cone caught his eye and gave him a thumbs up. The trailer that served as the home office was just ahead; he walked up to the front door and rapped on it a few times. When nobody answered, he opened it and went in.

Lou Fortune sat at his desk. He motioned for Cone to sit in the chair in front of him, looking the ex-con over.

"Rayland Cone," Lou Fortune said. "What kind of name is that?" He sat slackly, his hair mussed, his clothes rumpled. Several empty bottles of Jack Daniels lay in the wastebasket beside the desk.

"Cone? Scottish."

"No. Rayland."

Cone shrugged. "I don't know."

"Bo told us he went over the job with you."

Frank Fortune sat at the other desk in baggy sweatpants and a greasy shirt, ignoring them both. He opened a letter and began reading, seeming to struggle to comprehend it.

"No drugs. And no drinking on the job," Lou Fortune said. "If you do, you're gone. Any questions?"

"No," Cone said. And, simple as that, he'd been hired.

—

What Cone liked most about working carnivals was you got to watch people up close, the faces of many alert and curious. In a few of the strangest carnivals he'd worked there remained the vestigial remnants of a bygone era—brash lighting drawing attention to signs featuring sensationalistic portrayals of the weird and wondrous, advertising attractions such as the Alligator Man, the World's Smallest Pony, the Wolf-Woman from Borneo, and Claude, The Human Lobster.

Then there were the sounds of the carnival: the ride-music ranging from calliope to raucous rock, the waves of voices rolling and crashing through the sea of people. The savory smell of burgers, hot dogs, cotton candy, and kettle corn enticed and beckoned. There were games of skill and games of chance, for cautious couples on their first dates or faded lovers looking to win at anything to try to stir up the quickening stagnation in their lives. With fall at the doorstep and winter not far behind, the carnival rushed in like the last hurrah of the dying summer, everyone wanting to hang on to its dregs for as long as they could.

It was the final night of the St. Regis Carnival, one of Fortune Brothers annual gigs, a middling affair held at a Catholic school in Wilkes-Barre. Bo told Cone they always set up in and around the practice fields outside the football stadium, where there was plenty of room. They'd be packing up early tomorrow and heading out to the next venue in Hagerstown.

After everything at the fair had been shut down, Cone rushed back to the Winnebago, showered, dressed, and headed out the door in a flash. Most times he and Bo hit the bars together, but Bo's good looks and natural way with women had begun to get on Cone's nerves more and more lately, it cramping his own game. He wanted to go solo tonight.

Cone walked about a half-dozen blocks when he spotted the sign for the High Street Lounge. He entered and quickly surveyed the scene, deciding to sit at the bar. The barkeep, a bald, unsmiling man, took his order and poured him a frothy Yuengling draft. Behind the bar and in several other locations throughout the tavern were big-screen televisions featuring the Phillies-Dodgers game. Some patrons played pool or darts in the adjacent room, while in the main room a few diners sat at tables. Those customers who sat at the bar seemed steadfastly focused on drinking.

Cone understood them, the committed drinkers. There were different ways you could decide to kill yourself. Some took the short route, opting to eat a bullet or hang themselves. Others took the long road home, doing themselves in a drink, a snort, or a jab of a needle at a time.

That was when Tegan—the good-time girl who went any which way the wind blew—sat down on the stool next to his.

He bought her a drink and tried stringing her along with small talk until she started looking around for what seemed to be a better option. Flashing her a peek at the joint he had cupped in his hand—a birthday gift from Bo—he motioned with his thumb and a tilt of his head for her to join him outside to smoke it. She smiled and nodded, and they got up and left.

Cone coaxed her to walk with him around the block. They then continued on down the dark alley, the arc lights they passed casting no illumination, looking like giant, alien flowers with buds unbloomed, drooped over and dead, the night rendering the buildings ahead in fuzzy silhouette, even the few with a lone dim light inside otherwise engulfed in shadow. As they moved further on, the distance between the buildings ahead increased markedly.

"Here we go," Cone said, taking her by the hand and leading her into a backyard, thankful that no security light flashed on as he tried the knob on the side door to the garage. It opened. They entered, and Cone flicked his Bic, it casting enough light for him to make out the clutter that filled the garage, leaving no room for a car. He lit the joint and inhaled, then handed it to the girl.

After Cone took the second drag, the strange warp he felt taking hold in his brain made him realize the joint was spiked with something. They took a few more tokes each, she starting to tremble and babble nervously. Though he was zonked as fuck too, he tried to calm her down, giving her a hug to reassure her. She didn't pull away, so he took it as a sign that it was okay to make his move on her.

But then she began screaming, flailing at him with her fists before pushing him off and scrambling away. She barreled through the door and out into the night, he taking off after her. The wilderness crowded round this desolate end of town, the landscape primitive and forlorn under the moonless sky massed with looming clouds that seemed too close, the darkness bleeding out from the nearby woods to snuff out the light and signs of life at its edges.

Tackling her and pulling her down to the ground, he clamped his hand over her mouth, using his weight and strength to control her as she struggled. He couldn't have anyone come to hear fucking lies from a crazy bitch who couldn't handle a high, filming him with their phones and posting it for all the world to see, making him out as a monster to loathe and deride even before the police arrived to haul him off and lock him up again.

—

It wasn't over and done with, though. Screaming girls brought attention, but dead girls brought attention too. There were witnesses who'd seen them leaving the bar together, and any of his

DNA found on her body would give the prosecution a slam dunk case against him.

Cone got out his phone and called Bo, giving him directions as best he could to come pick him up. After what seemed an eternity, Bo finally rolled up in the Winnebago. Cone opened the passenger side door and got in.

"Cut the lights," Cone said. "I need to use the RV. You can hang out here and I'll come back and get you when I'm done."

"What the fuck happened?" Bo asked.

"I ... It was an accident."

Bo turned off the motor. "Show me," he said.

Cone sat quietly for a moment, then got out of the RV. Bo followed him into the yard next to the garage, where Cone lit his lighter to reveal the girl's body.

"Okay," Bo said. "Let's get her in."

No lights went on inside or outside the nearby houses. No cars approached in the alley. No people were to be seen or heard anywhere. A slice of the underworld seemed to have manifested on the Earth's surface before them.

They got her into the vehicle and drove off.

—

Bo drove the RV back toward Scranton, heading off into the forested hills and flatlands outside the city, swaths of land still ravaged and scarred in the aftermath of coal mining that had begun over a century and a half earlier. He knew the area intimately from the many summer days and spring and fall weekends in his youth, spent exploring the wilderness, riding his trail bike over the terrain, and, when he was older, scouting out secluded spots by car for parking and partying.

Slowing, then bringing the RV to a stop, Bo grabbed a flashlight and exited the vehicle, Cone following him. They walked up to the entrance of an abandoned mine, the entrance boarded up. Bo maneuvered some of the planks that had been pried loose enough to move and went inside. He turned back to face Cone. "Stay here," he said, disappearing into the mine.

When Bo finally returned, they went back to the RV and retrieved the dead girl, bringing her back to the mine. Bo removed the bottom plank from those covering over the entrance and took it with them as they carried the body into the mine. Stopping at a spot where the side of the dirt wall had partly collapsed, they laid the lifeless form at the foot of the wall. Bo poked and jabbed the plank repeatedly into the side of the wall, breaking the dirt loose to spill over the body, then used the plank like a shovel to cover over whatever remained exposed. When he was done, he shoved the plank underneath the loose earth and used his hands to further work the scene until it appeared natural and undisturbed.

As Bo was bringing his efforts to a finish, Cone watched him, thinking.

What did he really know about Bo Badman? Badman's indifferent attitude toward the matter of the girl's death and his coldly composed manner in carrying out her disposal painted a somewhat sinister portrait of him: a villain having a hand in making similar dark and dirty deeds go away, maybe even committing some of those deeds himself.

But the question that wouldn't go away was: what more was he capable of?

—

As Cone drove on, each mile he left behind faded into nothingness, the past a relative fiction existing only in memory. And memory itself was a selective uncertainty, shaped by the rememberer's areas of focus and interpretation, a process of erosion that lost grounding with the passing of time. He imagined everything disappearing into a cloud of obscurity, all memories of each event losing their solidity, his hold on them loosening before they slipped away to merge into the dense, dark mist that covered over the past, rendering it inscrutable.

The present was all. A mystery unfolding in time, with chance as the backdrop, shaped and driven by impulses and tendencies that remained elusive to his efforts to trace out their scope and ultimate meaning. A kind of sleep from which there was no awakening, in which the outline of things remained uncertain and unfocused, where there was neither redemption nor grace, but instead the ever-present specter of that eternal and awful cloud of unknowing from which everything originated, and into which everything ultimately would be swallowed up and disappear as if it had never existed.

THE SCARECROW

BY KAREN KEELEY

I first twigged to the guy when I saw him walking the hallways with attitude. Then dumb luck got me stuck with him in Geography class because old man Graham favored his students sitting alphabetically by last name. Whenever the Scarecrow bothered to show up, he lounged in his desk, one long lanky leg thrown over the desktop, a pointy-toed black leather Beatles boot pointed at the ceiling, him wearing Levi's and a faded tee-shirt, both about as appealing as my mom's old dishrags. Everything about the guy shouted rebel, even the ratty old navy pea coat he wore to class. It didn't take long to figure out school was a kind of prison for him—1967 and a time of free love, defying the establishment and flipping the bird at any and all who reeked of authority. The Scarecrow wanted to be out there—whatever out there meant.

Eventually I twigged to the fact that his name was Pete Lonigan but by then, what did it matter? We'd become friends. I helped him with his homework, and he provided the weed. He also provided me with my first introduction to Pink Floyd—he simply called them the Floyd, an up-and-coming rock band that was gonna change the world. I'd been a Stones fan up until then, caught up in their hype. One afternoon I was at his place and he introduced me to *The Piper at the Gates of Dawn*, the two of us sharing a big fat doobie. I then understood the relevance of his nickname, the idea of standing in a field of barley, field mice running circles around his pointy-toed Beatles boots, him without a care in the world. How cool was that?

Not long after, we were once again in old man Graham's Geography class, bored out of our gourds, me fantasizing about Helen Rose's big tits when a piece of chalk suddenly struck my forehead. "Damn it all," growled Graham. "I was aiming for Lonigan."

By this time, the Scarecrow had become plain old Pete to me. He was folding another paper airplane in his big catcher's mitt hands, making ready to launch it toward Helen. Old man Graham, reeking of booze and stale cigarettes, marched down the aisle, told Pete to get his head out of the clouds and back in the here and now. He then grabbed Pete by the collar of his shirt and pulled him from his desk. "Take a walk to the Principal's office," he growled, and shoved Pete toward the back of the classroom.

Pete took up his coat, shrugged, gave me a quick wink and departed. It wasn't until after school that I found him at the Moody Park little league ball diamond, listening to his transistor radio, a Sony small enough to fit in a shirt pocket. Somewhere during his travels, after leaving school, he'd bought a pack of Player's filter tips. He offered me one.

"So what happened?" I asked, taking the smoke and using Pete's Zippo for the light.

"Kicked out for two days," he said and then shrugged—telling me he didn't give a flying fuck. School was for losers.

I agreed but at sixteen, what else were we gonna do? It wasn't like we could get any jobs that paid decent wages. Hell, my parents were always going on about the importance of getting an education, reinforcing the notion I needed at least grade twelve to go anywhere in life.

Later, the two of us hunkered down in his basement, Pete's parents both at work and not due home until well after six o'clock, I rolled a joint while Pete put on *The Piper at the Gates of Dawn*. He dropped onto a couch littered with dozens of cigarette burns and started rambling on about Syd Barret, the face of Pink Floyd. He told me Syd was the creative genius behind the band, writing the songs, bringing the band members together. I'd heard about the fiasco with the Pat Boone special, how Syd just stood there, refused to play his guitar or sing—not when it came to rolling the tape for the final take, though he had played along during rehearsals.

"Well fuck, whaddya expect?" said Pete. "Syd's the man—no one's gonna tell him what to do." Pete, like Syd, hated rules. Breaking the rules also meant scoring the drugs and Pete's parents were mighty generous when it came to doling out the coin. They thought putting money in their son's pocket would help keep him out of trouble, especially with me there to help him with his homework. By then, Pete had started to identify with Syd Barrett. In the beginning, I could see the similarities—Syd, a likeable and charming guy, popular with the girls. But as the schoolyear wore on, Pete started to unravel, just like his hero. He became more disruptive in class, his moods became dark and gloomy, his attitude confrontational. He even embarrassed Helen Rose a few times— actually made reference to her big tits, something that simply wasn't done, not when the teacher was in the room.

Those comments sent him off to the Principal's office for a second, third and fourth time, and eventually he got a major expulsion, one that lasted a full week.

It wasn't until after Christmas break that we met up again. He seemed better, not quite as moody or snarly as he had been, and behind the baseball dugout at Moody Park, he told me he was on good drugs and left it at that. Later, I overheard my parents discussing his diagnosis, something called attention deficit disorder. According to my mom, Pete was on some drug called Ritalin. It must've worked because I eventually got the old Pete Lonigan back.

Toward the end of March, one Friday night, he told me, "We're going on a panty raid."

I sat up, the room spinning. If my parents had known what I was up to most nights, smokin' weed, droppin' acid, they'd have had my guts for garters—a favourite expression of my dad's. "What's that we're doing?" I asked.

"A panty raid," said Pete. "We're gonna nick a pair of Helen Rose's knickers."

"I don't think so," I told him. "She lives in lockup, you know that. Her father's a goddamn cop, for Chrissakes. We get caught and you can kiss your ass goodbye."

"We won't get caught," he said.

"How's that?"

"I scoped out her house," said Pete. "We simply push up her bedroom window, get in and get out. Her knickers are bound to be in some dresser drawer somewhere in the room."

"Jesus, you've been listening to that damn fool song again, haven't you? Believin' the hype about nickin' underwear."

Pete was laughing. He smacked his skinny thigh. "That and my signature tune—how can you not love the Scarecrow? It's time to put these bad boys to work."

"What bad boys?" I asked.

"Move my arms—get my head thinking. It's time I embraced my fate."

"Your fate, my ass! Your parents are gone, like always," I told him. "We got the basement to ourselves. There's food in the fridge, maybe even some beer. Knowing your old man, he'll never miss it. We do like we always do—we hang here, listen to the tunes on your badass stereo, pass around a fat doobie, drop a hit of acid."

Pete stood, raked his fingers through his matted curls. God only knew when he'd last had a decent haircut or had used an actual comb. Come to think of it, we were both beginning to look like Syd Barrett, which wasn't necessarily a bad thing. Smoke enough weed and drop enough acid and all things begin to look good, decorum and reason gone by way of throwing the baby out with the bathwater.

"Come on, asshole. You know you're up for it," he said. "You've been droolin' over Helen's tits since the beginning of the schoolyear. We'll nick a pair of her undies and you're in knicker heaven. You'll have a souvenir, something to treasure while whankin' off between the sheets."

That stopped me cold. He had a point there. Not something I would've thought of. Maybe a panty raid wasn't such a bad idea. "Lead the way, Macduff—I bow to your conviction."

Gaining entry to Helen's bedroom proved easy-peasy, just like Pete had said. No one was home, the place locked up tight like Fort Knox except for the windows, not even a porch light left on. What we didn't reckon on was the family pet—a Jack Russel terrier riding shotgun.

After finding an old wooden sawhorse in the backyard, we shoved it under Helen's bedroom window and Pete climbed aboard. The window rolled up smooth as butter slicked on a corncob. Pete then got one leg over the sill, was fumbling in the dark for a handhold on something to break his fall, when the damn dog grabbed his ankle, snarling like a wolverine. Thank Christ for the pointy-toed Beatles boots. He was bustin' a gut with laughter, shaking a leg, trying to get the Jack Russel to let go. Finally, freedom—and Pete came tumbling backward where he landed on me. By then, we were both giggling like a couple of school girls, laid out in the flower bed beneath the window, the wooden sawhorse, the tulips and the daffodils having taken a beating, the two of us higher than a kite, having failed miserably at nicking a pair of goddamned laced panties.

Pete's ankle was collateral damage, the little Jack Russel having gotten a good hold on his leather boot but luckily no blood and nothing broken. In our drug-induced haste to get away, we neglected to close the window. We could hear the dog barking as it made frantic leaps for the windowsill. I had no idea how high a Jack Russel could jump but if that puppy ever got its paws on the window ledge, it could leverage itself clear, jump through the open window and tear us each a new one, leaving Pete and I lookin' like a couple of Fraser valley scarecrows decimated by the Big Blow that blew through back in '62. We took off running. Pete was favouring his ankle but it didn't slow him down. We tore out through the back gate and raced down the alley. Eventually, back at his place, we flopped onto the couch, both of us out of breath.

"What's your next harebrained idea?" I asked.

"It never occurred to me we could've waited," Pete said, massaging his injured ankle while taking a good hard look at his Beatles boot, tabulating the bite marks.

"Whaddya mean?" I asked.

"When her old lady does laundry, whaddya wanna bet she hangs it outside on the line."

I smacked my own forehead. Of course! Why hadn't I thought of that?

In those days, we still had outdoor clotheslines, most moms using them when the weather was decent. We decided to scope out Helen's place throughout the coming week, randomly play hooky, skip school, take a powder from class, call it what you will. Helen's mom finally did the laundry on Thursday, a bright sunny day. We hid behind the garden shed, waited for the laundry to be done and Helen's mom to have disappeared back inside the house.

Our luck held, no sign of the Jack Russel but the problem then became, with the height of the clothesline, we could see Helen's knickers hanging in the bright sunlight but they were too high up for either of us to reach.

"Okay, Sherlock, what now?" I asked.

"Climb on my shoulders," said Pete. "I'll duck walk us over there, you reach up, grab a pair of Helen's underwear, and Bob's your uncle."

"Bob's your what?"

"Something my old man says—thought it might be appropriate for this caper," said Pete.

"Caper—Christ, you really are losing it."

Pete squatted down. I climbed onto his shoulders. I was a tad shorter than him but I still weighed a pretty penny and to this day, I still don't know how he did it. He must've been doubling up on his morning bowl of Wheaties because he duck walked to the clothesline where I grabbed a pair of undies, the wooden clothes pegs snapping off and hitting me in the eye, just like getting whacked by a couple of out-of-play foul balls. Hurt like hell.

Pete leaned forward, I jumped, landed on my feet and the two of us took off running. Back in his basement, Pete held up the underwear. "You think these are Helen's?"

"How the hell should I know? I just reached up and grabbed."

Pete tossed the underwear onto the couch. "I think they're her old lady's—look at the size of them. Helen's not that big—big tits but no ass."

"Jesus! We're a couple of clowns when it comes to being crooks. Maybe my parents are right—stay in school, get an education. At least with an education we don't have to resort to stealin' underwear as a means to an end."

"Whaddya mean by that?"

I then had an idea—a flash of brilliance. My sly grin told him

Little Red Riding Hood would always prefer the company of the woodsman. "Are you up for tryin' something different?"

The next day, during Geography class, old man Graham about busted a gasket when he found a pair of ladies underwear in his desk drawer. Pete and I both knew where he kept the booze—a fifth of Jack Daniel's hidden in his desk, in a drawer, in a paper bag. We were in the middle of an impromptu flash quiz—Graham loved to pull that stunt, all of us busy scribbling away when he pulled open his desk drawer. His big old hand reached in and what does he find but a pair of knickers.

I thought Helen Rose's eyes were gonna pop out of her head—maybe she recognized the panties, maybe they were hers after all. And the class broke up laughing.

Old man Graham went purple with rage. He couldn't exactly blame Pete directly but the way he was cursing, we could tell he was pretty damn certain who had done the dirty deed. It would never have occurred to him that it could've been me—not boring old Keller, not the golden boy who had all the answers, ever ready to zip through the class quizzes, the end result a hundred percent most of the time.

I didn't turn around and give Pete a high five. I wasn't that stupid. But I did feel him give me a shove between the shoulder blades, his way of letting me know, a damn fine caper! Somehow I needed that. High praise coming from him.

Over the next couple of years, the media would give us stories about the assassinations of Martin Luther King and Robert Kennedy. The Vietnam conflict would continue to rile young Americans looking for social change—hell-bent on stopping the war and bringing the soldiers safely back home. That same neighbor to the south would also land a man on the moon, hoping to gain a leg up on the world stage. Pink Floyd too, would reach new heights while embracing change. David Gilmour joined the band as Syd Barrett succumbed to his mental illness. Personally, I didn't have a problem with change—change was good, it was inevitable. As I grew older, the Floyd's music would continue to haunt me, them too, growing in creative expression, something we should all aspire to.

Pete Lonigan would also continue to haunt me. The night of our high school prom, two years after the panty raid, the weather turned nasty just like the night of the Big Blow back in '62, when the tail end of Typhoon Freda slammed the Pacific Northwest. A pineapple express roared up from the Hawaiian Islands and dumped a boatload of water across BC's lower mainland, all the way from Stanley Park in Vancouver out toward Chilliwack. Pete was driving his '56 Chevy Bel Air on Columbia Street in New Westminster, not far from Moody Park, windshield wipers slappin' time, when he and Helen Rose were both killed, Pete's beloved Chevy T-boned by a drunk driver. Couldn't even blame it on the weather.

Just Pete's dumb luck—wrong place, wrong time—and to this day, I still try to wrap my head around that, wondering if our destiny is written long before we are born, none of us ever knowing the timing of the ultimate ending. Take Syd Barrett. He certainly wouldn't have believed his short run with the Floyd would end so soon, other members of the band believing in the music, believing in the message, all of them rockin' on well into their seventies.

Whenever I think of Pete, I think of a tall lanky dude standing in that field of barley without a care in the world, his face turned toward the sun, soaking up the rays, field mice rootin' around in the grain, a man happily resigned to his fate. As for stealing underwear, that was our one and only attempt at wanting to be badass criminals. Helen told Pete when he fessed up six months later, her mom had no idea a pair of undies had gone missing from the clothesline. It was one of a dozen pair, black and green lace with satin trim, the underwear purchased at Woolworth's, the remaining pairs kept safe, tucked away in a bedroom dresser drawer, out of sight, out of mind.

WISH YOU WERE HERE

BY ANDY RAUSCH

Lou Lou had her blonde hair up in a pony and her makeup done the way Eddie liked. She even had on the too-tight cutoff jeans he liked; the ones he said were so tight he could read her lips. She'd done all she could to doll herself up, but none of this could conceal her shiny purplish black eye. When she'd stopped at a gas station on the way to the prison, the fuck-head behind the counter had joked about her looking like Rocky. Then the bitch he worked with remarked, "I'd hate to see what the other bitch looks like." Lou Lou wanted to tell them both they could go fuck a one-eyed squirrel, but she'd kept her mouth shut. She couldn't risk getting herself in trouble. Not today. Not before she saw her Eddie.

So here she was, sitting in front of a big glass screen, waiting for a guard to escort Eddie out so they could talk. As she sat waiting with her legs crossed, Lou Lou stared at the heart tattoo on her ankle; the blue heart with the yellow banner across it that read "Lou Lou Loves Eddie. This made her crack a cynical, tight-lipped smile. When she'd gotten that ink all those years before, neither she nor Eddie could have guessed where they'd end up. While

197

Eddie had always been a small-time hood, neither of them would have predicted Eddie's "once-in-a-lifetime" scheme to rob an old oil man's ranch upstate. Nor would they have predicted that Eddie would lose his temper and shoot the oil man. So, having not predicted any of that, they also would not have predicted that the dead oil man would have a surveillance camera that caught his murder on tape. But, prediction or not, that's what happened, and here they were.

Finally, after Lou Lou had waited longer than the running time of "In-A-Gadda-Da-Vida," a stocky black prison guard brought her husband in and sat him across from her. Then the guard went and stood with his back against the wall behind Eddie, overseeing both Eddie and another prisoner Lou Lou couldn't see at a window to her left. Eddie looked up with sad, wet eyes that were on the verge of real tears.

Eddie pressed his palm flat against the glass, and Lou Lou looked into his eyes. The damn broke, and tears streamed down his face. She raised her hand to the glass and pressed her palm against his.

They both cried. Eddie was the first to lower his hand. He then pointed at the red telephone on the wall beside him. He picked it up and put it to his ear. Following his lead, Lou Lou picked up the phone on her side of the glass.

"I love you, pretty girl," Eddie said.

Lou Lou cried hard and it took her a moment to respond. "I wish you were here, Eddie."

He nodded and started to calm her when he noticed her swollen eye. His eyes squinted and his head tilted a bit. "What happened to your eye, Lou? Somebody hit you?"

She looked down for a long moment, composing herself.

"Who did that shit?" Eddie asked.

She looked up with tears in her eyes.

He repeated the question. "Who hit you, Lou?"

"It ... it was Donnie."

Eddie's mouth fell open. The news hit him like a brick. *"Donnie?!"*

Lou Lou nodded.

Donnie was Eddie's best friend. His road dog. His ace. Eddie and Donnie had been friends since they were kids. Eddie used to tell Lou Lou that Donnie was his "brother from another mother." He said, "I got a real brother, but that prick ain't half the brother Donnie is." He'd always said Donnie was the one person, outside of Lou Lou, who would always be there for him, through thick and thin. And that had, until now, been true. Donnie had been there on the ranch with Eddie the day he'd plugged the old man. But Donnie was outside keeping watch, so he didn't make a cameo in the old man's snuff film. When the cops came for Eddie the next day, Eddie told them he'd been alone.

Lou Lou leveled her gaze at him. "Has he come to see you?"

"No, he hasn't," Eddie said, considering this.

"That bastard hit me, Eddie."

Eddie's expression changed to something that was equal parts pain, confusion, and disbelief. Lou Lou knew Eddie needed to keep hold of his disbelief; he *needed* Donnie to be innocent.

"You sure it was him?" he asked.

Lou Lou, still crying, became agitated and pointed at her eye. "You think I don't know who punched me in the eye? I was there, Eddie. I was the one who got punched."

Eddie stared at her, trying to reconcile this with the Donnie he knew.

Her eyes narrowed. "And that ain't all he done, Eddie." Her voice was sharp enough to cut steel.

Eddie stared at her with the same wounded look he'd had when she'd said it was Donnie. "What else he do?" But he already knew. "Did he . . .?"

She stared at him, sighing with tears in her eyes, just as tired and overwhelmed as he was. She cried harder, her chest heaving like a child. She looked down at the floor as if she might find answers there.

Eddie softened. "Lou," he said, almost whispering.

She looked up. Her eyeliner ran, making black streams down her cheeks that almost matched her eye. "I'm sorry, Eddie," she said. "He knocked on the door. When I answered, I just looked out at him through the screen. He told me he needed to come in and talk to me about the—" She caught herself and looked up at the guard. He wasn't paying attention, but she wasn't sure what to say.

Eddie nodded. *"The stuff?"*

She stared at him, wanting to be sure he meant what she meant.

He said it again. "You know, that *stuff* we got. The stuff me and Donnie got."

Now they were on the same page and she knew they were both talking about their share of the $330,000 Eddie had robbed from the dead oil man. She nodded. "Yeah, that was it. The *stuff*."

"Okay, then what?"

"He said he needed to talk to me about it. Said it was important."

"So what?"

She shrugged a little. "I let him in. Did I do wrong, Eddie?" Lou Lou said. "I didn't know he was gonna pull that shit."

"No, Lou," Eddie said. "This ain't your fault."

She leaned forward and cried into her free hand.

Eddie took a deep breath, trying to maintain composure. "Okay, okay. So what about the stuff?"

She looked up at him with fire in her eyes. "Is that all you give a shit about?"

Eddie knew he'd fucked up. In fact, he'd known it before she'd even responded.

"I'm sorry, baby girl," he said. "That wasn't fair. You know I love you. I love you more than anything in the world."

Her body relaxed a little. She was still crying but tried to rein it in. She looked at him and said, "You promise?"

"You know I do."

She nodded. "I do. And I'm sorry."

"I'm sorry, too, baby girl."

She stared at him with big eyes.

"So the stuff?" he asked.

"God Eddie. There was nothing I could do."

"It's *gone?*"

Lou Lou nodded, her mouth tightening and her chin jutting out some. "Half of its gone," she said. "The half that was in the house."

Eddie's face hardened as he clamped his jaws. Then he leaned forward, shaking his head. "You think you know a motherfucker. But you know, I don't think anybody really ever knows anybody. I've been road dogs with Donnie since we were playing little league ball. He was a pitcher and he kept throwing fastballs, trying to hit me every time I came up. After the game we got in a fistfight, knocked the shit out of each other, and after that we were friends for life." He paused and looked at her through teary eyes. "None of that means anything, I guess."

She put her palm against the glass again. "Please forgive me, Eddie."

He stopped himself, remembering their time was precious. "It ain't your fault, Lou. None of it. It's my fault for gettin' my dumb ass locked up here. It was my fault for trusting that motherfucker." He nodded, still staring at her. "I shoulda known, Lou. I shoulda known. You're the only person I got . . ."

He raised his hand and pressed his palm against the glass where hers was. "I'm sorry I got you into this, and I'm sorry about Donnie. I promise, when I get out I'll take care of it." He looked into her eyes. "I promise, baby girl."

She sighed. "You'll be old and gray if you ever get out of here."

Eddie nodded a sad, deflated nod. "I'll never get out."

"No matter what, you've got me. I'll never leave you, Eddie."

Staring past their hands, he said, "I know, baby girl. I know."

Staring back, she started to bawl again. She pulled her hand back to cover her face, smearing the mascara down her cheek. "I'm scared, Eddie."

He sat there with a pained expression, feeling helpless. "What are you scared of?"

She looked into his eyes. "Donnie wants the rest. He said he's comin' back to get it, and he threatened to kill me. He's crazy. I can't stay there anymore."

Eddie was confused and upset, unsure whether he should be more angry or hurt. He shook his head and said softly, "It'll be okay, baby girl."

"I don't wanna die."

"You ain't gonna die," he said. "Do me a favor. Just this one thing. Take what's left and go hide. Go somewhere safe and send me some postcards."

"No, Eddie. I am not leaving you alone here."

He looked at her and started sobbing hard. "You gotta go, Lou. You *gotta*."

Now the guard moved towards Eddie. Lou Lou looked at him and Eddie knew what was happening by the look in her eyes.

"I love you, baby girl," Eddie said. "Go and do what I told you."

The guard prompted him to stand. Lou Lou took one last look at her husband and said, "I love you, Eddie. I'm not going anywhere. I'll be back soon, baby."

They both cried as the guard escorted Eddie back to his cell.

—

Lou Lou wept as she made her way through the prison, all the way back to the exit. As she stepped out into the sunlight, she calmed herself and wiped away the tears, then reached into her purse and grabbed a pack of smokes. She extracted a cigarette, put it to her lips and lit it. Now, she smiled as she walked back to the stolen Corvette. She looked up at Candace, the pretty brunette standing beside the car.

Candace asked, "How'd it go?"

Lou Lou grinned. "Fine as blueberry wine."

"He bought it?"

She shrugged. "I'm a good salesman."

Lou Lou kissed her hard on the mouth.

Candace said, "You're kinda cute, you know that?" She laughed. "But you've got fucking eyeliner all over your face."

Lou Lou laughed. "Shit, I forgot all about that."

She reached up and wiped her eyes with her arm. "You know how it goes," she said. "You gotta go all in and play the thing 'til the end."

Lou Lou turned and popped the trunk so she could take another look at the money. She opened the cardboard box, eyeballing the money inside. Then she looked at Donnie's corpse stuffed in the trunk behind the box. "Can't wait to ditch his ass in the reservoir," she said. Candace stood beside her, eyeballing the money. "So that's what a quarter of a million dollars looks like."

"Yep." Lou Lou nodded. "That's what *our* quarter of a million dollars looks like." She closed the trunk and turned around to face Candace. They kissed again, this time a long, sweet one. Lou Lou pulled back so she could look into the other woman's pretty blue eyes.

"Anywhere in particular you wanna go?" Lou Lou asked.

Candace thought about it for a moment before saying, "I always wanted to see Disneyland."

Lou Lou nodded. "We're going to Disneyland."

CHILDHOOD'S END

A. B. PATTERSON

- 1 -

The bear was the only one smiling in the fetid motel room.

I remembered the fixed grin on the soiled, pink teddy bear, with a rainbow across its grubby white tummy. I dredged my whiskey-dampened memory. A synapse or two fired, reluctantly: it was called the Cheer Bear. She'd told me that in the interview room two years ago.

Wasn't so fucking cheery now.

—

A girl's naked body lay half on the double bed. It hadn't been a natural death. I didn't need forensics to tell me that. Semen and shit trailed down the inside of her parted thighs. Her vagina and anus looked like a baseball bat had visited.

I recognized the back of her head, with the short blonde bob: Clare Sarafian. Current, until last night, prostitute. Former child sexual assault victim.

I thought of that interview room, meeting Mister Cheer Bear during the rapport building. Before the sordid details spewed forth in a torrent of retold depravity.

—

One of the uniformed officers straightened from his slouch against the wall as I held up my badge.

"Detective," he nodded.

The casual attitude and the sneer at Clare's body pissed me off.

"Detective Sergeant," I corrected him.

The other constable grunted. "Junkie whore, risky lifestyle. Job over to you, Detective Sergeant. Can we go now?"

Poor tone begets itself.

"Yes, idiot. Go catch yourselves a traffic offender, or your half-priced McDonald's. Just get out of my sight."

My glare and my rank combined to stop any more lip.

Being hardened to crime scenes, even some off humor, I can handle. Disinterested contempt for a dead girl I can't stomach.

I gave them the bird as they pulled out of the car park, and I got on my phone to the duty crime manager. Forensics and the pathologist were being dispatched.

—

I looked at Clare.

She'd survived an appalling adolescence only to end up here.

Three different types of cigarette butts littered the dirty beige carpet. Clare's menthol remnants were in the ashtray on the bedside table.

So at least three guys had done her.

An empty, depressed syringe lay on the floor half under the bed. I wasn't going to need the pathologist to tell me she'd been given a hotshot.

What a tragic waste.

Could she have hauled herself out of her lifestyle? Maybe, maybe not. Two years ago, she'd told me she was trying to get off the game and the gear, that unholy duopoly of vice.

But there were too many predators out here. For a young, damaged girl trying to scrape by on her own resources, which really amounted to her orifices, these streets were a living hell.

I stepped back onto the concrete veranda and lit a smoke. There were days when I hated this job, life, the whole shitty shebang.

—

Twenty minutes later, a silver station wagon pulled up.

A looker in tight white coveralls got out. Late twenties. Copper-colored hair in a pony tail, and a bust Michelangelo would have been proud to sculpt. I'd seen her at another crime scene a while back, but had been too occupied to take heed. Couldn't remember her name.

She smiled. Utterly lovely.

"Detective Sergeant Harrington?"

"Yep." I held out my hand. "Call me Bruce."

She shook. Firm. "Maeve Slattery, SOCO."

"No team? I called it in as a homicide."

She looked guilty or embarrassed. "Sorry. Boss said it was just a dead hooker, so didn't warrant a team. Resources and all that."

I ground my third ciggie out and slapped the wall. "For fuck's sake! Somebody loves her." I wasn't sure of that, but I wanted it to be true.

Maeve looked at me, silent.

Time to retreat. "Sorry, not your fault. I'm having a shitty week."

"You reckon yours is shitty. I was supposed to be getting married on the weekend. Fucking bastard ran off with my maid of honor."

"Ouch. Sorry, Maeve. Wrong title for her, obviously."

"The maid or the honor?"

We both had a chuckle.

"I'll pay that," I said.

"And your crap this week? Apart from the job?"

"Divorce finalizing. I'm flat broke, living in a borrowed room, scrounging overtime, and she ran off with a fucking barrister."

Our eyes lingered together. What the hell. "Feel like a drink later, Maeve?"

"Are the Kennedy's gun-shy?"

—

Constable Slattery got busy with photographs and dusting for prints.

The pathologist arrived. Her money was on a hotshot, coupled with asphyxiation, and that the sexual penetrations were concurrent with the death. But she'd want to do the autopsy and get the toxicology before she confirmed it.

The doctor left as the government contractors arrived and went inside with their gurney.

Maeve had finished her work, but had a smoke with me until all was done.

"What's your number?" she asked, pulling out her phone.

I told her. My phone beeped with her message.

Clare's body was loaded in for its sad, lonely journey to the morgue. The anonymous white van departed.

"Call me when you knock off, Bruce."

"Cool. My local watering hole is excellent."

She nodded and smiled. "Good. We both need a night out." She moved towards her car.

"Sure. Any eating preference?" I called after her.

She half turned. "Cock."

- 2 -

I knocked off early, privilege of rank, and headed for my local pub.

I walked in out of the bright sunshine and dark world. My eyes adjusted to the subdued lighting. One of the owners, Zed, was behind the bar.

"G'day, Bruce. Bit earlier than normal?"

"Yeah, rough day."

"The usual coming right up then, mate."

I swallowed half my beer in one gulp. Needed that.

Zed, true professional, lined up a second, with a whiskey shot.

—

I turned my thoughts to Clare Sarafian.

They say you don't get to choose your family. Ain't that the bloody truth. Clare was at the bottom of the barrel when it came to bad luck in the ancestry stakes. Her father had started screwing her when she was thirteen. Went on for three long years until Clare did a runner.

I'd been working at the Child Exploitation Squad at the time. Clare's was an unusual case, in our books, because it was her natural father doing her. A good old-fashioned incest case. It wasn't unusual because a young girl was getting raped in her supposed sanctuary called home: that was dime a dozen. No, it was unusual because these cases invariably involved a step-father, or single mum's new boyfriend, or a sports coach, or the neighbourhood guy who offered to babysit, or even the local priest. Although that latter category tended to prefer little boys.

What wasn't so unusual, but equally as tragic, was how Clare's useless bitch of a mother didn't want to know when Clare finally spoke up. And so sixteen-year-old Clare Sarafian ended up on the street with a suitcase, her teddy bear and not a damned hope left worth pissing on.

And so any dreams she had cherished turned rapidly to nightmares, both awake and asleep.

—

I was just thinking back to my arrest of the father when Maeve sidled up next to me, a waft of Gaultier massaging my nostrils. Goodbye forensic overalls, hello short skirt and waist-tied blouse. Sizzling hot.

"You look gorgeous. Drink?"

"Bubbles, please."

She knocked two back in fifteen minutes as we made small talk. Sexual tension smoldered.

"Food's great here."

"Didn't come for food. Buy me another bubbles, though."

Two more. She got more voluble about her arsehole fiancé. Couldn't blame her. As she polished off her fourth glass, she turned to look at me.

"I'm going to the bathroom. Give me three minutes, then follow."

She kissed me, grabbed her purse and sashayed off to the ladies.

I watched her arse swagger as she moved. Sensational. Either her maid of honour was a supermodel crossed with a porn star, or the fiancé was a total fuckwit. I think I knew which.

I skulled my drink as three minutes came up. I told Zed I'd be back and headed for the bathrooms. No one looking and into the ladies I stepped.

A young blonde babe was fixing her lipstick and looked surprised in the mirror.

"Police, routine check." I held up my badge. Amazing what those words can do. Babe pouted at herself and me, smiled cheekily and left.

—

A cubicle door opened and Maeve was standing there naked except for her heels.

Wordless, she turned and bent over. We started fucking fast and hard.

She passed me her phone and told me to film her getting impaled. It was a gift for her fiancé. How thoughtful. Well, that's who I assumed she meant by "the fuckstain."

I hadn't had a shag in a bar toilet in donkey's years, but it felt great in that adrenalin-laced way, for its brief existence. Needs rule.

—

Back at the bar she had one more drink and kissed me on the lips.

"Thanks, a great evening. See you around."

"Ciao, bella."

Out of the corner of my eye, I could see Zed grinning as he watched me watching her departing arse.

Zed said nothing. Still smiling, he put a large whiskey in front of me.

- 3 -

I stared into the amber liquid.

Poor bloody Clare. I'd charged her father, George Sarafian, with twenty-seven counts of incest, indecent dealing, and administering a stupefying substance. All round father of the fucking year.

The prosecutor's office said it was one of the worst sexual abuse cases they'd seen. They commended me on the brief of evidence. Fat lot of good it did.

No confession, of course. The gutless bastard exercised his right to silence. But Clare's account was solid and there was the medical evidence.

I'd spent several sessions with Clare in the lead-up to the trial, getting her settled and ready to stand tall and give her testimony.

The night before, she cut her wrists.

She survived, but the trial was adjourned.

Three months later, a year ago now, she'd made it to court, but late, looking drug-fucked. Her testimony was rambling and uncertain, and the arsehole's top-shelf lawyer tore her to shreds. Like getting raped all over again. Made her story sound like an inconsistent fabrication and suggested she was chasing compensation money to feed her drug habit. The jury didn't exactly warm to poor Clare.

And then, for the icing on the defence cake, the delightful mother took the stand to say how deceitful, troubled, and promiscuous Clare had been as a teenager. That last compliment was concocted to explain the medical evidence that said Clare's vagina and anus had seen more traffic than a city freeway. Finally, a procession of society types gave glowing character references for the respectable businessman, and major charity benefactor, George Sarafian.

The jury took just twenty-five minutes to acquit him on all charges.

The bastard smiled at me as he walked free from the courtroom.

—

I found Clare back on her beat later that evening.

"See? I told you no fucker would believe me."

"I did, Clare."

"So? Didn't get me justice, did it? Didn't see that fucker get what he deserves, did it?"

She turned and walked off. She got into a car with a punter on the next block.

That was the last time I ever spoke to Clare Sarafian.

—

And the last time I saw her, until I looked at her naked, violated corpse this morning.

The only shred of karma in the whole sordid saga was that the loving mother got cancer and died six months after the trial. That left the arsehole father single. Single, but still without justice being done.

And now Clare's short and sad life had come to its brutal end. I didn't expect my colleagues at homicide, who would be taking over the case next week, to try too hard. Solving the murder of a prostitute would never be much of a priority, so Clare's memory wouldn't be getting any justice either.

I got stuck into another whiskey.

As I stared morosely at my glass, with my phone on the bar next to it, I remembered that there'd been a message from my divorce lawyer before Maeve had arrived. Time to listen to it now. Nothing better to do.

I hit play. I listened.

I wanted to scream at the walls. Un-fucking-believable.

The judge had handed down his ruling today on the bitch's petition for the house. She'd got the fucking lot. And what cash I had left in my starving bank account would get consumed by my lawyer.

My worldly assets, sparse company in the room I was boarding in, now amounted to two suitcases of clothes, four packing boxes of books, music, and photos, and two thriving addictions: ciggies and booze. What a winner! What a shitty end to a shitty day in a shitty life. Sex with Maeve being the fleeting glimmer of human joy.

I dragged my sorry arse out of my self-pity and thought about Clare again. She'd deserved some justice, somehow. And every dog deserved its day, in my books.

I had a thought . . . .

- 4 -

The next afternoon, I went into my office. It was Saturday so no other detectives were around.

I rummaged through my cavernous bottom drawer, what I referred to as Pandora's box, ignoring the green bottle loitering there. I found what I was looking for: my old notes for Clare's case. I needed an address and didn't need any traces on the police computer system. No point making life easier for those armchair wankers in IA.

Next I went to the exhibit room and got out Clare's diary from the motel room. I wanted to revisit a letter I'd seen stuck inside the back flap of it: a sanctimonious note from her father telling her that he forgave her—thoughtfully sent after his acquittal. Bet she got wasted that day.

Back to my desk and cotton forensic gloves on. Spent half an hour with a pen and about twenty sheets of paper.

Done. One sheet folded and into an envelope.

A couple of other items from Pandora's box. Old-school detectives like me have fascinating bottom drawers, believe me. That's why we're a dying breed. I pocketed those items, took the gloves off and added them to my inside jacket pocket.

—

The evening was warm and heavy with cloud. Perfect, as there was zero moonlight. There were some lightning flashes out over the ocean, and the first fat drops of rain were splashing down as I walked up the path at the side of George Sarafian's suburban mansion.

With the terrace door open and Wagner on full bore, the wanker was sitting in an antique leather armchair with a bottle of cognac and a half-full balloon next to him. A Cuban was in his mouth, seeping smoke.

I strode in, slipping on my forensic gloves again. With the "Ride of the Valkyries" pumping out from the stereo, he didn't have a chance to hear a thing before it was too late.

I slipped one hand over his mouth. The other pulled out my .38 Special service revolver.

He dropped his cigar. That would leave a nasty burn on the fine leather of the armchair. Shame, I hate to see beautiful things get ruined, but collateral damage happens.

"Hello, cunt."

His eyes looked at me, half arrogant defiance, half sheer terror.

"Now, if you make a noise when I take my hand away, I'll fucking kill you. Got it?"

He nodded.

I lifted my hand away, keeping the .38 pointed at his face.

"Clare's dead."

He grunted. No words. His eyes said he didn't give a fuck. He shrugged.

I hate shrugs, the ultimate in lazy contempt. I badly wanted to belt him, but that'd leave a mark. Not in the plan.

The rain started belting down outside. I stepped over and closed the door.

I came back to him. "She was your fucking daughter!"

My raised voice startled him, but he settled again. A sneer crept across his mouth.

"She was a loser. No daughter of mine."

"That why you fucked her for years?"

He smiled. "You can't prove that, detective. You tried, remember? And failed, remember? Another loser."

I badly wanted to flog him. I dug deep into my self-restraint reserves.

I took the envelope out of my jacket pocket. I handed it to him. He turned it over, but it was blank on the outside.

"Open it and read the letter."

He did. He frowned. He wasn't used to not having full control and understanding of a situation. It's a flaw the powerful have.

"Put it back inside and put it on the table there." I pointed to the space next to the cognac bottle.

He looked back at me, still frowning, desperately trying to solve the riddle.

"It's your suicide note. I think I've done a good job on copying your handwriting. Don't you?"

"And ... And you think you're going to persuade me to kill myself?" He looked incredulous.

"Of course not, arsehole. You're way too self-centred for that."

He relaxed visibly. The smug sneer returned.

"So what then, loser detective?"

I holstered my .38, and pulled a Beretta .22 pistol from my inside pocket. From that evil bottom drawer, you understand.

His confused look returned.

"No, but it's sure going to look like a suicide."

"But … But the gun …"

"Untraceable, at least to me or the police. It's what we call a throw-down. It'll look like you had it all along."

I grinned now. I pointed to the suicide note. "It reads perfectly, doesn't it? 'I'm sorry, Clare, I wronged you, and I lied. I'm so sorry. Please forgive me.' Fucking poetry, I reckon, Mister Sarafian."

"But …"

I didn't let him continue, couldn't stand any more arrogant tripe. I put the Beretta to his temple and pulled the trigger. His head flopped to the side, resting on the wing of the chair.

I took his right hand and nestled the pistol into it, putting his finger through the trigger guard. I fired one more shot into the cushion to get some residue on his hand. That, along with my beautifully crafted note, would be enough to satisfiy the lab people that the fatal shot was self-inflicted.

The box of Cubans was mine. I was going to suck on one of those babies later as I savoured getting young Clare some belated justice.

I legged it out of there and ran in the rain to my squad car parked two blocks away.

I towelled off in the car and put the Cubans in the glove box. I lit a smoke and put the window down a centimeter. It was bucketing down.

I turned the police radio on. It was a busy night on the area channel.

"Control to any vehicle free in the Oak Grove area, possible shots fired."

I picked up the handset. "Control from Charlie three-ten, I'm in the vicinity, can assist."

"Roger, Charlie three-ten. Locals are tied up at a robbery. This came in a couple of minutes ago. Caller wasn't too sure if they were gun shots but needs to be checked out."

"Roger, Control."

"Stand by for the address, Charlie three-ten."

"Roger that." I started the engine.

Time to go and get myself all over that crime scene, officially. I do love to tie up loose ends.

WAITING FOR THE WORMS

BY PAUL WILLIAMS

The Celestial Detective was my first, and only, visitor. I watched him on the Middle End Monitor, passing through jungles teeming with the dead, walking across seas and past unnecessary land barriers to arrive at my office on the ersatz beach. It looked a bit incongruous, two stories held up on white posts with a garage underneath. To reach it you had to climb a ladder and the Celestial Detective was the second, after me, to do that.

He entered, looking immaculate in his dark suit, glowing with an orange aura. Made him resemble one of the angels that humans on Earth said inhabited heaven. Most of them will never know if they were right because they're stuck here in the Middle End.

The Celestial Detective spoke, the first time anyone had spoken to me. I squealed then apologized. I learnt so many customs watching humans on the Earth Monitor. The Celestial Detective pointed at my trident and asked, again, if I had a license for it.

"I wasn't aware that I needed one," I said, leaving aside the practical difficulties of issuing.

"The agreement for the Middle End explicitly states that the dead who await judgment shall not bring weapons or personal items with them."

"I'm not dead," I said, feeling that he knew that and wanted me to confirm. That's what detectives do on some of those television shows that humans watch. I've seen thousands of them. Boring, after the initial excitement. Predictable formats.

"You admit it?" he said triumphantly. "The capacity agreement for the Middle End states that none of the living may enter."

I laughed. "It actually says that no living male or female may enter. That's why my father created me without gender." I stood up to show him my female bottom half. He started blushing beneath his aura, a show of emotion indicating that he wasn't entirely dead. He looked more alive than the other creatures waiting in the Middle End. His eyes moved for one thing, not just side to side but up and down. I think the humans call it blinking.

"And who is your father?" he asked.

This time I challenged him. "If you've read the capacity agreement, you'll know that the gates to my father's domain are in the East."

"Just as the gates to my master's domain are in the west," he said. "Why do you keep the trident?"

"Because my father left it for me."

"You've seen him?"

"Not since I was born."

The Celestial Detective wanted to search. On Earth he would need a warrant. In the Middle End I found the request amusing and showed him the copy of the capacity agreement that my father left with the trident. Took me a long time to figure out how to read; had to adjust the Earth Monitor to find lessons that matched the language in the capacity agreement.

The Celestial Detective read the agreement. I sensed he already knew then he said the last bit aloud. "When the allocated human capacity of the Middle End is reached the gates of heaven and hell shall open and the occupants of the Middle End be even distributed. The allocated human capacity of the Middle End is 150 billion."

He looked at the counter above the Earth Monitor. "025,000,000,000," it said. The zeros never moved. Only the first two digits which had been on six when it first arrived. The Celestial Detective stared at the planet floating in space. I used my mind to change the picture to a beach like the one we were on.

The Celestial Detective held up the capacity agreement. "Where is the next page?" he asked.

I feigned ignorance.

"And you have not spoken to your father recently?"

"I have not seen him since I was created."

"I must report this," he said. "Immediately."

"May I come with you?" He looked reluctant. "Please."

The Celestial Detective nodded. I followed him downstairs and we walked through places that I had not visited before. They all felt the same because the Middle End was predominantly an illusion sustained by Daddy's will and that of his enemy, once a friend. My feet didn't burn on the sand, sink in the mud or get wet in the waves. Some of the water is real. I drink it, from rivers not the sea.

The monitors did not convey the full beauty of the landscape. The colors of the dead, copied from life, were amazing. Little green frogs, yellow wasps with black stripes, blue butterflies, and tiny black beetles. It didn't matter if you stepped on them. I've touched creatures sometimes, birds and the little geckos that find their way up my stairs. They're more numerous than the humans but size is relative. All around us were human settlements based on the ones they used to live in. Inside them, hundreds of unmoving eyes watched us pass, the living and the angel.

Eventually we reached the gates of heaven, which were as impressive as the monitor showed them. They looked like someone had taken a pile of huge teeth and smashed them together. Daddy's were the same, only yellow. Decaying, which, I guess, is symbolic of the fate of those within. Permanent death. Some of the watching humans gave the impression they would prefer that to limbo.

The Celestial Detective approached the gates. I asked him what it was like inside.

"I am not allowed to discuss," he said.

"Then at least tell me what's different here."

"There are no worms," he said. Then he stepped towards the gates and they swallowed him. I tried to follow but smacked against the hard surface of the teeth. It was the same as my father's domain. Only the invited dead could enter.

When I got back to my office, I scanned the Earth monitor, then the Middle End one, zooming right in, and saw that the Celestial Detective was right. Earth had hundreds of species of worms, mingling in the soil, devouring bodies, and just lying around. Some even survived in fire. Not one of them were in the Middle End.

I have often wondered if animals have souls. The capacity agreement only speaks about humans. I read my copy regularly, including the final page, to pass the time. My equivalent of the Bible that those who believe read on Earth. Only a fraction of those go to heaven. The ones who don't believe, usually because they hadn't heard of it, come to the Middle End.

My father saw a serious flaw in God's plan, which is why their relationship and friendship broke up. If you're going to judge people by a set of rules, then you must make sure they all know them. You can't pick out a chosen race and condemn all the rest. God thought that segregation was okay. My father made him invent purgatory otherwise known as the Middle End. It's a boundary for the humans who are neither perfect followers of God nor his enemies. The majority. A land resembling the one they once knew, copying everything except the worms.

And on the final page my father explained that he created me to kill God when the gates of his domain opened.

—

Centuries later the Celestial Detective came back. He hadn't aged and nor, I think, had I. I saw him coming in the monitor and rushed to wash myself in the sea. Didn't want him blushing again.

"Why are there no worms here?" I asked.

"Because they consume the living and the dead. Apart from you the creatures here are neither. Have you noticed there are more of them?"

He showed me the sea. It contained more fish than ever before plus crabs and lots of litter. "It replicates current conditions on Earth," said the Celestial Detective. "Perhaps the images are actually taken from there. The permanent inhabitants are a greater concern."

The counter now had a one in the first column. "The population is increasing," said the Celestial Detective. "People may live longer but their time on Earth still ends. Plus, there is a decline in religious belief, people are worshipping pop stars now. Fewer and fewer get into heaven."

I delighted in telling him that I enjoyed a good concert when I watched the Earth Monitor. For a few seconds I imagined myself in the audience, dancing with the crowd. I must have smiled because he was smiling too. He changed his expression quickly. Inspired, I searched for music and found a band playing in a place called Brixton. It was a bit psychedelic for my tastes, but I started dancing, dragging my tail around the floor, and chanting the lyrics. The Celestial Detective continued smiling. Then he grabbed the trident and ran.

I darted after him, grabbing the trident back. For a moment, I thought he would strike me then he pulled away. My hand went through him, exposing him as an illusion like the others. I had been sure he was different. "I know," he said, reappearing. "Your purpose is to destroy God."

I laughed. "Both God and Daddy are immortal."

"Not so," said the Celestial Detective. "They cannot kill each other but can be killed in their own domains."

"Which no living creature may enter."

"Until the gates open and those in the Middle End will be divided between heaven and hell."

"That's not fair," I said. "An arbitrary decision, based on nothing except proximity." I guessed that the design of the Middle End was deliberate, the settlements resembling the area of Earth known as the West were placed closer to heaven.

"Is it fair to destroy God?" asked the Celestial Detective. "You have been waiting millennia for this moment but please consider repenting. In return you can live forever in heaven."

"My first loyalty is to my father," I said. He made me after all, the only creature to live in the Middle End. "Surely you understand that? Do you not have a father?"

The Celestial Detective stepped back then turned and walked into the sea. I took the trident home and waited for the day of judgment.

—

On his third visit the celestial detective ran the whole distance. I saw him a long way off and wished, for his sake, that angels had wings, like they said. I went to meet him on the beach, my feet swishing in icy cold water that had reached the second rung of the ladder.

The ground was shanking. The waves were splashing ferociously. And the bits of debris were larger. Amongst them were dead creatures. Fish, not even pretending to be alive. A dolphin flapped closer to shore than it had ever been.

The Celestial Detective grabbed my arm and said, "It's too late."

I took him upstairs. The first three digits on the monitor were 149, as they had been for a while. "Go to your father," he said.

I ran all the way to the gates of hell, splashing through water that suddenly felt wet. The dead humans were moving in the opposite direction, as if they knew. Animals and insects too.

As I arrived the yellow teeth parted, and I saw the inferno inside. Flames burning more brightly than anything I had seen on the monitors, even the asteroid explosions. There were charred bones and flesh everywhere. A creature emerged. A huge red human with pointed horns and a long tail. As the tail swished, I saw that it was a long worm. The creature faced me. His face was covered in worms, red hot ones eating out through the flesh. Only his eyes were familiar. I remembered them.

"The worms were not dead," he said. Then he collapsed.

The Celestial Detective stood behind me. His suit twitched. A worm crawled out. He touched the trident, more worms falling from his fingers. "Too late," he said. "My master knew that the worms would devour the dead and the living."

Carrying the trident, I ran to the gates of heaven, pushing through the souls in limbo. The gates opened, just a little. A worm crawled out.

AUTHORS

IN ORDER OF APPEARANCE

T. Fox Dunham lives in Philadelphia with his wife, Allison. He's a lymphoma survivor, a cancer patient, and a modern bard and historian. His first book, *The Street Martyr*, was published by Gutter Books. A television series based on the book is being produced by Throughline Films. His most recent work, *Destroying the Tangible Illusion of Reality* or *Searching for Andy Kaufman*, which explores what it's like to be dying of cancer, was released by Perpetual Motion Machine Publishing. Find him online at tfoxdunham.com, on Twitter: @Tfoxdunham, and check out his podcast, *What Are You Afraid Of?* at whatareyouafraidofpodcast.com

dbschlosser is an award-winning author who lives in Seattle, with his lovely wife and their dogs, and at dbschlosser.com. Find his story "Pretzel Logic" in *The Best American Mystery Stories 2020*. He's taught writing, crime fiction, and high-school debate; delighted and offended people in *New York Times*, *Wall Street Journal*, "Hard Copy," and "Inside Edition;" and delivers daily writing prompts via PromptInspiration.com.

Paul D. Brazill was born in England and lives in Poland. His books include Gumshoe Blues, Guns of Brixton,and Man of the World.

His short stories have been included in three editions of The Mammoth Book of Best British Crime, alongside the likes of Lee Child, Ian Rankinand Neil Gaiman.

When **Kimberly Godwin** isn't writing, her service with the US Navy takes her around the world. A lifelong learner, she completed her BS in Criminal Justice/ Forensic Science with American Military University and a MS in Geographic Information Systems from PennState. She is currently completing a MS in Strategic Intelligence from the National Intelligence University. Follow her latest projects at studiohnh.com.

Fraser Massey penned the liner notes (sleeve notes in America) to the CD and vinyl reissue of the soundtrack to the documentary film *Tonite Let's All Make Love in London,* which featured rare tracks from Pink Floyd's first studio recordings. An early draft of Fraser's yet to be published debut novel, the neo-noir thriller *Whitechapel Messiah,* was shortlisted for the New Voices award at the *Capital Crime Festival* in London. For more info, see the author's website www.frasermassey.com.

Linda Slater has held a life long wish to turn her imaginative, music-based, out of the ordinary stories into published works for others to enjoy. When she is not writing, she manages her youngest son's music career or is cooking for family and friends. She lives in San Antonio, Texas with her husband and their two dogs.

Phil Thomas is an author and screenwriter from the suburbs of Philadelphia. He is also the co-host of "What Are You Afraid Of?" a weekly horror and paranormal show, available on iTunes, iHeart Radio, Stitcher, and airs on Para-X radio on Friday evenings at 9:00pm. He is featured in *Monsterthology 2* collection, released in October 2019 by Zombie Works Publications with his story, *Tinfoil Bullet.* His short story,

Teddy Bear Kill! Kill! is featured in the upcoming anthology, *Nightside: Tales of Outré Noir*, released by Close to the Bone Publishing on October 30, 2020. *The Poe Predicament* will be released by Foundations Publishing in 2021.

Bill Baber's writing has appeared at Crime sites across the web and in print anthologies-most notably from *Shotgun Honey, Dead Guns Press, Close to the Bone and Authors on the Air Press*- and has garnered Derringer Award and Best of the Net nominations. A book of his poetry, *Where the Wind Comes to Play,* was published in 2011. He lives with his wife and a spoiled dog in Buckeye, Az. on the edge of the desert and sometimes just on the edge.

Tom Leins is a crime writer from Paignton, UK. His books include *Boneyard Dogs, Ten Pints of Blood* and *Meat Bubbles & Other Stories* (all published by Close to the Bone) and *Repetition Kills You* and *The Good Book: Fairy Tales for Hard Men* (both published by All Due Respect).

Mark Slade is the author of the evelina giles series and Barry London series, as well as writer/producer of the radio show Twisted Pulp Radio Hour. He currently created the publishing company Screaming Eye Press with Cameron Hampton, Lothar Tuppan, and Chauncey Haworth. He lives in Williamsburg, Va with his wife and daughter.

Kenneth W. Cain is an author, an award-nominated editor, and a graphic designer. His most recent releases have been through Crystal Lake Publishing, and his novel, *From Death Reborn*, is forthcoming from Silver Shamrock Publishing. www.kennethwcain.com

Jim Shaffer is the author of the novella Back to the World (Close to the Bone). His crime fiction stories have appeared in several anthologies (Nightside, Wrong Turn, Hardboiled, Dark Yonder)

and on line at Close to the Bone, Flash Fiction Offensive, Retreats From Oblivion, and Punk Noir Magazine. He's on Facebook at: Jim Shaffer.

C.W. Blackwell was born and raised in Northern California, where he still lives with his wife and two sons. He has been a gas station attendant, an auto mechanic, and a crime analyst. His passion is to blend poetic narratives and pulp dialogue to create evocative genre fiction. His recent work has appeared in Pulp Modern, Shotgun Honey, Switchblade Magazine, and Econoclash Review.

Morgan Sylvia is an Aquarius, a Mainer, a metalhead, a coffee addict, and a work in progress. A former obituarist, she is now a full-time freelance writer. Her publishing credits include a horror novel, *Abode*; a fantasy novel, *Dawn*; two poetry collections; and over a dozen short stories. Her most recent book, *As The Seas Turn Red,* an ocean-themed poetry collection, was nominated for an Elgin Award.

Renee Asher Pickup is a Marine Corps vet and mellowed out punk, living in Southern California. Renee writes fiction about bad things happening to flawed people, nonfiction that is critical of the status quo, and truly believes From *Dusk Till Dawn* changed her life. She is one half of Cult of One Media and her novel with Andrez Bergen: *Black Sails, Disco Inferno* is available from Open Books. Follow on social media or visit www.reneeasherpickup.com.

K. A. Laity is an award-winning author, scholar, critic, editor, and arcane artist. Her books, music, art and more can be found at KALaity.com. Check out her new podcast Is It Funny? and find her all over social media.

Joseph S. Walker lives in Bloomington, Indiana. He is an active member of the Mystery Writers of America and the Short Fiction Mystery Society. His stories have appeared in *Ellery Queen's Mystery Magazine*, *Alfred Hitchcock's Mystery Magazine*, *Mystery Weekly*, and a number of other magazines and anthologies. In 2019 he won both the Bill Crider Prize for Short Fiction and the Al Blanchard Award. Find his website at: https://jsw47408.wix site.com/website.

S.W. Lauden is the author of the Greg Salem punk rock PI series including *Bad Citizen Corporation*, *Grizzly Season* and *Hang Time*. His power pop-themed crime novelettes include *That'll Be The Day: A Power Pop Heist* and *Good Girls Don't: A Second Power Pop Heist*.

Kurt Reichenbaugh grew up in Florida and has lived in Phoenix Arizona for the past 30 years. He's is the author of the novels *Last Dance in Phoenix* and *Sirens*. His short stories have seen publication in various independent presses. He works as a financial analyst by day. He loves old movies, old books and old records. His first Pink Floyd record was *Dark Side of the Moon*.

Allan Rozinski is a writer of speculative fiction and poetry who has most recently had fiction and poetry accepted or published in *Weirdbook, Spectral Realms, and Star*Line*. His poems "The Solace of he Farther Moon" (short form) and "Cannibal Rex" (long form) were nominated for the Rhysling Award in 2020. He is a member of the Horror Writers Association and the Science Fiction and Fantasy Poetry Association. He can be found on Facebook and Twitter.

Karen Keeley is a twenty year cancer survivor; Stage IV Hodgkin's Lymphoma. She is thrilled part of the proceeds from the sale of the anthology will go to the Leukemia and Lymphoma Society to help with their continued fight on that front. Her short stories have appeared in numerous anthologies, the most recent *Peace, Love, and Crime: Crime Fiction Inspired by the Songs of the '60s* (Untreed Reads).

Andy Rausch is the author of more than forty books. His fiction includes the novels *Layla's Score*, *Bloody Sheets*, and *American Trash*. His newest nonfiction book is *My Best Friend's Birthday: The Making of a Quentin Tarantino Film*. He writes a regular column in *Screem* magazine and is a web editor for *Diabolique* magazine. He resides in Independence, Kansas.

A. B. Patterson is an Australian writer based in Sydney. He was formerly a detective sergeant working in paedophilia and vice, and later a government corruption investigator. He mainly writes hard-boiled crime fiction, and is the creator of PI Harry Kenmare, an old-school man of rough justice featuring in the Harry Kenmare novels and short stories. He can be found at: www.abpatterson.com.au

Paul Williams is a writer from the UK, living in Australia. He's best known for his book that discussed 333 Jack the Ripper suspects and has also written books on mystery animals and the folklore of wolves, plus short fiction and articles. His work is usually inspired by Doctor Who but this piece is from lyrics written over 40 years ago with terrifying contemporary relevance.